the
unicorn
hunter

the
unicorn
hunter

the
unicorn
hunter

che golden

Quercus

New York • London

Quercus

New York • London

© 2013 by Che Golden
First published in the United States by Quercus in 2015

The quotation on page 19 is from *The Second Battle of Moytura*,
translated by Whitley Stokes in *Revue Celtique*, vol. 12, Paris, F. Vieweg
(1891), sourced via CELT (www.ucc.ie/celt)

Any member of educational institutions wishing to photocopy part or
all of the work for classroom use or anthology should send inquiries
to permissions@quercus.com.

ISBN 978-1-62365-874-8

Library of Congress Control Number: 2014918568

Distributed in the United States and Canada by
Hachette Book Group
1290 Avenue of the Americas
New York, NY 10104

This book is a work of fiction. Names, characters, institutions, places,
and events are either the product of the author's imagination or are
used fictitiously. Any resemblance to actual persons—living or dead—
events, or locales is entirely coincidental.

Manufactured in the United States

10 9 8 7 6 5 4 3 2 1

www.quercus.com

For India and Maya.
I hope you always see unicorns.

A Note from the Author

IN THIS BOOK, SOME OF THE CHARACTERS HAVE unusual names. To find out how to say them, turn to page 305.

prologue

As soon as the dart hit the mare's shoulder, the world solidified around the stallion. The air enveloped the gleaming white beast in a damp cloak, and sounds shattered against his ears. He watched as his mate sank to the ground, her nose settling upon her knee. Dark clouds rushed in overhead as birds flew up from the trees. For a fraction of a second the earth shuddered on its axis, throwing wind patterns into chaos and aiming a stream of cold air at one small country in the western hemisphere. The stallion started as the blare of a car horn in the distance reached his ears, but as suddenly as the sounds of the mortal world had battered him, they retreated as the snow began to fall. Big, soft flakes swirled lazily from the gunmetal sky to coat her body and hush the air. The ground was soon blotted out with white, and drifts formed against the mare's sides. The stallion bent his head and tried to move her, but she did not stir. Her chest and eyelids were still, and her mane was plastered to her head and shoulders with melted snow.

He lifted his head and called for help. There was no answering cry in the forest; no one came. The woodland creatures hid and tucked their faces into their tails. He looked at her with agony in his breast, and then, as the sun went down, he turned and fled toward a presence that called him, a presence that would surely help them both.

The unicorn stallion ran from the forest until he reached a muddy lane that ran behind a little row of cottages. Smoke spiraling from their chimneys stung his eyes and nostrils, and the scent of people nearby terrified him. Still he ran, eyes and nostrils flaring red, running toward that soothing presence. He turned sharply and leaped over a wooden gate, his knees buckling briefly as he crashed down on to a graveled path. He ran up to a green wooden door and frantically beat at it with a hoof, as cats gathered on the roof above him, staring at him with golden eyes.

His sides heaved as he panted and waited for the door to swing open, his hoof scraping at the gravel to leave a wound of bare brown earth. Then she was beside him, her cool hands on his face and the soothing sound of her blood thrumming against his body as she pressed herself to his flank. He lowered his head, confused and exhausted as the Feral Child combed her fingers through his tangled mane and whispered words of awe. The purring of the cats rose to a hum above his head, and the stars spun as his world became a dark and dangerous place.

chapter one

MADDY WOKE UP SLOWLY AND STARED AT HER bedroom ceiling. Her stomach clenched with dread as she realized it was cold, much colder than it should be. The old wound in her shoulder ached, and that only happened on cold mornings. But it was early autumn— that ache should not have been bothering her for at least another month. She rubbed at the scar through the thin cotton of the T-shirt she slept in and frowned. A memory flickered deep in her mind, unraveling in flashes before her waking eyes before she had a chance to shut the lid on it. A blade of ice, sliding clean and blue into her flesh, the hot red blood that flooded the air with a scent of iron, and a white face with boiled white eyes twisting into an evil smile as she shrieked.

It had been almost a year since Maddy had gone into the faerie realm of Tír na nÓg to rescue little Stephen

Forest, a child that in the mortal world slept just beyond her bedroom wall. He had been snatched by a faerie when the mounds had opened at Halloween, the one night of the year faeries could cross into the mortal world freely. The Feral Child, the faeries had called her, when she had fought, starved and frozen, to get him back. But she was no such thing. She just wanted to forget, but the horrible, roiling tension in the pit of her stomach told her they were not going to let her do that. The faeries of Tír na nÓg were back, and it had something to do with the unicorn stallion she had locked in the coal shed.

She listened as the clock in the sitting room begin to strike the hour, and she sat bolt upright in horror as she counted the chimes. Ten o'clock! How had she slept so long? She threw back the duvet and scrambled into her clothes, combing her fingers through her tangled brown hair.

She looked around her room as she stuffed her feet into her sneakers, waggling them from side to side to push past the straining laces, knots forced so tight now only long fingernails could pick them apart. Her grandparents had made an effort to make the spare room feel more like her own since she had come to live with them, but that hideous wedding-wrapping-paper wallpaper was everywhere, and so far she had failed to persuade Granda to take it down. Granny liked it too much, and Granda wanted his money's worth out of it before he got rid of it. Her eyes rested for a moment on the picture of her parents, dead eighteen months now in a car crash in Donegal, and her lips thinned with the dull pain it still brought her.

"Why did you let me sleep so long?" she asked Granny as she walked out of her bedroom.

"And good morning to you too," said Granny. "I was just about to wake you up so you saved me the bother. Sit down there and eat your breakfast. We have to leave for Mass in half an hour."

Maddy thought of the unicorn in the shed, who was probably wondering where his breakfast was. "I just . . ."

"You just nothing," said Granny, with a do-not-mess-with-me look on her face. "Breakfast, make yourself presentable, Mass. You have time for nothing else."

Maddy looked down at her crumpled jeans and scuffed sneakers. "What's wrong with the way I look?"

Granny rolled her eyes up to the ceiling. "What am I rearing?" she sighed.

Sunday was the day Maddy's hideous Aunt Fionnula and her revolting brood paid a duty visit to Granny and Granda. Maddy couldn't stand any of her cousins, apart from Roisin and Danny. They had risked their lives with her last year trying to get Stephen back, and she couldn't forget that. They might not be best friends, but they had a bond no one else could share, and it made Maddy just a little less lonely in Blarney.

As soon as Aunt Fionnula launched into one of her monologues (Aunt Fionnula never had what you would call a proper conversation, where the other person talked back), Maddy herded Roisin and Danny into the kitchen.

"I am going to show you something I don't want anyone else to see, so just stay calm," she whispered.

"I don't like the sound of this," said Roisin as they snuck out the back door and over to the coal shed. Maddy threw open the door, and Roisin and Danny's jaws dropped as they stared at the unicorn. The animal was so white he was almost blue, and he shone ghostly in the dark and dusty coal shed. His horn scraped against the roof as he turned his head to look at them with an anguished expression in his sapphire-blue eyes.

"Oh, no," said Danny, who had gone almost as white as the unicorn.

Roisin stretched out a hand to the animal, which snuffled her palm with a velvety nose.

"He's so lovely," she breathed. "Can we keep him?"

"What, one of the pillars of old magic that keeps the world propped up?" asked Maddy. "Don't be soft."

"Oh no," said Danny. "Oh no, oh no, ohno, ohno, ohno."

"Will you *please* get it together?" hissed Maddy.

"I am not going through all this again," said Danny. "Get rid of it, get it out of here! How are we going to explain a unicorn in the coal shed?"

As soon as the words were out of his mouth, the back door opened, and they heard the crunch of feet on gravel. They looked at each other in panic. "Now what?" squeaked Roisin. Granny was walking toward them holding the coal scuttle. She frowned when she saw them.

"Don't be thinking of playing in there now—it's filthy," she warned. "Danny and Roisin, your mother will scalp the pair of you if you ruin your clothes, and I won't be too happy with you either, Maddy." Roisin and Danny looked on in amazement as Granny walked straight through the unicorn, filled the scuttle and walked back out again, closing the door in the animal's face. "I mean it—play either in the garden or in the house, but stay out of here."

They trudged obediently behind her in stunned silence, and then they huddled in the kitchen to talk in private. The unicorn had nudged the shed door open, and they watched him sniff around the garden while George stared at him from the safety of his kennel with all the intensity of a short-fusing terrier brain.

"How come Granny was able to walk through him like that?" asked Danny.

"She's been doing it all day," said Maddy. "Remember what Finn said? They are more symbol than animal, and if you don't believe in what they stand for, then you can't see them."

"But we can see him and touch him?" said Roisin.

"That's because we're faerie touched," said Maddy. "We see things like him whether we want to or not."

"What's he doing here? Why is he hanging around?" asked Roisin.

"I don't care. I'm having nothing to do with this!" said Danny as he began to walk toward the sitting room door. "It can't be good; it never is. This lot doesn't just drop in for a visit. It wants something, and I am not getting dragged into anything this time."

"It's not an 'it,'" yelled Maddy, just as the door was yanked open.

Aunt Fionnula stood framed in the doorway, her pastel-pink shell suit throbbing faintly in the soft glow of the sitting room lamps. Her gimlet eyes were fixed, as usual, on Maddy. "What are you making all this racket for?" she barked. "We can barely hear ourselves think in here!"

"I'm not in here on my own, you know," said Maddy.

Aunt Fionnula leaned down to glare into Maddy's face. *Amazing*, thought Maddy. *The old wagon already looks like she's sucking on a lemon. Pucker up a bit more and she'd look just like a cat's butt.* She bit the inside of her cheeks to stifle a nervous giggle.

"*My* children have been properly raised," said Aunt Fionnula, hiking a thin eyebrow so high in her disapproval and contempt that it almost disappeared into her solid mass of hair. "*My* children know better than to run around shouting and roaring and making a show of themselves. The fact that you cannot says something about you, young lady." She raised a bony finger and began to poke Maddy in the chest, a painful jab emphasizing each word. "You. Are. An. Ignorant. Bad-tempered. Little. Brat."

Maddy gritted her teeth. Her legs shook and her blood boiled as she stared up at Aunt Fionnula. Out of the corner of her eye she could see her grandparents and her cousins looking around to see what all the fuss was about. Granny sighed and came over to them, as Aunt Fionnula raised her finger for another jab.

"Maddy, love, why don't you take George for a walk around the square and leave us to talk for a little while?" she asked.

"I haven't done anything! Why is it every time someone starts on me, *I* have to take the dog for a walk?" said Maddy. She jerked her chin in Aunt Fionnula's direction. "Make her walk him."

"Please, Maddy, just for a little while," soothed her grandmother, as she took Maddy's jacket from a hook behind the back door and ushered her out into the backyard. "Stretch his legs before dinner."

Maddy looked over her shoulder at Granny, her green eyes brimming with tears.

"Why don't you ever take my side?"

Granny sighed. "It's not a question of sides, love."

Maddy gritted her teeth against the tears that threatened to spill, yanked a rather surprised George out of his warm kennel to tie the collar around his neck, and then stormed out of the back garden. She scowled and scuffed at the ground with her tatty sneakers, dragging the terrier along on his lead. George, his brown eyes bulging, kept trying to twist his body around to stare at the unicorn that followed them. The stallion was oblivious to the odd person that walked through him. Maddy didn't bother to look back at the little horse. Instead, she hunched her shoulders underneath her jacket and lingered beneath a tree overlooking the square. The wind was bitter, and the low village buildings cowered beneath needles of icy rain that began to hammer down from the leaden sky. Maddy sighed and zipped her jacket tighter to her throat. The front of her hair was already soaked where her hood crept back from her forehead. Soon Roisin and Danny came panting up.

"We got away as soon as we could," said Roisin.

"It wasn't easy—Mom's not too keen on us hanging out with you," said Danny. Roisin glared at him and rammed an elbow into his ribs. He gave a yelp of pain.

"What's your problem? She knows Mom doesn't like her," he said.

"There's no need to spell it out," said Roisin. "Anyway, Maddy, what's going on? Any idea why our friend here has shown up?"

"Are you interested?" said Maddy.

"Of course we're interested," said Roisin, looking at Danny, who was studying his feet. "*Aren't* we?"

"Yeah," Danny mumbled, shamefaced. "Course I am."

"Good," said Maddy. "I think we need to have a chat with Seamus. And we need to find out why the mare isn't here."

chapter two

Seamus was one of the Tuatha de Dannan, the powerful faerie gods. He used to be worshiped as Cernunnos, the Horned God, by the Celts. The Tuatha de Dannan had ruled Ireland thousands of years ago, before the Celts drove them beneath the mounds, banished them from Ireland for their cruelty and greed, and confined them to Tír na nÓg except for Halloween, when time and magic fell into chaos. Maddy figured Seamus's ego was having a hard time letting go of being worshiped as a god, because he still hung around the mortal world in a vastly reduced form when he could have been living it up in Tír na nÓg with the other Tuatha. Humans fascinated him, even if they didn't worship him anymore. But looking at his house, Maddy thought he was taking the whole idea of being human just a little too far.

His house was on a dull housing estate on the edge of the village. Every house there was the same red-brick, plain box. The only thing that set his apart was that it didn't have a car parked on a pitted and stained concrete driveway. As Lord of the Forest, Seamus was big into saving the environment, so he walked everywhere.

Maddy rang the doorbell while Roisin and Danny huddled behind her, the tips of their noses red with the cold and damp. The unicorn had trailed along behind them all the way through the village, and he was now nibbling half-heartedly at the grass in the neglected front garden. Maddy could only guess what Seamus was going to say when he saw she had one of the unicorns in tow.

He didn't have to say anything. He wrenched the door open before her finger had even left the bell and stared at the animal behind her. The unicorn slowly raised his head and gazed back at the Lord of the Forest. Seamus lowered his head in a bow, and the unicorn dipped his in return, before turning back to nibble at a dehydrated fuchsia bush.

"Inside, the lot of you, now," Seamus growled.

Maddy swallowed and stepped inside, with Danny and Roisin shuffling in her wake.

The three of them perched on a brown leather sofa, trying to huddle away in the necks of their jackets as they listened to the door slam and Seamus's heavy tread in the doorway.

He was a big bear of a man, and Maddy felt a little claustrophobic as he paced the little sitting room, one hand tugging at his thick graying curls. She didn't have to turn her head to know that, like her, her cousins were staring at the huge spread of antlers that sprouted from Seamus's head, waiting for one of the points to catch on the cheap paper that hung loosely on the walls. She *knew* they were there, but she still found it hard to get used to.

Seamus stopped pacing and loomed over them, the shadow of his antlers throwing a lattice over their faces. They shrank back into the squeaky leather as he glowered at each of them in turn.

"Why did he come to you? What did you do?" he snarled. *"What did you do?"*

Roisin gasped, outraged. "We haven't done anything!" she said, before her face clouded over and she turned to look at Maddy. "You haven't, have you?"

"No, I haven't!" said Maddy. "He turned up in the garden last night and practically kicked the back door in. I put him in the coal shed . . ."

Seamus's eyes rolled back in his head, and his voice was a horrified whisper. "The holy of holies—in a coal shed . . ."

"Yes, the coal shed," said Maddy. "And I came to see you as soon as I could. I have no idea why he's here, but I'm guessing it's not good."

"No, it's not," said Seamus grimly. "The Tuatha de Dannan and the rest of faerie kind have been out looking for him for hours—some have even endured terrible pain to cross over into this world to find his tracks— and you've had him *locked in a coal shed.*"

"Well, what was I supposed to do with him?" asked Maddy. "Ring up the local stables and book him in as a livery? My Invisible Pony?"

"The important question is, where is the mare?" interrupted Roisin. "She hasn't turned up."

Seamus threw himself down in a battered armchair and drew his hand across his tired face, scrubbing at his stubble with his palm. "We have no idea, which is a big problem because they would never leave each other's side. Not willingly. Something has happened."

They stared at him and waited for an answer. Outside, the unicorn stallion snuffled at the diamondpane-effect window.

"Well?" said Danny, as the silence stretched taut. "Where is she?"

Seamus sighed. "Mortally injured and hovering on the brink of death."

Maddy gasped.

"How do you know?" she asked. "Have you found her?"

"Do you really think that a unicorn could be struck down and the people of magic would not know it?"

asked Seamus. "We all felt it as soon as she was hurt, and as her life force ebbs, she pulls us all closer to the abyss."

"Who would do such a thing?" cried Roisin.

"Is it even possible?" asked Danny.

"It's hard to do, but it's possible, given a powerful enough weapon," said Seamus. "As to who would want to . . ." He shook his head and looked at the floor.

"What abyss?" asked Maddy. "What exactly do you mean that she is pulling us all closer to the abyss?"

"She is balance to her mate, and together they are the symbol of the forest, of life in all its forms. She is summer and fertility," said Seamus.

"I'm probably being thick, but could you spell it out for me?" asked Maddy.

Seamus sighed impatiently. "The unicorns are a physical manifestation of magic, the very life force of the forest and nature, which is why they exist in Tír na nÓg and in the mortal world at the same time," he explained. "A faerie once made a prophecy as to what would happen should the unicorns die:

> *Summer without flowers,*
> *kine without milk,*
> *women without modesty,*
> *men without valor;*
> *captives without a king,*
> *woods without mast,*
> *sea without produce.*

"Famine," breathed Roisin, her frightened eyes round.

Seamus nodded in agreement. "Famine. Cold wet summers, long, long winters, and a land that sickens until it dies." He looked out of the window. "It's started already."

"'Long, long winters,'" echoed Maddy. "Now, who do we know that would be pleased about that?"

"Liadan," said Danny, his voice flat with anger. "Who else would benefit but a Winter Queen who never wants her power to end?"

"No!" said Seamus. "She wouldn't do this. No faerie could do this!"

"She's *insane*," said Maddy. "And the mare's dying is exactly what she wants. Think about it—famine, chaos. An eternal winter, here and in Tír na nÓg, for the Winter Queen and her court to reign over. If not her, who?"

"One of you," said Seamus. "A mortal."

Danny snorted. "Yeah, right!"

"How could it be one of us?" Maddy objected. "Most mortals can't even see the unicorns, and the Sighted ones are too scared to go near them. Let's face it, you have them all pretty much under your thumb—no one says squat to the faeries around here, even if they're burning the house down around your ears."

Seamus let out a roar and banged his fists on the arm of his chair, his fury sending the unicorn squealing and spinning in the front garden. "No faerie would commit such a horror—none! Only you mud people could do such a thing."

Maddy snapped her mouth shut, her lips thin and white with rage. *Mud people.* Now she knew what Seamus really thought of mortals. What he really thought of *her.* His angry words rang in the air as they glared at each other.

"We have to find the mare," said Roisin, rubbing her forehead with the tips of her fingers. "Can we please just find the mare and sort all this out later?"

"That's easy enough, now that we have the stallion," said Seamus. "He'll lead us to her." He dug into the pocket of an old waxed jacket slung over the arm of the chair he was sitting on and pulled out a cell phone. Maddy knew she shouldn't be surprised, but it was still a bit of a shock to watch an ancient Celtic god struggle to dial numbers with his big meaty fingers.

"Bat, it's me, Seamus." Maddy realized Seamus was talking to her grandfather, and an icy trickle of apprehension ran through her. "Call everyone you can, and get them to meet outside my house. Try not to draw too much attention to yourselves."

He snapped the phone shut and fixed her with another glare. "Now we'll get to the bottom of this."

He stalked over to a massive, ornate mirror that looked completely out of place in the room and muttered a few unintelligible words as he stared into its surface. It clouded over and then cleared enough for Maddy to see strange faces in the glass mouthing silent words at Seamus. She couldn't get a good look as she tried to peer around Seamus's bulk, but one of those faces was framed by a sweep of straight hair that was as black as a raven's wing.

"What's he doing?" whispered Danny.

"Talking to the other Tuatha," said Roisin.

"What for?"

"He's calling them here," said Maddy.

She turned and looked out of the window at the unicorn in the front garden. The stallion stood unnaturally still, staring out into the village. He was waiting.

chapter three

MADDY HAD KNOWN SINCE THE EVENTS OF THE PRE-
vious year that the village of Blarney and the surrounding
countryside were full of people with the Sight, the ability
to see the faerie world. But Granda hadn't been keen to tell
her who they were, and tonight was her chance to see who
made up the net of conspiracy that kept the faeries a secret
and allowed their bad deeds to go unpunished. Maddy was
still angry that no one had wanted to go after her next-door
neighbor, two-year-old Stephen Forest, when he had been
abducted by a faerie. Even angrier when she thought of all
the children who had been lost over the years that no one
had dared to rescue, letting mothers and fathers bring up
stunted changelings in their place. Tonight she was going
to fix the name and face of every one of the cowardly
adults in her mind.

And there were so many. Some knocked softly on the door and came into the house. A few waited in the street, exchanging small talk, like neighbors who had bumped into each other on an evening stroll. The only thing that betrayed their anxiety was their eyes flicking to the house every few seconds. Roisin and Danny drifted over to join Maddy, their faces set and white. She knew they were thinking the same thoughts as hers. Roisin gripped Maddy's hand and gave it a squeeze.

There was the local doctor who had treated her wounds last Halloween when the Winter Queen and her faeries had almost killed Maddy. *No wonder no one thought to question how banged up I was when the local GP was covering it all up,* thought Maddy. There was Mary O'Brien, who worked in the Blarney Castle shop, the boy who delivered their newspapers, and the butcher. . . . As Maddy stared through the window, she could see endless faces of adults who had been nice to her since she had come to live in Blarney, people she thought of as friends. These adults knew that faeries existed and did nothing when they stole children. *How many of them would have just abandoned me, if I had been taken?* she wondered. *How many would have turned a blind eye to a changeling in my place?* Tears of anger and self-pity stung her eyes, and she dug her fingernails into her palm as she got a lump in her throat. She saw the worried face of her grandfather making his way to the front door, and the anger coiled in her stomach.

Granda knocked on the door, and Maddy kept staring out of the window at the rest of the Sighted while

Roisin ran to let him in. She heard him mutter a greeting to Seamus, and then he came and stood behind her. She could hear him breathing, and if she raised her eyes a little, she would see his face reflected in the glass in front of her. But she didn't. She kept her gaze fixed on the people in front, the useless, impotent Sighted, and rolled the taste of her rage around in her mouth, enjoying its battery-acid sting.

Granda stared at her. "I know that look on your face," he said after a few minutes. "You might as well let it all out."

She looked at him then, her stare hard enough to scratch glass as she flicked her green eyes up to meet his.

"You don't want to know," she said, the words barely escaping the click of her teeth.

"I do," said Granda, looking sad but wary. "I always want to know."

"Fine," said Maddy as she swung around to face him, fixing him in place with her glare. "I'm just trying to do the math—twenty adults in this village, *twenty*, who know full well what the faeries get up to, what horrible things they are capable of, and no one says anything."

"You know why no one says anything—" Granda said.

"Yeah, I know, so they don't end up in the funny farm," Maddy interrupted. "But what's been stopping any of this lot from forming a Neighborhood Faerie Watch group and trying to stop bad things from happening? Do you even talk about this stuff among yourselves?"

Granda looked at her, his mouth pressing into a thin line as anger and frustration battled it out across his craggy face. "I don't know what you want me to say," he said eventually.

"Do you ever?" asked Maddy, shouldering her way past him, her arms still folded tightly to her chest.

She walked over to the fake coal fire and gazed sightlessly as the red and yellow light flickered. She slipped her fingers inside her jacket and rubbed the knot of scar tissue that adorned her shoulder. She could feel its puckered, wrinkled lips beneath the cotton of her T-shirt, and she shuddered at the memory of the ice that pierced her through. The red-painted lips of the Winter Queen flickered in the electric glow as Maddy remembered her faerie-cruel smile. She could still see that shard of blue-white ice protruding from her shoulder, the way her hot blood cooled as it flowed over the frosty blade. The only thing she could now hear in that room full of people was the sound of her own breath quickening as the panic rose in her belly. She still dreamed she was being pinned to a board like a butterfly while Liadan and her court of nightmarish faeries drove spikes of ice through her joints. The nightmares that woke her screaming and thrashing in sweat-soaked sheets sometimes crept up on her during the day, sinking icy claws into her ribs and exhaling their fevered breath in her ears. Fear and remembered pain chased each other through her now, and the teeth of the Winter Queen's cold gnawed at her chest.

She jumped as a soft, warm hand clutched her arm and the sounds in the room roared in her ears. Roisin's pale face peered into hers as Maddy blinked her panic away.

"The stallion is walking away," Roisin whispered. "We need to follow him."

"We can't all go charging down the street at once," said Seamus, peering out the window. "Let the others walk on ahead, and we'll catch up with them."

They waited a few minutes while Seamus switched off the fire and the lights, before slipping out into the dank autumn air. The Sighted were fanned out on either side of the road, walking in groups or alone, laughing and chatting as if out to enjoy an evening walk despite the weather. But they cast glances back over their shoulders at Seamus, and Maddy could see their pale faces and frightened eyes in the glow from the streetlights. The unicorn was far ahead, the intense white of his hide gleaming in the cloud-tossed moonlight. As he went, the October wind snatched fire-red and yellow leaves from the trees and spun them around his feet so the tarmac seemed to boil.

On he led them, through the quiet, sleepy estate and out on to the busy road to Cork city. There was no one about to see where the group of villagers was going, and none of the motorists in their cars stopped to ask them where they were headed. Only the Sighted could see the little unicorn walking on with dying leaves entangled in his mane.

He reached a chain-link fence that separated a scrubby field from the busy main road, and he walked right through it the way a ghost would. An overgrown hedgerow dipped low over the neglected soil, the rain swelling into big fat drops as it spilled from twiggy branches. The earth beneath was bare and mucky. A gleam of white that matched the hide of the stallion lay on the ground a few yards ahead in the gloom.

The fence was old and sagging on its supports, flapping loose and baggy in its frame like forgotten washing. The first of the Sighted to reach it pulled up its aging skirts and ducked underneath. Maddy reached out and clenched the gritty cold of the links in her fist. Before she could pull it up over her head though, Seamus held her back, his fingers digging into her scarred shoulder.

"Mind your tongue tonight, Maddy," he growled. "This is a bad business, and all the courts will be here. Now that the stallion is out in the open, they will be drawn to him like a moth to a flame, and when they see how the mare is, they will want answers. You're about to see the Tuatha de Dannan and the faerie courts in all their glory. Very few mortals can stand for long in their light and not be scorched to a crisp because of an ill-thought word. Don't be a smart mouth."

A smart remark was exactly what came bubbling into Maddy's mouth, but she closed her lips against it and gave Seamus a curt nod before ducking underneath the fence.

chapter four

It was a sad, pathetic place for such a magical creature to be brought to bay. The unicorns existed in both the faerie and the mortal worlds at the same time, and Maddy fervently prayed that if the mare was aware of what was happening, then she thought she was somewhere far more green and pleasant.

The wet, slimy roadside was littered with sad, weather-faded trash that careless drivers had thrown from their cars. Cookie and cracker packets, sodden candy wrappers, and drink cans had been pushed by persistent winds through the fence, and they had skipped and danced to the stricken unicorn, resting against her too-still flanks and entangling themselves in her sodden mane. The cruel rain had not let up. Around the mare, the air gave a hiccup, and a brief flurry of snow fell about her head. Melting clumps of dirty slush dotted the browned grass around her. Lying among the junk of the mortal world, the mare looked neglected and disrespected. It made Maddy's throat ache with tears to look at her—the mare should be covered in flowers and her head laid on a pillow of silk. Roisin could not help herself and began to cry. Maddy could hear the sobs among the Sighted as some knelt in the mud, hands outstretched, not daring to touch the stricken creature. Her nose lay on her knee, and her eyes were shut tight. A dart stuck out from her shoulder, and black poison was beginning to work its way through her veins, spreading down her leg.

The stallion nudged at her neck and blew his warm breath against her wet mane. Her eyelids did not even flicker. The stallion raised his head and wailed, a low mournful sound closer to a whale's cry than a horse's neigh. It ached and throbbed in the damp air before trailing off into silence.

There was a clump of trees toward the far end of the field, and a light began to glow among their trunks as the stallion's cry broke apart on the sharp autumn breeze.

Maddy clapped her hand to her cheek as she felt a puff of air kiss it, warm as the desert, carrying the rich, heavy scent of tropical flowers. "Can you feel that?!" exclaimed Danny, as Roisin gasped beside her.

Granda bent his head down to the three of them. "Show no fear, no matter what happens next."

The glow grew brighter and the breeze stronger until a warm wind blew over them, smoothing their hair from their faces with balmy fingers. Another golden light joined the glow, and together they pulsed toward the group of the Sighted ones. Seamus went and stood close to the unicorns, his shadow antlers stretching huge across the ground.

Maddy squinted against the glow. There were shapes moving about in it and more shapes gathering beyond it. A bright blue butterfly came swooping toward her, dusting her cheeks with its wings. The golden light grew so bright that she gasped and closed her eyes for a moment, spots of red sparking against the lids. When she opened them again, she nearly fell to her knees.

Walking toward her, at the heart of the pulsing, golden glow, were two couples, arm in arm. The women were blond and blue-eyed, so alike they could have been twins. One man was dark haired, the other fair. Warm air rippled out from both couples, and butterflies flocked around them. Where one couple trod, the grass turned lush and emerald green, while flowers of every color sprang from the feet of the other couple and lapped like a perfumed tide around the unicorn and against Maddy's grubby sneakers. A white butterfly landed on the cherry-pink lips of one woman and beat its wings there like a pulse. Behind them, walking silently from the trees, was a host of people who looked similar but lacked the intense light that shone from the arm-linked couples. Pennants fluttered in the air, and men and women with the faces of angels sat astride white horses. Smaller, odder shapes could be seen behind them, shapes that capered and tumbled, and there were flickers of wings in the shadows cast by bright faeries.

Seamus in mortal form was a shadow of these creatures. *The Tuatha de Dannan,* thought Maddy. *How did Granda ever think I would be scared?*

She wanted to get down on her hands and knees and crawl to touch the hem of the Tuathas' cloaks, as dirty and ugly as she was. She could hear sweet music, joyful and aching at the same time, and she turned her head from side to side as her ears strained to catch the notes that always seemed to be on the edge of her hearing. The hedgerow and the trees were full of whispers and giggling, and the air was thick with the thrum of gossamer wings. Her eyes were dazzled . . .

She was brought back to her senses with a jolt as Granda grabbed the back of her jacket and yanked her to her feet as she tried to lower herself on to her belly. He wrapped his long arms around her and around Roisin and Danny, who looked as moonstruck as she was, and he hugged his three grandchildren so hard she could feel their ribs grinding together.

"Don't be fooled," he growled. "They are putting a glamour on you! It's a magic that makes you see only what they want you to see."

He squeezed them harder, and Maddy heard Roisin and Danny yelp as she did from the pain. Their faces were pressed so close together she couldn't see their expressions, but she felt her mind become a little clearer as the pain doused her like cold water.

"Look at them now," said Granda. "*Really* look at them."

As the couples drew closer, they dimmed the light that radiated from their bodies. It settled around them like a cloak, and Maddy could see them clearly for the first time.

They were still beautiful, but their beauty was hard and unnatural to mortal eyes. The color of their hair was more than blond—it looked as hard and cold as beaten gold. The darker man's hair was as rich and as unyielding as ebony. They were impossibly tall, nearly eight feet, Maddy guessed, and like many of the faeries, their fingers were triple-jointed and unnaturally long. Their faces were triangular, narrowing down into a chin a baby could cup in its palm, while their eyes were huge and round beneath a bulging brow. But it was their expressions that sent a shudder down Maddy's spine— cold and cruel.

"They look like . . . they look like . . ." stammered Roisin.

"Aliens," babbled Danny. "They look like aliens out of one of those sci-fi comics, like that guy that landed at Roswell, only medieval, with lots of hair . . ."

"Shh!" whispered Granda. "Keep thoughts like that to yourselves. Don't offend them, and don't, whatever you do, get them to notice you. We want to walk away from here tonight without a single glance in our direction."

"Who are they?" asked Maddy.

"The monarchs of the Spring and Summer Courts," said Granda. "The blond couple are King Nuada and Queen Sorcha of the Spring faeries. The dark-haired man is King Aengus Óg of the Summer Court with his wife Queen Niamh. The monarchs are the most powerful of the Tuatha de Dannan."

"Aengus Óg?" asked Roisin, her brow puckering as she thought. "I've read stories about him. The god of love?"

"Among other things," said Granda grimly.

"God of love doesn't sound that scary," said Danny. "It sounds a bit girly to me."

"There is *nothing* girly about Aengus Óg," warned Granda. "Call yourself a boxer, but I'm almost tempted to let you say that in his hearing just to teach you a lesson. I think we would all prefer that the skin on your back *stayed* there."

Danny swallowed and went quiet.

Maddy winced as a blast of cold air hit her right cheek. The terror she had left behind in Seamus's house jumped on her back and squeezed her throat with icy fingers. She forced her fear-stiffened neck to turn her head and see the faerie that haunted her nightmares.

Liadan, the Winter Queen, who had hunted Maddy, Roisin, and Danny across Tír na nÓg last year, was shuffling across the grass with her crippled, dragging step. Her long black hair was piled high on her head, and her crown of ice perched on top. Frost and ice radiated from her feet and petrified the ground. Bitter arctic air from her lips blew against the warm air of the Spring and Summer Courts. The clouds of butterflies spiraled into the air in panic, a few stragglers dropping to the ground as the cold iced their tissue-thin wings and stopped their tiny hearts. The Spring and Summer monarchs frowned, and their warm golden glow roared into life in a solar flare to clash with Winter's chill. The air sizzled and steamed, water pattering to the ground and marking a boundary line in mud between them and Winter.

Now that Maddy could compare Liadan to the Tuatha de Dannan, she could see how weak the crippled Winter Queen really was. Liadan was no Tuatha de Dannan but a bloodthirsty elf who had been given the Winter crown and had married to Seamus in an attempt to bring peace to the war-torn faerie realm when the last Winter Queen disappeared. But it is not easy wearing the crown of a Tuatha. Liadan was an old and powerful elf, but she did not have the strength of a god. As soon as the High Queen of the faeries, the Morrighan, had placed the crown on Liadan's head, the cold of winter entered her body, and it had twisted and warped her, ruining her beauty and her mind. Maddy shuddered as the elf sent a cruel smile her way. She would never forget the look of joy on Liadan's face when she had stabbed ice through Maddy's shoulder. Or the way her painted lips had curled in a snarl when she had knelt over Maddy and sent waves of ice into her chest in an attempt to stop her heart.

The leader of Winter's war band, Fachtna, towered behind Liadan. Maddy felt the world spin around her and her knees buckle as the field roared away. The memory of Fachtna standing over her, lightning flickering over her bone-white skin as she raised her silver sword to drive it through Maddy's throat, washed over her and drowned her senses. Maddy heard her own voice screaming in her head—*"You can't kill me!"* And Fachtna, cocking that long head at her, the fire in her red eyes glowing bright. *"Let's find out."*

Fachtna was as tall as the Tuatha, and every inch of her skin was covered in gray tattoos. Her white hair was stiffened with lime and formed a high Mohican, her teeth were filed into points, and her red eyes burned in her pointed, hook-nosed face. She bristled with weapons and scars. and as Maddy stared at her, the faerie grinned and an unnaturally long tongue curled out and licked her pointed teeth. She had no doubt Liadan still wanted her dead and that Fachtna was tasked to do the deed. The war faerie was probably still furious that Maddy had outrun her hounds last year and that she, Fachtna, had failed to hunt her down for the Winter Queen. She could not boast that she always catches her prey, not anymore. Fachtna enjoyed killing, and Maddy was under no illusions that if Fachtna caught her, her death would be slow and painful. The dark faerie gained nourishment in some weird way from the darker human emotions. She would take great pleasure in making Maddy scream and would drink in every drop of her agony like a fine wine. The back of Maddy's throat burned, and she felt Granda's arm tighten around her as he held her up, bringing her back to the here and now.

"Breathe, Maddy," he said. "Don't give her your fear—it will only make her stronger."

The howling of the faeries brought Maddy back to her senses, and she wrenched her eyes away from Fachtna's glowing red orbs and listened in horror as the courts taunted and threatened each other. Steam billowed up where the warm and cold air fronts twisted and fought against each other, cloaking the field in fog. Through the half-light she could see the faeries of all the courts brandishing weapons in paws, claws, and hands. Demon hounds, their shapes shifting to flaunt paws, claws, fur, and scales all at once while red eyes glowed in shadowy faces, bayed on all sides as the monarchs faced off. You would never know what they truly looked like until they were close enough to bite.

A woman behind Maddy cried out, and that one sound was enough to spread fear through the Sighted ones like a contagion. Maddy could practically smell the panic rising behind her. The golden-haired armored men of the Spring and Summer Courts began to round up mounted warriors and line them up in battle formation, facing the Winter Court. Fachtna drew her sword and turned to bellow something at the seething dark mass that was the Winter Court faeries. She pointed with her sword, and Maddy watched as trolls, dark-haired gancanagh, their beauty deceptive, and fir dorocha began to form themselves into ranks. The fir dorocha, the "dark men" of Celtic legend, were a shifting faceless mass, terror whispering from them and oozing over the ground toward the opposing courts. Their shadow hands held the silver chains that restrained the hounds.

"They're going to charge!" screamed Roisin.

Maddy twisted in her grandfather's grip as she tried to look behind her. Steam obscured her vision, and she couldn't even see if the Sighted were still standing behind them or if they were alone in what was about to become a battlefield.

"Stand your ground!" barked Granda, as Maddy, Roisin, and Danny squirmed like puppies.

"We need to go!" said Danny, his voice high with fear. "We need to go right now!"

"Remember the rules," said Granda. "Never run. If we run, they'll chase, and we won't make it as far as the fence."

Maddy froze, her chest hitching with dry sobs, her hair plastered to her head with the condensing steam. She couldn't think, and she could barely see—her whole body shook as she fought the urge to flee.

"Faeries!" spat Seamus. "You can't have them in the same space for five minutes without their trying to tear each others' heads off!" He drew the shadows of the ground into himself, and suddenly his mortal form grew and expanded until he was eye to eye with the other Tuatha. A spread of shadow antlers with too many points for Maddy's terrified brain to count uncurled through the air and pierced the steam.

"ENOUGH!" he roared, his booming voice rolling across the courts and ending with a clap of thunder that made everyone, mortal and faerie, cover their ears with their hands.

The silence was immediate and deafening. The Summer and Spring monarchs dimmed their glow, and the butterflies rested, trembling, on their clothes. Liadan smiled, a bitter offering, and drew her cold back into herself.

Maddy heard Danny and Roisin let out a shuddering breath. She could make out whimpers and mutterings behind her. It seemed the Sighted had stood their ground.

"What now?" she whispered in the quiet.

"Now we wait," said Granda.

"For what?" asked Roisin.

"For Autumn to arrive."

chapτer ɼive

A PERFECT SILENCE REIGNED FOR A FEW HEART-
beats before the assembled courts began to grumble
among themselves. Aengus Óg drew himself up to his
full height and looked down his long nose at Seamus.

"How diminished you are, brother, that you have to
construct your true form with shadows and air before
you can face me," he sneered. "Has clinging on to the
mortal world weakened you so much?"

"Not so weak that I cannot remember who gave you
that crown, *brother*," growled Seamus. "Shall we see if I
can take it away?"

"Why do you argue?" cried Queen Niamh, her hands
fluttering around her face. "How can you argue when
such a tragedy has befallen us all?" She pulled at her
long golden tresses, but Maddy couldn't help but notice

that instead of tearing at them, she sort of fluffed them up so her hair would look fuller.

Sorcha rolled her eyes. "Luckily the mare isn't dead yet. A reasonable discussion about what we are going to do would be preferable to bickering as if we were only a few centuries old, but that's not possible, is it?"

"What are you implying?" hissed Niamh, her grief forgotten and her blue eyes narrowed to slits. "We're not the ones who blocked treaty after treaty—"

"But *you* are the ones who made the air burn and nearly ripped Tír na nÓg apart, trying to become the dominant court instead of sharing power as we are supposed to do," snapped Sorcha.

"And what would you have done if you had been winning?" asked Niamh. "How noble would you have been, sister, if you had had the upper hand?"

"Peace!" said King Nuada. "We must put aside our enmity and join together to face this bigger threat. Someone has done this to the sacred unicorn. Someone who does not care about tearing apart the fragile fabric that holds our world together."

"Nuada is right," said Seamus. "Now is not the time to rake over old fights and hurts. The mortal world and Tír na nÓg are already changing. It is growing too cold too quickly, and if the mare dies, we will not see summer again. An eternal Winter of starvation faces us all."

"And wouldn't that be wonderful?" said Niamh. "For one of us at least." She glared at Liadan.

The Winter Queen's face remained as impassive as granite. "My sister queen wrongs me. I rule for the good of Tír na nÓg, as does she. I live for balance and prosperity. It would not serve my court for the Land to be thrown into chaos."

"You lie with every word you speak!" screeched Niamh. "Your whole rule is nothing but disorder and riot! You are not fit to wear a Tuatha's crown, and I will never be your sister."

"Spare me from the spite of females," groaned Seamus.

"Do *not* include me in those words. I can show a measure of self-control," snapped Sorcha. Yells and insults began to rise in the courts as faeries on all sides traded insults and Liadan cocked an eyebrow at Sorcha. Aengus Óg laid a soothing hand on his wife's arm while glaring at Nuada. "Control your wife," he said.

The Spring monarch let out a humorless bark of laughter. "I'm not the one who cannot put a rein on my wife's passion. Or had you forgotten?"

Aengus Óg's face turned black with anger. There was clash of swords on shields as the Summer warriors began a menacing beat, faces set as hard as stone as they reacted to Spring's insult. The glow around the Summer and Spring regents began to swell again as they faced off, with Seamus shouting at them to be calm. A wind began to rise, whipping dead leaves into the air. The wind smelled of rain, and it tore around the Sighted, tugging at their clothes and howling in their ears. Maddy began to shiver as it blasted full into her face, its icy touch numbing her skin as if her clothes were made of tissue. Dark clouds rolled in overhead, and the air was ripped apart by lightning. Bolts leaped from the purple-black storm clouds and stabbed at the ground, scattering faeries and leaving a stink of ozone in the air. The dead leaves began to form a shape, a whirlwind between the courts that spun faster and faster, rising higher and higher. A clap of thunder crashed, and the whirlwind exploded in every direction, scattering leaves, the speed turning them into knives that slashed soft human faces. Maddy screamed and squeezed her eyes shut, and she felt Granda curl his long body over herself, Roisin, and Danny to shield them from the worst of the blows.

For a second time there was a perfect silence. Maddy opened her eyes and saw another Tuatha standing where the whirlwind had raged only a moment before. Her hair was as red as fire, thick and matted, and it was so long that it reached to the ground behind her. Her huge eyes were a bright, bright green, and she had draped her body in red plaid over a white under-shirt, pinned at the shoulder with a golden brooch. Gold armbands gleamed against her milk-white skin, and a torc hung heavy around her long neck. A huge shaggy black dog pressed itself against her thigh, its yellow eyes like lamps in the dim light. Three hideous women in greasy gray rags huddled behind her, their scabbed scalps pocked with limp strands of hair, each with one eye gleaming with malevolence in her blue-black face.

"Meabh," said Niamh, her eyes blazing with hatred. "So good of you to join us. And you must be feeling brave to bring only your storm hags and the Pooka."

"I did not realize I had anything to fear," said Meabh with mock innocence. She gazed around her at the assembled courts while the Pooka, a faerie that took the shape of a giant dog, bared his teeth at Niamh. "I thought I was coming to council, not war. Am I not safe here?"

Seamus stepped forward and offered his arm. "Of course, dear sister. We are under a banner of truce—no blood can be spilled. And your skills of witchcraft are much needed."

"Let me guess," whispered Maddy. "The Queen of Autumn?"

"The very same," said Granda.

"Where's the king?" asked Danny.

"Meabh's husbands have a nasty habit of dying in battle," said Granda. "She has been widowed for the second time since taking the Autumn crown, and there are not many volunteers to be her third husband."

Seamus walked Meabh over to the body of the unicorn mare, with her mate still standing forlorn by her side. The Autumn Queen bowed her head to the stallion, who lowered his in return. Then she crouched and drew the dart from the mare's shoulder. The unicorn did not move as the barb was pulled free of her skin;

not so much as a ripple shuddered through her silver hide. Meabh pressed her hand to the wound and closed her eyes. She stayed still and silent for a while, and the Sighted ones and the faerie courts pressed closer and watched her face.

"What is she doing?" asked Roisin.

"Meabh is a necromancer," said Granda. "As well as having power over the elements, like all the Tuatha, she can walk in the realm of the dead and talk to them there. The unicorn is hovering on the brink of death, and Meabh is the only one who can travel to her."

"So why is she touching the cut?"

"She is looking for the poison," said Granda. "Poisons are a bit like bombs—the people who make them often put their own stamp on them. If Meabh recognizes the poison, then we find the poisoner and we can all go home."

Meabh pulled her hand away and shivered. "Dark arts did this. Dark arts and a twisted, evil creature to hurt one so pure," she said, her eyes darkening in her face. "It will be safe nowhere, welcome nowhere, no guest rights can it claim. It is a thing transformed by the horror of what it has done."

"Can the mare be helped?" asked Sorcha.

Meabh nodded. "I can turn back the poison, but she is weak and will not survive a second attack."

Sorcha paled. "*Another* one? Why do you think there will be another attempt?"

"Whatever creature attacked her, the mare read the whispers of its heart before it struck her down," said Meabh. "It meant to kill her. I see no reason why it would not return to see the job finished."

"Why kill a unicorn?" asked Aengus Óg.

Meabh shrugged. "Whoever did this is clearly insane. I cannot fathom the reasoning of a mad creature."

"But *who* was it, Meabh?" asked Seamus. "Who did this thing? Faerie or mortal?"

"I cannot say—the mare did not see it before it struck, and these things are hidden from me," said Meabh as the faeries muttered angrily. "But the earth will burn beneath its feet. This thing can be tracked, in this world or in Tír na nÓg. It must be brought to bay, and it must be tracked by one who can walk above and below the hollow hills." She turned, and her bright green gaze settled on Maddy. "One such as you, Feral Child."

"NO!" shouted Granda. "Leave her alone!"

Maddy clutched at his coat and felt herself transfixed as the cold, predatory gaze of the assembled faeries focused on her. Her breath froze in her throat, and tears pricked at her eyes. Seamus walked over to her, his face set with anger. Panic rippled through the Sighted as the faeries began to advance.

Seamus stood over Maddy, and the shadow of his antlers blocked the rising moon, casting her into darkness. Granda's warm hands tightened on her, and she felt Danny and Roisin wind their arms around hers, locking her in tight. She looked up at Seamus, her mind blank with fear and her eyes wide in her white face. "Give the girl to me, Bat," said Seamus. "Do not make me ask twice."

"Don't do this," said Granda. "For the love of God, Seamus, how long have we been friends? Leave her out of this—she's just a child. Why does it have to be her anyway?"

"The Feral Child has the courage to walk in the mortal land and in Tír na nÓg, something no other Sighted has attempted to do for hundreds of years," said Meabh. "Wherever the hunter tries to flee, she can find it. And as you love your granddaughter so much, she will be a hostage for the Sighted's good behavior."

"You don't need hostages for that," said Granda. "We've kept the truce for centuries. You and I have even become friends, Seamus . . ."

Seamus smiled, but it was cold and cruel. "It's because we are friends that I don't take the girl by force. Look behind me. How are you going to stand against all four of the courts? I have a host of Tuatha and other faeries at my back willing to kill to avenge the hurt done to this mare, and they will slaughter each other and everyone in the village until the hunter is found. Meabh is right. Maddy can find it and save countless lives. You are selfish, old man, if you do not hand her over. Especially when you have two other grandchildren standing with you whose lives hang in the balance."

Maddy's heart sank as she listened to Seamus, and she waited for Granda to push her forward, but his hands stayed on her arms, and Roisin and Danny pressed closer to her sides.

"This is your problem to sort out," said Granda as Seamus loomed over him. "This is the work of a faerie or a Tuatha, and it is for the Tuatha monarchs to find them and punish them. None of the Sighted would dream of doing this, and none of them has the skill. Ask which of you has the skill of a poisoner. Meabh, with her black arts? Liadan, who is the only monarch who stands to gain from the mare's death?"

Meabh barked a harsh laugh.

"We would not do this, nor would any of our subjects," said Sorcha. "We have more honor. Only your kind, that pollutes and destroys the earth you stand on, the very air that you breathe, would raise a hand against the unicorn that brings new life into the world. Only your kind would think that killing her would be worth more than that."

"This isn't going to go away," said Aengus Óg. "The barrier that keeps us apart from the mortal world was forged in the same primal source that the unicorns sprang from. As she weakens, so does the magic that keeps us beneath the mounds. The boundaries are breaking down, and we will pass through day and night as both worlds weaken. This crime will not go unavenged. You cannot hide in your houses when the sun sets and pray we pass you by. Find the mortal who did this, or we punish you all. If the world must pass into eternal night, then we will feast on mortal flesh while we wait for our end."

"I would listen to him, old man, if you love this child and the two that stand beside her," said Meabh. "The barrier is failing already. How long will it take for the courts to rampage? How long before your door is broken in, and your children's doors? Will you see your grandchildren dead or in chains? And if the hunter does return and kill this mare, then both worlds will plunge into winter and famine. Think of it, when it happened here. All those people dead, and this time there will be no ships on which to escape to other countries, because everywhere else will be dying too. You would risk war and famine to avoid giving up one child?"

"This is a trick! Not even you, Meabh, Witch Queen, can say whether it was a faerie or a human who raised a hand against the unicorn," said Granda, his voice shaking with fear. "You cannot prove it was us. You're not using my granddaughter as a pawn in Tuatha battles."

Meabh smiled again, her eyes cold, while Niamh drew herself up to her full height. "This is no trick, you mortal worm," Niamh said. "The Tuatha already stand before you on mortal soil, and the Samhain Fesh—what you call Halloween—is still seven nights away."

"You are the strongest of your kind, called by one of the oldest of your people. You can overcome the barrier—"

"The monarchs are capable of breaching the barrier for small amounts of time, but their entire courts?" asked Meabh. "Face the truth—the barrier is already weakening. By the night of Samhain, it will have collapsed completely, and if I cannot cure the mare in time or protect her life, it will stay gone. And every faerie in the land, the courts and the solitaries who can be controlled by no one, will come pouring out of that mound, hungry for human flesh."

"Why wouldn't you want that, Meabh?" asked Granda. "You, who always reveled in war?"

"It's true, I would like to have back my mortal throne in Connacht, and I would like to have Ireland divided among the Tuatha again, rather than having only a season to govern," said Meabh, "but not to rule over the dead. You may not feel it, but the land is sickening. I take no pleasure in ruling a mortuary and watching my own people waste away in it."

"Do you want to risk another war, Bat? Another war between mortal and Tuatha, the likes of which have not been seen for thousands of years? Another famine that will spread across the world?" asked Seamus, his voice soft and cold. "The destruction of everything you love, for one child?"

"For this child?" asked Granda. "Yes." Maddy felt tears prick her eyes as she twisted the rough fabric of his coat in her fist. "I will risk another war. But will you? When the last one saw us the victors and your people driven beneath the hills?"

"Then you were a single army with a single purpose," said Seamus. "Who will persuade your kind to look away from their computer screens and televisions and see the threat that walks among them? Who will persuade them to believe in faeries again? You, old man?"

"We are wasting time in debate. There is a way to settle this," said Meabh. "Bring the child to the Blarney Stone. Let the Stone decide the part she is to play—or not."

"Will you accept this, old man? Will you stand by the Stone's judgment?" asked Seamus.

"No one is taking *any* of my grandchildren, and what a lump of rock has to say about it doesn't make any difference," said Granda.

Seamus stepped closer and lowered his horned head to talk softly in Granda's ear. "You will come, old man, and put yourself at the Stone's mercy, or else I give the order to slaughter every mortal who stands in this field but Maddy." Seamus turned back to the faeries and raised his voice. "We seek the wisdom of the Stone. Let a representative from each court accompany the Feral Child so all may know its judgment!"

As the faeries turned away from them and began to argue over who should be sent to the Stone, Maddy wrapped her arms around Granda's waist. "They noticed me," she whispered, her voice thick with the tears that were poised to scorch her face. "They saw me. I wish I could have hidden."

Granda stroked her hair. "I know, love, I know. But I'm not letting them take you."

chapter six

WHEN SEAMUS TALKED ABOUT GOING TO THE
Blarney Stone, Maddy didn't think he had meant right
now. Not when it was dark and cold and the sky was so
thick with clouds she could not see her hand in front of
her face once she left the glow of the streetlights. Cut off
from the rest of Blarney village by high stone walls, the
grounds of Blarney Castle might as well have been the
surface of the moon.

They had argued for ages in the field about who
should go to hear the Stone's judgment. Maddy was
beginning to understand that, for the Tuatha, fighting was a bit of a hobby. None of the monarchs could
be bothered to go themselves, and all their subjects
fought for the honor of representing them. Knives had
been drawn, despite the truce banners, and at least one

of Niamh's admirers had been dragged away unconscious. Maddy had watched them in silence, shivering
in the rain, surrounded protectively by Roisin, Danny,
and Granda. She could smell the wet wool of Granda's
heavy coat, and Roisin's chilled fingers were entwined
with hers. Danny watched the Tuatha with a grim, set
face that was the mirror of Granda's expression.

Maddy was confused about what was going on.
She had no idea what the Blarney Stone was going to
tell them, if anything at all. Hundreds of thousands
of tourists had kissed it, hoping for the gift of a silver
tongue, and Maddy doubted any of them had gotten
more than chapped lips. She wanted this whole nightmare to go away, for the unicorn to get up and walk off,
and for the Tuatha to go back to Tír na nÓg. Most of all,
she wanted Granda, Roisin, Danny, and herself to walk
out of here and go home for dinner. These thoughts
marched dully round and round in her head until one
faerie strode up to Seamus and injected fear straight
into her blood.

"NO!" Maddy yelled, her voice climbing an octave
with panic. "Not her!"

Fachtna had turned her blood-red gaze on her and
bared her filed teeth in a parody of a smile. "You have
no right to deny me, Feral Child," she rasped. "I am the
sword arm of the Winter Queen, her representative in
all things."

"She is right, Maddy," said Seamus. "She is Liadan's
captain. No one has the right to tell her no."

"I don't care!" said Maddy. "The last time she got me alone on the grounds of the castle, she tried to stick a blade in my throat."

"We are under a banner of truce. She cannot harm you, Maddy," said Seamus.

"She'll find a way!"

"Maddy, be reasonable," warned Seamus.

"Reasonable? That would be like, being mature, right?" asked Maddy.

"Exactly!" said Seamus.

"Well, maturity comes with age, and if you send her into the castle with me, I won't ever mature more than a couple of hours," said Maddy, folding her arms and jutting her jaw. "If you want me to go along with all this, then: Pick. Someone. Else."

Seamus sighed and turned away. Fachtna snarled and strode over to Maddy, her huge wings standing stiff from her back, quivering with her rage. Granda, Danny, and Roisin stepped closer to Maddy so she was partially shielded from the war faerie. "I will not forget this insult, Feral Child," she said. "You will pay for this, in blood and pain."

Maddy's knees shook as she glared back, but her voice was strong and low. "Just add it to the list of things I have done to make you angry, Fachtna," she said. "But I won this round."

Fachtna's tattooed skin rippled as she tensed every muscle in her body. Her fingers flexed on her sword hilt, and Maddy tried not to swallow as she wondered if Fachtna was angry enough to violate the truce and draw her sword anyway. After a long moment, Fachtna whirled away to stalk back to the Winter Court.

So that was how Maddy ended up climbing the steps in the tower of Blarney Castle with Tuatha before and behind her. Light glimmered around their bodies and lit the narrow stairway. Maddy hated these stairs. They were narrow and steep, their edges worn to slippery pouty lips from centuries of feet running up and down them. There was a rusty iron rail bolted into the wall, and she clung to it with white-knuckled fingers. The tall Tuatha were bent almost double as they squeezed up the narrow stairwell, the shadows on the wall scuttling on ahead of the living bodies. Maddy paused, puffing, and she snatched a look over her shoulder. She could see the white face of Connor, Liadan's gancanagh, behind her. He had been picked in Fachtna's place, and while Maddy wasn't wild about any of the Winter Court, she felt safe enough from Connor as long as he didn't try to touch her.

Granda and Dr. Malloy had been the only Sighted ones allowed to come with Maddy. Granda had sent Roisin and Danny home. They had both protested loudly at the sight of Maddy's white and fearful face, but Granda had insisted. "There is nothing you can do here. Go away home, and spin your granny a tall tale until we come back."

Maddy's breath misted faintly in front of her face. The inside of the castle was always a few degrees colder than the outside world, and its walls wept night and day as if in despair at the ruin it had become. The stone smelled like the damp earth of a freshly dug grave even though only faint smears of grime could be seen on the steps. Weeping water gathered in every pit and dip, making it treacherous underfoot. Maddy's rubber-soled sneakers squeaked from time to time as they skidded on the gray stone.

Her own labored breathing and that of Granda and Dr. Malloy roared in her ears. Nothing of the outside world could be heard inside the narrow stairwell. The grounds had been pitch black as they hurried through them, the only sounds being the nearly bare branches rattling in the wind, the deep rushing of the river that cut the estate in half, and the tortured rasp of a fox's bark. But in the castle, all she could hear was the sound of mortal breathing; all she could see was the stooped Tuatha ahead of her, and all she could feel was the weight of all that stone piled above her head.

On and on the stairs went, until Maddy could feel the panic of claustrophobia clawing into her throat. Sweat beaded her brow, and when at last cool night air opened over her head, she threw herself forward gratefully to cling to a tooth of the battlements.

The wind at the top of the castle was a different animal. It shouldered its way past her, howling in her ear as it went. Below her she could see the pavilions of the Tuatha courts spread out, and sounds of music and laughter drifted up to the lonely battlements. Liadan's white tent alone was silent.

"Do you know why we are here?" asked Seamus as everyone gathered around Maddy, the Tuatha surrounding her with a glowing nimbus.

"Haven't a clue," said Maddy.

"Do you know what the Blarney Stone is?"

Maddy shrugged. "I've heard a few legends. It was the gift of a goddess, or it's part of the battlements they used as a privy hole so the Irish could have great fun watching the English kiss a toilet. That's about it."

Seamus sighed. "When are you going to learn not to speak lightly of things you know nothing about? The Blarney Stone was a gift from the Tuatha to the Celts. It's a Seeing Stone of the Coranied—it links this world directly to Tír na nÓg. Every time someone presses their lips to the Stone, the Coranied harvest their dreams and their nightmares, for their mistress the Morrighan. Their Stones around Ireland are what feed the dark faeries and keep Tír na nÓg alive. For allowing the Coranied to tap into their minds, the ancient Celts were given a promise that Tír na nÓg would stand forever and the Tuatha would have no need to find territory in the mortal world."

"What's this got to do with me?" asked Maddy.

"The Coranied are seers and prophets. They can see into the future, and if you have a part to play in bringing the attacker of the unicorn to justice, they will know. They answer only to the Morrighan, and they want what she wants—balance. Balance keeps both our worlds safe. Tuatha and mortal alike can trust what they say."

"Will the Coranied know who attacked the mare?"

"They might. But they see the past only in fragments."

"And if I do this, I can go?"

"That depends on what the Stone judges your fate to be. The Stone will speak through you, and we will all know its judgment."

Maddy looked at Granda. His eyes were dark in his face, and his lips were pressed into a straight line. He gave a slight nod. Maddy sighed. "Fine. Let's get it over with."

The floors in the middle of the castle tower had crumbled away, and the battlements were a mere catwalk around a yawning pit. There was a thin iron rail fencing her off from certain death, but Maddy kept one hand on the stone skin of the battlements and walked as close to them as she could. The empty space that gaped just inches from her feet was an impenetrable black that gave no hint of the vertiginous drop and bone-shattering, organ-crushing landing that awaited her if she fell.

She walked cautiously to the area where the Blarney Stone was built into the battlements. It was a bit of a family tradition to kiss the Stone. Granny and Granda's house was full of pictures of her cousins doing it in their Holy Communion clothes, but this would be Maddy's first time. She peered down through the gap in the wall to the pale ribbon of the concrete path hundreds of feet below and gulped.

"It's easy enough," said Granda. "Just lie flat on your back, hold on to the bar in the wall, lean out, and kiss the battlements. I'll have a tight hold of your legs."

"Do I have to kiss it?" asked Maddy, wrinkling her nose. "It doesn't look very hygienic."

"It hasn't killed anyone yet," said Seamus. "Just put your hand on it, if you have to, but get a move on."

So Maddy, not without a small amount of trepidation, lay on her back and dangled her torso out over the dizzying drop. She screwed her eyes up to ignore the sight of treetops far below her and put her palm flat against the Blarney Stone.

chapter seven

For a second, nothing happened. Maddy felt the blood in her head rush to her eyeballs, and she thought, *Well, this makes me look really stupid.*

Then she felt a tugging sensation on her hand, and even though she could still see her own pink flesh against the Stone, she could definitely feel her hand being sucked into the Stone, the rock closing over it as tight as a vice.

She forgot the massive drop below her as panic took over, and she twisted and bucked to pull her hand free. Seamus leaned down hard on her legs to keep her steady and said, "Relax, Maddy. Don't fight it. The sensation will pass in a moment, but you have got to relax. Your hand is fine—it's not really inside the Stone. It's just the way the Stone makes you feel as it makes a connection with you. Look at your hand, Maddy. You can see it!"

"You come down here and relax!" she yelled, as her hair whipped around her face and her head began to throb.

As suddenly as it came, the sucking sensation was gone, and Maddy could not see or hear anything. The world went black for a split second, and then it was like someone had switched on a light. She was standing upright in a round stone room. She lifted her shaking hands in front of her face and then plucked at her clothes. Nothing was sealed in stone, no one was holding on to her, and she was definitely the right way up. She looked around her and noticed *who* was in the room with her.

Twelve black-robed figures drifted toward her. She could not see a hand or hear a footfall, and their faces were shrouded with such large hoods that all she could make out was pinpricks of light glittering in the rough vicinity of their eye sockets. The room was dimly lit by candles that smoked greasily. Cauldrons bubbled all around, books were stacked in every nook and cranny, and a raven cocked its head to glare at her with its bright black eye on a perch that looked suspiciously like it was carved from bone.

The Coranied. Maddy felt like she had been dropped into a snake pit.

Feral Child, whispered a dozen sibilant voices in unison, the words blooming inside her head. *Welcome.*

"Where am I?" asked Maddy. "How did I get here?"

Your body is still at the castle, flesh joined to stone. Only your mind has traveled to speak with us in the Shadowlands of Tír na nÓg. Your body is no more than an illusion.

Without taking her eyes off the Coranied, Maddy reached out to touch a nearby stack of books. Her hand passed right through, and she could feel nothing.

Why do you disturb us? Do you still seek death?

"No, not anymore," said Maddy.

Ah, your heart does not tell it so, child. Anger and hate still run through your veins, and lies drip from your tongue like snake venom. Why lie, when we can so easily give you what you want?

"I *don't* want it," said Maddy. "I'm not that girl anymore."

You will always be that child. Always. The Coranied tipped their heads to one side and then the other in a mechanical gesture. The raven fluttered on its perch and cawed. The hissing voices continued. *Then if not for death, why come you? What does your head desire you to seek that it ignores the cries of your heart?*

"An answer," said Maddy.

To what?

"A question," said Maddy. "Someone has attacked the unicorn mare . . ."

We know, said the Coranied with an impatient twitch of twelve pairs of shoulders. *The whole world knows and hides its face in horror.*

"Who did it?" asked Maddy.

That we do not know. It is hidden from us.

"Was it a faerie or a human?"

It is a thing that is neither one nor the other but with stripes of both.

"Superb," muttered Maddy. Louder she asked, "Can it be caught?"

The laughter that limped around the room sounded as dry and dusty as a corpse's cough. *That is not your question, Feral Child.*

"What *is* my question?"

WHO must track it, WHO must bring it to bay? And is that "who" you?

Maddy ground her teeth. "I know the answer to that question," she said. "It's not going to be me. Not this time. I've done enough."

There is no such thing as enough. It will be you, whether that pleases you or no.

"Why?" asked Maddy, her angry tone ringing against the stone. "Because of fate? Destiny? I don't believe in that!"

Nor do we.

"Then why?"

Balance. We live for order and peace. You bring balance between the mortal world and Tír na nÓg. The Morrighan charges us to maintain balance so that the Land never changes and her people are always safe. Some seek to disturb that balance. By your very nature, you are the counterpoint.

"Why me?"

When their need is great, your people have a Hound that watches them in the night and guards against the Tuatha. Once there was a Hound in Ireland so fierce he dared to bark at Meabh and bar her way, when she craved a bull so pure and white that she would have soaked the ground with the blood of men to have it. You are the new Hound. As we say, it is your nature. What kind of Hound you will be remains to be seen.

"I won't do this!" said Maddy.

You will. It is your nature. Nor will you be alone. There is one who lives in Tír na nÓg who can help you. See . . . The Coranied stepped to one side and raised cloaked arms to point at a cauldron.

Maddy walked over and gazed down at the water that bubbled away inside it. As she looked at it, the water smoothed to soft ripples. An image began to form just beneath the surface, of a man with long shaggy black hair, dressed in blue plaid. His hair was plastered to his head with water, and a massive sword was gripped in his hand. He was staring ahead of him, his face heavily lined by grief and anger. By his side sat a huge Irish wolfhound, its coat so wet with rain it seemed to drag its shoulders down. It turned its head to look at Maddy, and its eyes were human, blue, and sad. But the water began to bubble again, and the image shattered and dissolved in front of her.

"Who was that?" she asked.

That is Finn mac Cumhaill, the greatest hero Ireland has ever known. A man whose legend is so powerful it has taken on a life of its own, and he lives now in the Shadowlands with his Fianna, his tribe. A powerful man still and a dangerous enemy.

Bodiless or not, Maddy felt giddy with relief. "Even I have heard of him. This is going to be easy! I can explain what is going on, and *he* can find the unicorn hunter."

It is not mac Cumhaill who will help you, but the wolf-hound at his side, Bran. She is the gentle huntress, the only animal that will bring the hunter to bay and allow you to take it alive. Bran always brings her prey back alive. You must persuade mac Cumhaill to lend her to you.

"Would it not be easier all round to get Finn mac Cumhaill to find this hunter?"

Mac Cumhaill turned his back on the mortal realm long ago. He cannot walk above the mound. The hunter could hide from him too easily.

"All right then, how am I supposed to get him to hand over Bran?"

It is your task to find out. We can help you no more.

"Great." Maddy sighed. "Have you shown me all that you can See?"

We have shown you all that we think you should *see.*

Maddy looked at the cauldrons that bubbled with the hopes, dreams, nightmares, and everything else that could lurk in the corners of a human soul.

"The Tuatha are threatening war with humans over this," said Maddy. "Can I balance things out enough to stop it? Can you see if the war will happen? Will famine come again?"

You have as many futures as you have choices, Feral Child. And your choices will tip the scales between war and peace, famine and plenty.

"So what choices should I make?"

No one can dictate your conscience. You are a free creature, but we can see a day coming where you will need to decide where your loyalties lie.

"What do you mean?" said Maddy.

You have the future of two worlds resting in your hands. Who knows how each decision you make will reverberate through the lives of millions?

Exhaustion swept over Maddy's mind. It had been a long day, and she really wasn't ready to be responsible for a hamster, never mind millions of people. "I can't do this," she whispered.

You must.

"Send me home, please," said Maddy. "I need to rest."

As you wish, Feral Child, said the Coranied.

"I wish everyone would stop calling me that," she muttered, as a gray mist obscured the tower room and the Coranied, leaving her in a swirling no-man's-land.

Chuckling drifted around her in the fog, a low evil laugh.

What shall we call you instead? What will please your ears? Walking curse? The doom of Tír na nÓg?

"Who are you?" called Maddy.

You mean what *am I?*

"You're the Stone, aren't you?" said Maddy. "What do you want?"

What do I want? I am merely a humble servant of the Coranied, the stone sentinel of Tír na nÓg. I have no wants, no needs, no desires.

"Are you passing judgment on me?"

Done. You are the new Hound. What the Coranied See and speak, I also See and hear.

"Then let me pass," said Maddy. "Unless the Coranied have told you to keep me here."

That whispering laugh sounded in her ears again. *Tarry a while, Feral Child. For I also See far and wide, and I can speak prophecy too. I am no inert tool, cold and dead when not in its master's hands.*

"I've had a prophecy," said Maddy. "One's enough, so let me back into my body." The mist boiled around her as the Stone hissed in anger. A grinding pain started in the wrist of the hand that was trapped in the mortal world. Maddy gripped it and moaned with pain. She looked at her hand in shock. How could the Stone inflict pain on a body that didn't exist? *It's all in my head*, she thought. *Don't think about it, and it can't hurt.*

It seems the Hound is an arrogant puppy who would go from me and not ask my wisdom, said the Stone. *For such things have I Seen. You would be wise to know your future, Feral Child.*

The bones in Maddy's hand ground together as if stone teeth were chewing on them. Maddy screamed in pain. It was no use; she couldn't think it away. "What are you doing?" she yelled. "Let me go!"

Listen first and know your future. I See fear advance before you and blood bubble through the ground where your feet touch. All who know you will be laid low by grief and pain. Fire and flood will be your companions. War is your new mother, and she will kiss you with cold, cold lips. This is your future, Hound, as it was the future of every Hound before you. Men may sing of your deeds when you are long dead, but they will curse you while you live!

Maddy hugged herself as the agony flamed up her arm, setting nerves and tendons alight. She closed her eyes and screamed as the world went black again.

The next thing she knew, she was back on the top of the dark, cold castle, and she scrambled away from hands outstretched to help her out, clutching her own tortured hand to her chest. She backed up until she was crouching against the iron railings, her clothes clinging to her back in a cold sweat, with no thought of the drop behind her. She shivered and spread her fingers out and stared.

They were perfect, unharmed. She turned her hand over, searching for bruising, blood, any mark that had been left by the pain the Stone had inflicted on her. There was nothing, and the pain was gone. It had all been in her mind.

She looked up at the white, set faces that surrounded her and almost spat with rage. "You wanted me to put my face against that thing!" she said to Seamus, as he looked down at her with an unreadable expression. "It made me feel as if it were chewing on my hand! Did you know it was going to do that?"

No one answered her. She looked from face to face. "What?"

"Maddy . . ." began Dr. Malloy. He choked on his words and stumbled to a halt before starting again. "We heard, we all heard . . ."

"What? Me screaming my head off?"

"No, not that," said Dr. Malloy. "We heard . . ."

"We heard the Stone's judgment," interrupted Seamus, and the other faeries nodded in agreement. "Its words poured out of your mouth when you were joined with it. It declared you the new Hound."

Maddy looked back at Seamus. "Did it now? That's news to me," she said.

"Don't you lie, Maddy. We all heard it," growled Seamus. "You are the new Hound, and it is your task to find the creature who attacked the unicorn mare."

Maddy looked at Granda who stared at his boots, the picture of misery.

"I don't remember any of this," she said.

"You can't deny it," said Connor. "The Stone spoke through your lips."

"How do you know it was the Stone?" said Maddy.

"What?" asked Connor, looking bewildered.

"How do you know it was the Stone?" repeated Maddy. "I was in so much pain I could have been yelling in Arabic for all I know."

"Of course it was the Stone!" said Seamus, his voice rising in irritation.

"Prove it," she said, climbing to her feet and dusting her hands off on her jeans.

"What?" yelled Seamus, looking so angry she thought his head was going to explode.

"Go on, prove it," said Maddy, folding her arms across her chest. "Prove it was the Stone and everything it was saying was true and I'm the new Hound, rabbit, whatever, and that it's my job to sort out this mess with the unicorn."

The mortal men and the faeries alike stared back at her as she looked from face to face, a mixture of anger, frustration, and, in the case of Granda and Dr. Malloy, fear, chasing across their faces.

"You can't, can you?" said Maddy cheerfully.

"Faeries cannot lie!" said Connor.

"That doesn't mean you know what the truth is in the first place, does it?" asked Maddy, glaring back at him. "Until the lot of you can prove you know what you are talking about with this Hound nonsense, you can find someone else to do your legwork for you and take all the risks. Someone taller, older—you know, a *grown-up*. And until you can do that, I'm going home." She turned and strode off toward the stairwell, Granda and Dr. Malloy following closely behind.

chapter eight

THEY MANAGED TO WALK THROUGH THE TUATHA camps and the castle grounds with no one trying to stop them or harm them. Seamus and the faeries representing the courts made no attempt to follow them. As far as Maddy could tell, they stayed up on the battlements after Maddy, Granda, and Dr. Malloy had left. Probably too busy discussing a problem none of them had ever encountered before. Maddy would bet money that no one had ever asked the faeries to prove they were telling the truth. Everyone just took it as gospel that they did and that they never got things wrong.

Still, her skin crawled as they walked through the Tuatha camp. Most of the faeries were feasting, drinking, and capering about to their wild music, but a few stopped and stared after them with frowns marring their beautiful faces. She waited for a shout to go up behind them telling them to stop and for a long, triple-jointed hand to clamp down on her neck, but it seemed that the faeries were content to let them go if Seamus had done so. But that did not stop cold sweat from trickling down her back or her legs feeling shaky and hollow with fear. Her eyes strained to achieve the impossible and look behind her without her turning her head or snapping the ligaments that held her eyeballs in their sockets. As the tension grew too much for her, she began to turn ever so slightly, but Granda saw her and grabbed her elbow.

"Don't look back," he hissed through clenched teeth. "Don't give them any reason to follow us or stop us."

So she stumbled on between the two men, their breathing harsh in the blackness of the night that cloaked the grounds. She almost cried with relief when they finally reached the car parking lot and its streetlights. But as they turned to face each other and she saw the expression on Dr. Malloy's face, she shrank back into her jacket. He looked frightened and just a little bit angry, as if Maddy were a bomb waiting to go off.

"Do you know what you have done, girl?" he said, keeping his voice low. "You can't trick the Tuatha and get away with it!"

"Leave her alone," Granda warned.

"You heard what she was saying when she was connected to the Stone—we all did!" said Dr. Malloy. "We can't shelter her. The Tuatha will come for her sooner or later."

"Thanks to Maddy's trick it will be later, and that buys us time to think," said Granda.

"Time to think about what?!" Dr. Malloy struggled to keep his voice down, but his face was reddening with rage. "She can't get away from them, and you can't keep her!"

Granda's face turned a red to match Dr. Malloy's, and he opened his mouth to answer back, when a tiny snowflake fluttered lazily down between them and came to rest on the toe of his boot. The three of them stared at it, as it melted on the black leather. Maddy looked up, but only drizzle drifted down to coat her skin.

The fury drained out of Dr. Malloy's face. "It's started."

"Nothing has started," snapped Granda. "You heard Meabh—she can cure the mare, given enough time."

"Can she stop her from being killed though?" said Dr. Malloy. "Because apparently they need your granddaughter to do that. I have family of my own, Bat. I'll not see them die so you can keep one child. You have plenty of other grandchildren."

Maddy gasped at his callousness. Granda stared hard at the doctor, a muscle jumping in his jaw as he ground his teeth. Dr. Malloy stood his ground, but his eyes began to dart about. He had the expression of a man who knew he had gone too far.

"Go home, now," said Granda. "We'll talk later."

"That we will," said Dr. Malloy. "And don't think I won't be telling the other Sighted about tonight," he said over his shoulder as he scuttled away.

Granda stood next to Maddy and carried on grinding his teeth, his hands clenched into fists at his sides. He eyes roved over the village, and Maddy knew she should just give him time to calm down. But it was cold, and the tips of her fingers and toes were beginning to ache.

"Granda?" she asked in a small voice.

"What, love?" he said, his eyes still staring into the distance.

"Can I have fish and chips?"

He looked down at her then and unclenched one hand to stroke her hair. "Course you can."

Granda said nothing more to her, not even when they were waiting for their fish and chips. Not on the walk up the lane to the little cottage on the square, with the smell of vinegar tickling their nostrils and the wrapped paper parcels hot in their hands. He was going to think for a while about what she had done, she knew, and then she was going to cop an earful. She was just relieved that he looked worried rather than furious.

chapter nine

SHE *did*, HOWEVER, USUALLY TELL ROISIN EVERY-thing, and she was now getting nagged to within an inch of her life.

"I cannot *believe* you lied to the Tuatha, and Seamus, Cernunnos, whatever he's calling himself at the moment . . . of all the Tuatha," said Roisin, as they flicked through reference books in the school library the next day. "You're never going to get away with this."

"Why not?" asked Maddy.

"Have you ever gotten away with lying to Granny and Granda?" asked Roisin.

Maddy thought about this. Granny had an uncanny ability to know when Maddy had done something wrong. "No."

Roisin pushed her glasses back up to the bridge of her snub nose and glared at Maddy through smeared lenses. "Then what makes you think you are going to get away with this?"

Maddy shrugged. "I dunno. Luck?"

Roisin snorted. "Yeah, because that's what I always say about you, Maddy: you're lucky." Her voice dripped with sarcasm.

Maddy sighed and leaned back against the book-shelves. They had hidden themselves at the back of the library, and her skinny butt was going numb from sitting on the paper-thin carpet tiles. Roisin was panicking and doing what she always did in a tight spot— research. The school librarian would have had a fit if he had seen all the books that lay scattered on the floor around them.

"I told you, I'm not getting involved, not this time," said Maddy. "Someone else can sort this out."

"But you *are* involved," said Roisin. "Every bit of trouble around here always seems to involve you. And because, for some strange reason I haven't worked out yet, we're friends, that means I get involved too."

Roisin went back to leafing through a reference book, while Maddy seethed quietly. It did not help that Roisin was right as usual. "Besides, the Tuatha *know* you are lying, and as soon as they can prove it, they are going to have all three of us running around Blarney or Tír na nÓg, avoiding the pointy bit of a sword," continued

Roisin. "Personally I would like to be prepared with some kind of plan before that happens."

The library was overheated as usual, and Maddy's eyelids were heavy with tiredness and boredom. She let them droop and listened to the slow whisper of the pages turning beneath Roisin's fingers.

Roisin let out a deep sigh. "But how can we plan for this?"

Maddy's eyes snapped open, and she saw Rosin's big brown eyes fill with despair.

"Don't, Ro," she whispered. "Let's not talk about it."

"We have to," said Roisin. "You probably didn't hear much about this stuff in England, but this is what we are facing." She slid a heavy hardcover book on Irish history on to Maddy's lap. Maddy didn't want to look, but she dropped her eyes to the print anyway, turning the pages with trembling fingers.

Phrases floated in front of her frightened eyes. *An Gorta Mór*, the Great Hunger . . . one million people dead from hunger and disease . . . one million more fled on ships to other countries . . . evictions . . . bodies lying dead of starvation by the roadside . . . mortality rate of 30 percent on "coffin ships" from malnutrition and disease . . .

Maddy thought about what Meabh had said. *This time, there will be no ships on which to escape to other countries, because everywhere else will be dying too.* Tears began to slip down her own cheeks, and Roisin crept over to her and wrapped her arms around Maddy's shoulders.

"If the barrier fails completely on Halloween, then the Tuatha will pile war on top of famine," said Roisin. "It will be the end of the world."

"I can't do this," said Maddy. "It's too much."

"You have to try," said Roisin. "I'll help."

"That makes me feel so much better," said Maddy.

"Wiseass," said Roisin, imitating Maddy's London accent.

"Did you find out what it meant when they said I was the new Hound?" Maddy asked.

"Not exactly," said Roisin. "But I did find out who the Hound was that got into a fight with Meabh."

"And . . . ?" prompted Maddy, when Roisin fell silent.

"Well, it's pretty well documented that when Meabh went to war over a bull, Cú Chulainn stood in her way. Meabh still got the bull though."

"Cú Chulainn—the Hound of Ulster?" asked Maddy, hiking an eyebrow with surprise. "They're saying I'm like him? That I'm a muscly superhero of Celtic legend, with a big sword and shield and everything?"

"Uh-huh," said Roisin, watching Maddy's face carefully.

Maddy stared at Roisin for a moment and then both girls burst out in peals of hysterical laughter, drawing the attention of an irate librarian, who shushed them into silence.

"Maddy?" whispered Roisin a few minutes later.

"Mmmm?"

"What if you are the Hound?"

Maddy glanced up at her quickly. "Don't you start!"

"But it would explain a lot, wouldn't it? Why all this stuff with faeries started happening when you came to live in Blarney . . . why they all seem to be drawn to you in a weird way."

"Ro, do I really look like some ancient Celtic warrior with mythical powers of strength, who can sort out a war between faeries and humans?"

"Honestly? No."

"There you go then. Trust me—this is someone else's mess to sort out. There is nothing we can do about it."

At 5 p.m., it was time to go home. Aunt Fionnula had left an irate message on Roisin's cell phone to say that Roisin was being picked up for her dinner *right now*, so Maddy helped her put the books back on the shelves.

"Granda will sort everything out," said Roisin. "They can't leave it all up to us."

"I hope so," said Maddy, although her insides warmed a little at the fact that Roisin had said "us."

Aunt Fionnula was waiting at the school gates, and she honked her car horn with impatience as soon as she saw Roisin. She did not smile or wave or give the slightest sign that she could see Maddy. Maddy knew that she did not have a chance of being offered a lift, so she said goodbye to Roisin and she walked off quickly in the direction of home.

Autumn was really biting down. The air was crisp and clear with the smell of rain. The last of the light was already fading from the sky, and the trees had ragged holes in their russet and gold finery. Maddy hunched her shoulders as the wind looked for gaps in her clothes with long cold fingers.

The walk home was divided into light and dark. On her left-hand side, the castle rose into the sky, its grounds guarded by a gloomy line of mature evergreens, thick and impenetrable. Only the occasional streetlight punctured the gloom. But on her right was an inviting pavement lined with houses where families were getting ready for dinner in glowing rooms. Maddy walked quickly toward the heart of Blarney village, forcing her eyes not to flick to the silent trees on her left. The thought that the barrier was breaking down between this world and Tír na nÓg gave her the creeps. If any faeries were watching from beneath those dripping branches, she was not going to give them the satisfaction of thinking that she cared.

She did dart a quick glance as she passed the entrance to the estate where Seamus rented his house, but his was the only one dark and silent. She wondered if a Tuatha could ever feel comfortable in that modern box, or if he was just sitting there in the dark while another world played out in front of his eyes. Or perhaps he was somewhere else, finding a way to trap Maddy into doing what he wanted. She shrugged off the prickle of apprehension that tiptoed down her spine on spider's legs and hurried on.

She tried not to give into the temptation to run on the wet pavement, all the while straining her ears and watching from the corners of her eyes for any sign of faeries around her, but all was quiet and perfectly normal. There was the usual traffic around the village— drivers were pulling into the supermarket to get some last-minute shopping done, and bus laden with off-season tourists was trying to squeeze its bulk around the narrow country corners of the village square. She could see the waiting staff in the local hotel setting up the restaurant for dinner and a smattering of customers in the local pub having a quiet game of pool.

She turned left and could see a little plume of smoke coming from the chimney of her grandparents' house. She was feeling chilled to the bone now, and she was looking forward to a cup of hot chocolate in front of the fire and a bit of TV before dinner. Granda would be home soon.

She smiled and could almost taste the sweetness on her tongue. Her stomach rumbled at the thought of a hot dinner.

But as she walked around the corner of the wall to the square, she saw a dog lying against the rough-cut stone, directly opposite her grandparents' front door. It was huge and black and shaggy, and it was no breed that she could name. It turned a massive square head to look at her, and Maddy nearly tripped over her own feet as she looked into yellow eyes as big as headlights.

It's just a dog, it's just a dog, it's just a dog that shouldn't be off the lead, just a dog . . . she thought as her hands shook and the tip of her front-door key skittered and scratched the lock as she tried to guide it home. She was desperate to turn around and face the animal, and her body was tense as she listened for the sound of a growl rumbling in its throat. But it stayed still and quiet, and she nearly wept with relief as the key shot home and the door opened as she turned it.

She should have kept walking. As the door swung open straight into her grandparents' little sitting room, a woman in plaid with red hair that tumbled around her and brushed the floor looked up from her granda's chair by the fire.

The Queen of Autumn had come for a visit.

chapter ten

MADDY STOOD FROZEN WITH SHOCK IN THE DOOR-way while Meabh smiled slyly at her. A few fallen leaves took advantage of the open doorway and scampered in around her ankles.

"Come in out of the weather, Maddy, for goodness sake, and close your mouth," fussed Granny, as she bustled out from the kitchen with a cup of tea in her hand. "Our guest will think you have no manners at all!" Meabh smiled up at Granny as she took the saucer from her hand, wrapping her long thin fingers around the delicate china.

"Thank you so much," she purred, her teeth hard and white against her ruby-red lips.

"Will you have a bit of cake with that?" asked Granny.

"I would love some," said Meabh graciously, and she smiled as Granny bustled back out to the kitchen.

Maddy looked over her shoulder at what was obviously, now that she took a long hard look at him, the Pooka. She stepped carefully into the house and closed the front door behind her, before sliding into a chair at the square dining table in the center of the room and glaring at Meabh.

"Who does my granny think you are?" she asked, cringing inside as she heard her voice give a little wobble with fear.

"A missionary collecting for the starving babies in Africa, a cause I understand is close to her heart," said Meabh.

A bark of laughter escaped Maddy's throat before she could shut her lips against it. "She's never going to believe that!"

"She's glamoured," said Meabh. "She will see whatever I tell her to see, and then she'll forget I was ever here."

Granny came out from the kitchen with a slice of fruitcake on a plate.

"Can I have some?" said Maddy, and she peered at Granny's eyes when she looked in her direction. Her pupils were reduced to pinpoints.

"Not before your dinner, Maddy. You know the rules," said Granny.

Not that glamoured, is she? thought Maddy.

"Well, this all looks lovely," said Meabh as she glanced down at the untouched food and drink cradled in her white fingers. "But I really need to have a little chat with Maddy all by myself so would you mind leaving us alone for a little while?"

"Of course!" said Granny, smiling away at Meabh like a loon. She walked back to the kitchen, shutting the door behind her without so much as a glance at Maddy.

"You'll fry her brains, doing that to her," said Maddy.

"She'll be fine," said Meabh, putting the tea and the plate on the corner of the table and pushing them away from her with the tips of her spindly fingers. They sat there in the silence, staring at each other. Maddy could hear Granny singing to herself as she washed dishes. The fire popped and crackled, and the clock ticked loud, but not a sound crossed Maddy's or Meabh's lips.

After a minute or two, Meabh threw back her head and roared with laughter.

"Oh, I do like you, Maddy!" she said. "You really are beginning to learn our ways, aren't you? Sitting there, waiting for me to say the first word, to give a hint as to why I am here, what I want."

"I have no idea what you're talking about," said Maddy.

"Yes, you do," said Meabh, still smiling. "You know, I never thought you could be this clever. All the time I've been watching you, I thought Roisin had all the brains, and you and Danny were just bringing along brute force. But you are learning, and that gives me hope that you can play the game."

"What game?" asked Maddy.

"The best game of all," said Meabh. "You're going to help me play a game of chess, with real kings and queens and knights and castles. If you're nice to me, I won't make you a pawn."

"Chess is boring," Maddy said.

"Maybe in your world," said Meabh. "But in our world it's life and death. Four courts, equally matched in power—what stops us from wiping each other out? We play games."

"I don't understand," said Maddy, shaking her head.

"Do you know the story of Oisín and Niamh?" asked Meabh.

Maddy frowned. "I think so. He was a musician and a singer, thousands of years ago, and he was taken to Tír na nÓg by Niamh, the faerie queen—"

"The Queen of the Summer Court," interrupted Meabh. "Go on . . ."

"But after three hundred years, he grew homesick and wanted to return to Ireland to see his friends. Niamh didn't want to let him go, but he insisted. So she gave him a white horse, and she told him that as long as he didn't get down from the saddle, he could leave and still come back to her. But when he was in the mortal world, he leaned down to help some men move a rock, the girth broke, and he fell to the ground . . ."

"Where the most beautiful man in Ireland turned to dust before their very eyes," finished Meabh in a sing-song voice.

"That really happened?" asked Maddy.

"Yes, but not quite the way the storytellers say," said Meabh. "Niamh did indeed fall in love with the mortal Oisín, and she did spirit him away to Tír na nÓg. But her husband was not impressed by how besotted she was with her new pet."

"Her husband was Aengus Óg—the god of love?" said Maddy.

"Exactly." Meabh nodded. "And didn't it make him look foolish, his wife infatuated with a creature far inferior to himself! But what could he do? Niamh is a bubblehead, but she's still a Tuatha regent. Aengus did not want to provoke his queen's anger by killing her mortal lover.

"What the storytellers do not say is that Aengus Óg looked outside his court for someone who would help him and keep it a secret, one who owed no oaths of loyalty to his wife," continued Meabh. "Niamh would never have let her lover leave, so it was I who brought Oisin that pure white horse—Embarr, my very own mount—and I told Oisin that he could leave and be back before his queen even knew he was gone. All would be well, I promised, as long as he did not get down from the saddle."

"But the girth snapped," said Maddy. "It was an accident!"

"Well, it doesn't take a genius to fray a girth to the point of breaking," said Meabh, spreading her fingers out and admiring her nails. "And even if it didn't break, I could trust Embarr to throw him to the ground."

"That's murder," said Maddy, her voice flat with anger.

"No, it was a convenient accident," said Meabh, wagging a finger playfully at Maddy. "Because now I have a monarch of a rival court who is in my debt. The point I am trying to make here is that when you are equal to your opponents in raw power, being clever, even devious, is the only way to get the upper hand. It is also a useful weapon when you are weaker than your opponents, as you are. As the new Hound, you're going to need all the help you can get."

"I'm not the new Hound," said Maddy. "None of this has got anything to do with me."

"That's how I know you have a talent for this game," said Meabh, smiling. "That was a very clever trick you played on Cernunnos, asking him to prove he was telling the truth. And I saw the way you looked at Niamh. Saw right through her, didn't you?" She stood up and had to bend her neck against the ceiling of the little cottage, she was so tall. The room suddenly got darker, and the flames rose higher in the fireplace, throwing the Tuatha's shadow huge against the wall. "But I'm not Niamh," Meabh said, her voice darker and thicker, with a rumble of thunder along its edge.

She moved so fast Maddy didn't have a chance to call for help. She saw a white blur, and then the Autumn Queen was bending over her, her long white fingers wrapped around the back of Maddy's skull, her palm pressing against her chin. Maddy kicked out and clawed at Meabh's hand, gasping for breath as Meabh lifted her from the chair to dangle in the air, her feet inches above the carpet. The Tuatha was so strong that her fingers didn't even twitch as Maddy's body jerked like a fish on the line.

"Quiet, little one," crooned Meabh, her green eyes glowing. "Have you ever seen a rabbit break its own neck trying to get loose from a trap? Hush, hush!"

Maddy gasped and then hung still, her fingers white at the knuckles where she clutched at Meabh's wrist. Her neck ached as her head tipped back on her spine, and the muscles in her jaw and cheeks burned where the bones of Meabh's fingers dug in.

"There is a war coming, but it will come at a time of my choosing and when it benefits my court most," hissed Meabh. "But this time I will have the Hound on my side."

Maddy tried to speak. "I'm not . . ." she began to mutter through clenched teeth, but Meabh squeezed tighter and cut the words off.

"Don't lie to me, child," said Meabh. "*I can smell your blood.* I *know* you're the Hound. But you're only a pup, and you won't last long in a Tuatha war, not without friends. Bend the knee, swear fealty to the Autumn Court, and I can help you find the unicorn hunter."

Maddy would have loved to reply to that, but gravity was keeping her jaw clamped shut in Meabh's hand. Meabh cocked her head and looked at her for a moment as the muscles in Maddy's neck and face screamed with pain. Then, without warning, she opened her fingers and dropped Maddy back into her chair.

Maddy gasped with relief and flexed her neck. She glared up at Meabh. "How exactly are you going to help me out?"

Meabh laughed, a throaty chuckle that excited the fire to leap and dance. "See how you negotiate the terms of your capitulation," she purred. "No words of defiance or anger—you play well. I am the Witch Queen—my court as your ally will strengthen your hand enormously here and in the Land. Not to mention the protection my faeries can give your loved ones. Especially those without the Sight—like your lovely granny."

Maddy's blood ran cold to hear Meabh talking about Granny. "I need to know your help is worth having before I hand over my allegiance."

"Do you now?" asked Meabh, settling herself back down in Granda's chair by the fire. "Well, I can't tell you *who* you are looking for, but I can tell you *what*."

"And?"

Meabh cocked her head again and looked at her with just one green eye, a bird-like movement that gave Maddy the creeps. "What do I get if I tell you?" she asked.

"My word that I will think about bending the knee," said Maddy.

"Is that all?" sneered Meabh.

"Trust me—it's more than you're getting right now."

Meabh stared at her, tapping her teeth with one long fingernail. "You have sharp teeth for such a little Hound."

"What does that even mean?" asked Maddy. "What's so special about being a Hound?"

Meabh shrugged. "In truth, nothing," she said. "It's just a title. It simply means you have the blood of heroes running through your veins, although it is much diluted these days. But you have seen the rest of the Sighted—timid, cowering creatures. So when one such as you comes along and dares to defy us, they get all excited and brave and call you the Hound, thinking back to Cú Chulainn. And some of the weaker-minded Tuatha think of him too, and they get nervous, thinking the Hound has returned to give us all a beating. It's only a title, and yet at the same time it's a nuisance for the feelings it whips up. So if you are going to go round calling yourself the Hound, girl, and causing ripples, I'd rather those ripples flowed out from my court and not into it."

"From what I've read, Cú Chulainn gave the lot of you a run for your money," said Maddy.

"Cú Chulainn was brave and unnaturally strong," said Meabh. "He could have married, had children, and lived a long and peaceful life, but he was told that if he picked up a spear, he would live a short one, full of glory, and his name would live on forever. He was too vain to resist. If anything is the mark of a Hound, it is stupidity. You've all been a little bit thick."

"So?" asked Maddy.

"So what?" asked Meabh.

"You were going to tell me what, but not who, I am meant to be looking for?" prompted Maddy.

"So I was," said Meabh. "Right after you swear an oath of fealty."

"Nice try."

Meabh grinned at her. "The Coranied told you the hunter was neither human nor faerie, but something with stripes of both, correct?"

"Yeah. So?"

Meabh tutted. "Patience! No child with both faerie and mortal parents has been born for centuries, so that leaves only one other possibility—a split soul."

"What's that?" asked Maddy.

"It is what is left behind when mortals have near-death experiences in Tír na nÓg. They seem to hold on to a sense of themselves, and they gather in the Shadowlands of the Coranied, listening to the whispers of your kind."

"I thought stolen children didn't come back," Maddy remarked.

"Do you always believe what you are told?" said Meabh. "And it's not just children who get taken—Liadan isn't the only one who likes to play with mortals."

Maddy gave Meabh a sharp look but decided not to ask any questions about that. "Nothing you have said explains why I need the dog Bran."

"Have you ever seen a soul?" asked Meabh. "Ever felt the weight of it in your hands? How it feels, how it *smells*?"

Maddy nodded as the obvious dawned on her. "The hunter has no scent. So why do I need a hunting dog to track it?"

"The unicorns are magic made flesh; *they smell*."

Maddy was confused. "But we know where the mare is. She's five minutes up the road."

Meabh rolled her eyes. "Give me strength. We know where she is *here*, in this world, but we have no idea yet where she fell in Tír na nÓg."

"I don't get how they are in both worlds at the same time," said Maddy.

Meabh sighed. "They are old magic, girl, older than the Tuatha. They are the life force of the earth, the male and the female, the yin and yang that keep *balance* within and between all living things. They are the magic that breathes life into this world, made of flesh, and into Tír na nÓg, the realm of dreams. They are the foundation stones our worlds are built on, so they exist in both at the same time." She leaned forward. "And someone has decided to take away one of those foundation stones. Now do you understand?"

Maddy nodded. "How can you be so sure the hunter will attack her again?"

"The mare is sure it wanted her death—that's enough for me. Mortal-side we can ring her with Tuatha guards and fend off an attack. But we still don't know where she is in Tír na nÓg, and sending ordinary hounds to track her is risky. Their instincts might take over, and they might attack if they find her vulnerable."

"But Bran never would, right? She always brings her prey back alive. Why is that?"

"Bran has certain qualities that make her a bit special," said Meabh, a sly smile playing about her lips.

"So you want me to go into the Shadowlands of Tír na nÓg to persuade Finn mac Cumhaill to hand over Bran, and then you want me to go chasing the unicorns around in the hope of catching the hunter on its next attempt?" said Maddy.

"Bravo! The penny drops . . ."

"And time is obviously a factor, seeing as the hunter might already be looking for the mare and I'm still sitting here?"

"Obviously."

"So why are the Tuatha not going straight to Finn mac Cumhaill? He's in your world—it would be a lot faster than trying to force me."

"Ah," said Meabh, sitting back in her chair and steepling her fingers in front of her face. "There we have a tiny little problem."

"Which is?"

"Oisin was Finn's son," said Meabh. "And Finn's wife was a Tuatha who disappeared under strange circumstances."

"Did the Tuatha make her disappear?"

"That would not be an unreasonable assumption to make," said Meabh. "But regardless of who did what to whom, the fact is mac Cumhaill hates the Tuatha, and he will never listen to us. But he might—*might*—be persuaded by a mortal. He might have respect for the Hound, although you do not make a very awe-inspiring figure."

Maddy sat back in her own chair and stared at Meabh through narrowed eyes. "You're frightened of him, aren't you?"

Meabh lowered her hands to grip the armrests of her chair. "What makes you say that?"

"You've got an ancient Irish hero sitting in Tír na nÓg who could sort all your problems out, and you're telling me that there is not a single Tuatha who dares to go near him? No one who can make him do what you want, no matter how desperate you are?" said Maddy, a smile lighting up her face. "He has made the Shadowlands his own territory, right under everyone's nose."

"Do I look frightened of *you*, Feral Child?" asked Meabh, her voice soft with menace.

Maddy gulped. "No."

"Remember that," said Meabh as she stood up, the crown of her head brushing the low ceiling of the cottage. She gathered her plaid around her shoulders to keep her warm while stray shadows climbed her body to nestle into the folds of the cloth. She walked to the door of the cottage and opened it on to the night. The Pooka sprang to his feet and padded to her side, nuzzling her palm.

"What are you?" asked Maddy. "God or faerie?"

"Your people have so many names for us," said Meabh, as she scratched the Pooka behind the ear. "You used to call us the Fair Ones, and that is where the word *faerie* came from—did you know that? Your names mean nothing to me. I am Tuatha, and that is enough. But again, Maddy, you're not asking the question you really want to ask."

"Which is?"

"'Which would be safer to anger—a god or a faerie?'" said Meabh. "That is what you really want to know. And the simple answer is that making any Tuatha angry, especially me, would be a very, very big mistake. And it would be a mistake to fail with mac Cumhaill, so tread carefully."

"He is *never* going to hand Bran over!" Maddy was practically yelling with frustration.

Meabh tutted, her eyes sparkling with laughter. "There's always a way, Maddy."

"Care to explain how?"

"Care to swear an oath of fealty?"

Maddy ground her teeth while Meabh laughed, her fingers buried deep in the shaggy fur of the Pooka. It wagged its tail as it gazed adoringly at its mistress.

"Why would I care about keeping the hunter alive? I know it's a faerie that did this—the Sighted are scared of their own shadows!" said Maddy.

"Because you want to know who sent it, don't you, Maddy? You have all sorts of theories buzzing around that busy little mind of yours, and you won't be happy unless you find out who gave the order to poison the mare."

"How do you know someone else besides the hunter is involved?" asked Maddy.

Meabh shrugged her shoulders. "I don't. Join my court, Maddy, and you will have all the help you need," she said. "All my faeries, all my powers, all my riches, will be at your disposal."

"But only for your advantage," Maddy pointed out.

"Of course," said Meabh. "That is the nature of the game we play. Why should you be given all the power of a Tuatha court for nothing? Think on it."

She turned to go.

"Wait!" said Maddy. "How will I find you again, if I change my mind?"

"Just swear your oath, Maddy," said Meabh. "Say it to the air, and I will hear you. But I must admit, you've disappointed me tonight."

"Why?"

"Because there is one very important question you have forgotten to ask."

"What's that?"

"Well, if the boundaries between our worlds have broken down so much that I am able to walk among mortals outside the Samhain Fesh—who else is here?"

chapter eleven

IT WAS THE CLICK OF THE LOCK ON THE KITCHEN door that woke her, just a small sound that was almost drowned out by the dull tick tock of the clock on the mantelpiece. But she was so tense that her mind had not surrendered to a deep sleep, and that small sound had cracked like a gunshot to her straining ears.

She lay in the bed, blankets wrapped tightly around her, her eyes searching the empty gloom of her room for something to do while her brain panicked, her ears pricked for another telltale noise. She was almost wondering if she had imagined the sound of the door being opened, if she should risk getting out of bed to see if there really was anyone prowling through the sitting room on soft feet, when she heard the softest scratching.

Her mind raced through its memory banks, frantically trying to match the sound to anything it had on file. It was so soft, so tiny a sound, it could only be . . .

. . . hair! Stiffened with lime, combed into high spikes on the head of a creature that was too tall for the low cottage ceiling. It must have brushed against the plaster as she turned her head to look from one door to the other, wondering which one to open.

Maddy lay in her bed, as clear and light and frozen with terror as an icicle. Her breath caught in her throat and blocked any screams or cries for help. Her eyes widened as she watched the doorknob of her bedroom door turn slowly, the stiff mechanism chuckling sleepily.

The blade came in first. The silver sword gleamed softly in the pale moonlight that filtered through her thin bedroom curtains, before the door was pushed wider and the faerie ducked her head to make her way into Maddy's tiny bedroom. There was the soft scratching noise again, as her stiffened Mohican rippled against the door frame. Her blood-red eyes burned in her bone-white tattooed face, and her huge wings filled the door behind her, ice-frosted and transparent. They snapped shut like a flower as Fachtna stepped all the way into the room, the hollow bones and gossamer skin folding in on themselves to avoid injury in the tight space.

She grinned, baring her shark's teeth, and prowled toward the bed, every muscle tense and her eyes waiting for the slightest movement. But as Maddy lay motionless, her grin grew wider.

"Such a little thing you are," she crooned as she slid on to the bed, her bony knees pressing deep pits in the soft mattress. "I won't be needing this." She lifted her sword blade to her lips and kissed it, its keen edge piercing the white skin above her mouth. Bright blood welled up in the cut, trembled, and then burst its banks to roll slowly down her chin. She laid the sword on the quilt and leaned forward, her blood splashing on to Maddy's face. She heard a hiss as Fachtna drew a short, curved dagger from her belt. Fachtna pressed the point of the blade against the hollow of Maddy's throat, enough to make the skin dimple, but not enough to break it. She lowered her face until her hooked nose was almost touching Maddy's and her blood-red gaze was all Maddy could see.

"You're no Hound, girl," she sneered.

Maddy shook with fear and struggled to push the scream in her throat out into the room, but her mouth was locked shut.

"You're a rabbit. And I'm going to cook you and eat you, just like a rabbit. But first I'm going to slit you open from throat to groin and I'm going to pull your intestines out and wind them round and round my dagger like spaghetti. Ready?"

Fachtna's wings flared open and rattled as she pressed down hard with the knife . . .

Maddy screamed and sat bolt upright in her bed. Her blood thundered in her ears, and her pajama top was glued to her back with cold sweat. She gulped in lungfuls of air that turned her panicking brain as light as a bubble, while her eyes roved around the room and assured her that everything was normal. There was all her stuff piled haphazardly on shelves next to her bed, the curtains were drawn tight against the night, and there was *nobody* standing between the bed and the door, grinning at her.

It was just a dream, she thought, as she hunched over in the twisted sheets and slowed her hammering heart. *It was just a bad dream. Fachtna wouldn't know what spaghetti was!*

A nervous giggle escaped her lips before she clamped them shut. She listened for any sounds coming from her grandparents' room. Surely they had heard her yelling? But all was quiet and still, and the ponderous ticking of the clock in the living room just outside her bedroom door was the only sound in the sleeping cottage.

She slipped out of the warm bed and peeled her sweat-soaked pajamas away from her body. Her skin goose-pimpled in the chill predawn air as she grabbed jeans, a long-sleeved T-shirt, and a hooded sweatshirt from the chair beneath her window. She dragged them on and gently eased the door of her wardrobe open. Three jackets hung inside: her school jacket, a fake leather bomber she had begged Granny to buy her, and a denim one. All of them hung lopsided on the hangers, and out of habit she flicked her fingers against the pockets closest to her. Each time her fingertips hit dull metal, and she smiled. Faeries hated iron, and all of the Sighted ones kept a piece of iron on them at all times. Granda had his iron cuff, and he had once given Maddy a little iron crucifix to hang around her neck, but Maddy had wanted something with a bit of bite for when the sun sank and the faeries were stronger. So she had persuaded Granda to have three dull iron knives made for her. Then she had raided Granny's sewing box and had carefully unpicked the stitching in one pocket of each jacket, slipped a knife into the lining, and stitched a thin band of Velcro into the opening so that she could easily grab the weapon if she got into trouble. It had taken her hours and patience she didn't know she had; the lining of each pocket was spotted with rusty bloodstains where she had stabbed her clumsy fingers over and over with a needle. But it was worth it. She never left the house now without feeling for that comforting weight on her right hip.

She shrugged on her favorite, the fake leather bomber jacket, and slipped out into the living room. She peered around the curtain at the sky. It was still too dark to go anywhere; faeries were stronger in the dark, and dawn was only a faint silver smudge on the horizon. Stepping outside now, with the veil between the worlds so fragile, would be suicidal. She sighed through her nose and settled into Granny's chair by the fire. It was a bony, comfortless thing, a thin wooden frame with foam pads tied to it. It was horribly old-fashioned, but Granny refused to part with it.

Maddy leaned her head back against it and forced her eyes wide open in the dim room, fighting sleep. Her head rang with tiredness, and her stomach roiled, but the adrenalin the nightmare had woken in her still crackled like wildfire through her veins. There was no way she was going to get any decent sleep before the alarm went off for school, and experience had taught her that she functioned better on no sleep at all than with a couple of hours of fretful dozing.

Granda hadn't been too impressed last night when he realized a Tuatha de Dannan had made a house call. He had come in from work and immediately sniffed the air, which did have a tang of ozone to it, like the after-effects of a lightning strike. He lost it completely when Maddy told him it had been Meabh.

"There's a reason why she rules alone!" he had yelled, banging the table with the flat of his hand. "She's had two husbands, and both of them have died on the battlefield! Rumor has it she helped along the blades that did the deeds. Do you know how hard it is to kill a Tuatha de Dannan, never mind a monarch? But Meabh seems to have managed to do it twice. Out of all of them, she's the most treacherous, the most bloodthirsty . . ."

"What on earth are you shouting about?" asked Granny, as she bustled in from the kitchen, looking stern.

Granda had stared at her for a moment with his mouth open, probably trying to think up a good lie in a nanosecond.

"It's OK, Granny. We're not shouting at all," said Maddy in a soothing voice.

"Yes, you were. I just heard you," said Granny, looking confused.

"No, you didn't hear anything, anything at all," Maddy had said, still in a low, singsong tone. "You're not going to hear anything either, are you? Me and Granda are just having a nice, relaxed conversation."

Granny had relaxed, her face went slack, and her eyes glazed over. "No, you're right, love. I didn't hear anything. I'll just get dinner ready."

Granda had peered suspiciously after her before looking over at Maddy. "Glamoured?" he asked.

"To the eyeballs," said Maddy. "Meabh did it when she was here, and it seems to be taking a bit of time to wear off. Granny believes anything you say at the moment, which could be handy."

"What's that supposed to mean?" asked Granda.

"Well, it's a shame it's not parents' evening."

"Don't be a smart mouth," he had growled. "You're playing a dangerous game, Maddy. Clever as it was, the Tuatha will find a way around that little trick you played on them at the Blarney Castle, and then they'll come looking for you again. When they catch up with you, they won't be happy, and what are we going to do to stop them from taking their anger out on you? The Tuatha and the rest of the faeries are not something out of a Walt Disney film, singing silly songs all day while making daisy chains. They like the fear and pain and death of others, and you are just drawing them on to you."

"Oh, that's right, blame me!" yelled Maddy. "How is this my fault? What, because I did the right thing and went off to Tír na nÓg after Stephen when he was kidnapped last year? Because I'm not saying sorry for that!"

"Nobody is asking you to," said Granda.

"Oh no, nobody is *asking* me to," said Maddy. "But you were all thinking it when that unicorn turned up and then all the courts came trooping in. 'If it weren't for Maddy, we'd be tucked up safe in our beds.' What all of you Sighted should be thinking about is how to keep us all safe from them instead of scurrying around wearing ugly iron jewelry and hoping that they don't touch any of you when another kid goes missing."

Granda had looked at her for a long moment, an angry pulse beating in his jaw. "So I scurry, do I?" he had asked in a low, dangerously quiet voice.

Nervous, Maddy had crossed her arms over her chest. "I didn't say you personally."

"You didn't have to," said Granda. "I told you the reasons why no one ever goes after the children who disappear into the mound, and the adults too. They're gone, and drawing the wrath of the Tuatha down on the Unsighted in Blarney, like your granny, would be a terrible thing to do."

"Only they're not gone, are they?" said Maddy. "I proved that when I got Stephen back."

Granda snorted with contempt. "You got Stephen back because they let him go, remember? It was a trap all along, Maddy, and it nearly closed shut on you for good."

The scar on Maddy's shoulder burned as she remembered the fear and the smell of her own blood in her nostrils. She heard Liadan's voice in her head, soft and evil as a snake's hiss. *Look into my eyes, and I can give you your life back.*

Maddy had given herself a shake. "I still proved my point," she said. "We can get people back."

"No, you didn't!" yelled Granda. "How many times do I have to tell you? You got lucky. And so now, what are you saying—that because you got Stephen out, you're going to find whoever hurt the unicorn?"

"I never said that," said Maddy. "Going after Stephen was the right thing to do, the thing that all you adults should have done. This unicorn stuff has got nothing to do with me—"

"Then what are we arguing about?!" yelled Granda in exasperation.

"We're arguing about the fact that I GET BLAMED FOR EVERYTHING!" Maddy yelled back. "It is NOT my fault someone hurt a unicorn, and it's NOT my fault that Meabh decided to turn up on our front doorstep, so why am I being yelled at as if it were my fault?!"

"Stop being such a baby! I TOLD you not to go after Stephen. I made myself very clear on why it was a bad idea," said Granda. "I told you not to draw attention to us when the courts were meeting. You ignored me both times, and now I find Meabh has been in my house. You should have known better than to let her stop for a minute under this roof or to get into any kind of conversation with her."

"What was I supposed to do?!" said Maddy. "Granny let her in—she gave her food and drink. Doesn't that give her guest rights? I couldn't have thrown her out!"

"But you could have called me," said Granda. "You could have called me and gotten me to come home, and *I* could have dealt with her. Instead, you sat down and had a conversation with her. God only knows what she thinks you've promised."

Maddy had flushed with guilt. She hadn't told Granda about Meabh's demand of allegiance in return for protection. "I'm not thick . . ."

"Maybe not, but you do a good impression of it!" barked Granda.

They had stopped yelling for a moment and glared at each other, both of them enraged. Then Granda had taken a deep breath, and he tried very hard to speak in a calm voice.

"This is the way it's going to be," he said. "You have ignored everything I ever said to you about dealing with faeries. And whether it's down to you or not, the fact is that there have never been so many faeries around Blarney, certainly not in my lifetime. And Tuatha walking among us, threatening war, prophesying another famine . . ." He shook his head. "This is a bad business, and they seem to want you in the middle of it. I'm calling your Aunt Fionnula in the morning, and you are going to stay with her in Cork city . . ." Maddy began to interrupt, but Granda had held up his hand, his eyes flashing with anger. "You'll be safe in the city, surrounded by iron. This crisis will pass, and the Tuatha will be drawn back beneath their hollow hills. When everything is back to normal, you can come home."

"You know Aunt Fionnula hates me," said Maddy.

"This isn't a punishment, Maddy. She's the only one in the family who lives in the city," said Granda. "You might actually get to know each other better."

"You can't—" protested Maddy.

"There's a lot of things I can do, Maddy," said Granda, hitting the table so hard that Maddy had jumped in fright. "The only person around here who tells me I'm weak is you. But by God, you're going to learn! I admit it, Granny and I have spoiled you. We've been too soft. We didn't want to go too hard on you after you lost your parents. But now it's time to buck your ideas up. You *will* go and stay with Fionnula, whether you like it or not. You will be polite and you will make the effort to get along with her. And if doing so chokes you, then remember you brought it on yourself because you refused to listen to someone older and wiser! When all this dies down, you can come back. And maybe by then you'll have learned a bit more respect for me."

Maddy had glared back at him, tears threatening to spill from her eyes. "Don't do this to me," she whispered, her voice cracking.

"It's for your own good," said Granda. "Cry all you like, love, I'm still sending you to the city. I'm not having you sneak off to the mound behind my back. You might not find your way home this time."

"What if they don't give up?"

"They will. Faeries are easily distracted. The unicorn will recover, this crisis will pass, our world will return to normal, and the Tuatha will go back to fighting among themselves."

"They think I'm the Hound," whispered Maddy.

"You are NOT the Hound," said Granda fiercely. "You don't want that, Maddy, believe me." He looked toward the kitchen, where Granny was singing cheerfully. He and Maddy had been yelling at each other for ages, and normally she would have stormed into the room by now, all five feet nothing of her, to spread a bit of shock and awe and make them SHUT UP AND GIVE HER HEAD PEACE! But thanks to the glamour, she was in her own little world.

"You're right," Granda had grunted. "Her being glamoured does have its advantages." And he had sat down to the read the newspaper, leaving Maddy standing numb and hollow, her fists clenching and unclenching by her sides.

Maddy jerked awake in Granny's chair. The hollow feeling was back in her stomach, jostling for room with the nausea. Being sent away was what Maddy had always secretly dreaded. She knew her grandparents were old and it was hard work looking after a child. They had probably thought they were finished raising their family and they could enjoy themselves a bit, before her parents' car had spun off an icy road in Donegal and left her orphaned. Granda had said it was only for a little while, but what if they decided it was easier to leave her at Fionnula's? She hated her aunt, and she hated Danny and Roisin's three older brothers. Life there would be unbearable.

She got up and stretched in an effort to keep awake. The room was cold, and she thought longingly of her warm, soft bed, but she walked to the window and peeked around the edge of the curtain at the silvering sky. A few small birds had woken early, and they were singing sweet, bubbling songs that were full of summer. Crows huffed in sleepy, messy balls—it was too early for them to stir themselves and drown out the dawn chorus with their grating calls. Maddy waited until she saw the first yellow rays of the sun stretch chilled fingers across the village square, and then she crept quietly toward the kitchen.

The linoleum on the floor was slick and cold even through her thick socks. She stuffed her feet into the sneakers she had carelessly tossed beside the back door, working them from side to side to force them in without undoing the laces. She covered the bottom bolt on the back door with her free hand as she slid it open to disguise the sound of iron grinding on iron. She carried a kitchen chair over so she could reach the top bolt and hushed that with one hand as well. Next she felt under the china shepherdess on the kitchen shelf to find the back-door key. She slid it gently into the gleaming brass lock and turned it slowly, steadying her wrist with her other hand—each noise the tumblers made as they turned over in slow motion cracked in the dark. A sheen of sweat coated her upper lip as the door swung free of its frame and she escaped into the cold morning air.

She tiptoed across the gravel in the garden, cringing at each crunch under her feet, convinced that at any second the back door would be flung open and a furious Granda would spot her sneaking out on her own. Or even worse, an irate Granny—the glamour had worn off by bedtime, and she was back to being herself. Maddy crept over to the dog's kennel and called softly to George. The elderly terrier wasn't impressed at being woken up, and she practically had to drag him out, smelling to high heaven of dog, rumpled and warm where he had been lying in his blanket. Granda's hounds, Pedlar and Bewley, snored on, oblivious to the world outside their kennels. She snapped a red lead on to the collar around George's neck and opened the garden gate.

She picked George up and held him in her arms until she had jogged quietly around the corner, past the huge bed-and-breakfast inn that sat next to her grandparents' house and out into the square. George shivered and looked up at her grumpily as she set off across the grass, before heaving a huge sigh and trotting after her dutifully. The grass was bleached with dew, and her footprints left emerald wounds across its surface. Wisps of early-morning mist clung to the ground and drifted about like the last stragglers from a party. It looked very Celtic and romantic, and Maddy was sure it was the sort of scene that would have tourists reaching for their cameras, but it reminded her of faeries and made her nervous.

She looked at the grass and flicked glances out of the corners of her eyes to see if she could catch any sneaky movements. Her hand went to her pocket, and with the tip of one finger she eased the Velcro apart as quietly as she could and closed her fingers around the dull, rough iron knife. It was light, and all faeries should be tucked up beneath the mound by now—but the faeries in Blarney were not behaving as they should.

A crow swooped overhead and cawed, making her jump. They were close to the wall on the opposite side of the square from her grandparents' house now, and just as Maddy put her hand on the piled stones to climb over, George peeled his lips back from his teeth in a rumbling growl, the hair on his back and neck standing stiff with alarm.

There was a slight sound from the other side of the wall, just a few inches from where her hand rested. It sounded like the dull clink of glass, and Maddy froze, her mouth drying with fear. George crept forward on his belly, his growl getting louder. There was a funny smell in the air, and Maddy sniffed. It smelt like . . . oh, yuck, pee and sweat and dirty clothes.

A bearded head with a shock of dirty yellow hair popped over the wall. *"BANG, BANG!"* it shouted. Maddy squealed in fright and stumbled backward, at the same time as George launched himself at the scruffy, dirty figure that was clutching the brown beer bottles it had stolen from the trash left out by the pub.

"BAD BOY, GEORGE!" Maddy yelled as she dived for the little black and white terrier as he tried to climb the wall, his claws scratching furiously at the gray stone. The figure squealed and shrank away from the bristling terrier. Maddy wrapped her arms around his squirming body, the claws on his front paws raised ugly red marks on her hands as he struggled to get down.

Maddy grinned and shook her head when she saw who it was. "Bang, bang," said the little man again. "You're dead."

Bang Bang was notorious around the village. He wore the same clothes winter and summer—greasy black pants, shiny at the knees with age, filthy sneakers, a huge gray overcoat belted with a piece of rope, and a scarf knotted up to his chin. He stank because it seemed he never took anything off to wash it or himself. He lived in a cottage outside the village and shuffled around all day, picking up bits of trash and eating the food that the villagers gave him. At least, that's what

Maddy assumed—she had never seen him grocery shopping. Everyone called him Bang Bang because that was how he greeted people. He thought he was a cowboy, among other things.

Bang Bang stuck his tongue out at George, whose sharp barks were beginning to hurt Maddy's ears. "Nasty doggie," said Bang Bang.

"Sorry about him, Bang Bang. He's being a bit daft today," said Maddy, clamping her hand around George's muzzle.

"I've got a right to be here, you know," said Bang Bang, glaring at her. "I'm doing the queen's business, clearing up all this mess."

"I know, I know," said Maddy. "It's all right, Bang Bang. You gave me a bit of fright is all. I didn't know you were there."

Bang Bang looked at her suspiciously, and then his eyes cleared a little. He shuffled a bit closer, bottles clanking, and his particular body odor wafted over Maddy in a big, curling wave thick enough to surf.

"I got lots of things today," he said, rattling the bottles in his arms and looking at them fondly. "I can share some, if you want."

Maddy swallowed and breathed through her mouth as she took a step backward, George's growls muffled by her hand. "No, you're all right. I don't want to take your stuff from you," she said, smiling apologetically. "I need to get back now anyway and eat my breakfast. I've got school today."

"More for me then so," said Bang Bang, jiggling his treasures. He turned away, blowing a raspberry at an outraged George before he walked off.

Maddy put the terrier on the wet grass, and he looked up at her, tongue lolling from his mouth in a wide doggy smile.

"Happy again, are you?" asked Maddy. "What on earth is wrong with you, you eejit of a dog?" George thumped his tail in response. Maddy sighed. "We'd better get home. You've probably woken half the square up."

chapter twelve

"I COULD HAVE HEARD THAT DOG BARKING IN Dublin!" yelled Granny as Maddy opened the front door. Maddy groaned as she saw both her grandparents were up, and Granda was giving her the hairy eyeball, that stomach-clenching look that said, *I'll deal with you later.*

"It wasn't really his fault. Bang Bang was in the square, and you know the way he always sets the dogs off," said Maddy.

"I'm not blaming George, and do *not* you be blaming Bang Bang," said Granny, as she put cereal and a bowl on the table for Maddy. Granda got up to open the back door and whistled. George shot through it and out to his kennel—he knew better than to stick around when Maddy was getting a tongue-lashing.

"You shouldn't have been out on your own this early in the morning on a school day in the first place," scolded Granny. "Instead of walking that fool of a dog, you should have been getting ready. Now you're going to have to rush."

Maddy poured milk over her cornflakes and began to spoon them into her mouth. "Yeah, but why is it that every dog in the village runs at him barking whenever they see him? It's horrible."

"Poor unfortunate," sighed Granny as she settled into the chair opposite Maddy and began buttering some toast. "He was a lovely lad when he was younger—bright and cheerful and always a smile on him. But he turned funny around the age of twelve, and he's never been right since. Broke his poor mother's heart, so it did."

"What's the matter with him?" asked Maddy.

"Nobody knows," said Granny. "His mother had him in and out of the hospital, wore herself out going up and down to Dublin to see specialists with him, and not one of them could tell her what was wrong with him. But he seems happy enough in himself, and he's managed to keep body and soul together since his mother died, God rest her soul."

"Still doesn't explain why all the dogs go mad when he's around though," said Maddy.

"Well, doctors say a brain that isn't well gives off different brainwaves than usual," said Granny. "Animals are meant to be sensitive to brainwaves—they can often tell when someone is ill, like if the person has a tumor. Whatever is wrong with poor Bang Bang, they know something isn't right."

Maddy chewed on her cornflakes and thought about it for a while.

"Some of the things he comes out with though, they're a scandal," said Granny, her mouth a thin line of disapproval.

"Like what?" asked Maddy.

"Well, I went up for Communion one day at Mass, and there was Bang Bang sitting in the front pew with his great long legs stretched out in front of him, so I had to step over him to get to the altar. The priest was handing me the wafer, and when he said, 'Body of Christ,' Bang Bang leaned forward and said, 'Gander poo!'"

Maddy choked so hard on her cornflakes some of them wedged in her sinuses. She coughed and sputtered as she tried not to laugh. Granny fixed her with That Look over the top of her glasses. "Isn't it time you got ready for school?"

Maddy nodded and shoveled the last of her cereal into her mouth before heading off to her bedroom, avoiding Granda's glare. She changed quickly into her school uniform, checked that she had everything she needed in her backsack, and went to the front door. "Roisin and I have to do some more studying after school today so I'll be home a bit later than usual," she said.

"You've no time. You need to be home before dark," said Granda.

"But—" began Maddy.

"No buts. Come home straight after school, and no messing on the way," said Granda, flicking the morning paper open.

Granny looked at her and shook her head ever so slightly. *Do as you are told.*

Maddy sighed and let herself out the front door. She zipped her jacket up tight against the sharp air and began the ten-minute walk to school. Blarney had woken up and was bustling about. People were doing a bit of early-morning shopping in the Co-op while sales assistants hid their yawns. Cars whizzed past, taking people into Cork for work or dropping children at school, brushing the crumbs of breakfast eaten on the run from their uniforms. She crossed the bridge, and the river that ran beneath her feet was swollen with autumn rain, its voice deeper and more self-important than usual as it tumbled over its rocky bed. A truck thundered past, the slipstream created by its grimy metal sides puffing against her hair.

Maddy took a deep breath. She loved this time of year. The trees were turning every shade of red and gold before their leaves dropped and they went into a deep sleep. The whole world seemed to burn with the trees' last surge of sap, and the air was as crisp as an apple. The warmth from the sun was weak, but the light was molten yellow. The earth would turn, and Maddy could hope things would be better next year, as she seemed to do every year since her parents had died. The wool of her school tights prickled against her skin, and the air was still just a little too warm to justify wearing them. Maddy longed to scratch at her thighs, but Granny would have a fit if she was seen doing something like that in public.

She groaned as she spied Bang Bang up ahead, on the pavement-less side of the road, muttering away to himself and rooting around in the row of evergreens that marked the boundary of the fields that surrounded Blarney Castle. He was raking away with his hand, stuffing bits of paper and bottle tops in the cavernous pockets of his coat. Maddy fixed her eyes on the ground and pretended the pavement was the most fascinating thing she'd ever seen. If she caught his eye, and Bang Bang was in the mood to talk, she'd never make it to class on time. Bang Bang seemed to have days when he would jabber for hours on end, and he really didn't have a preference as to whom he talked to. Anyone who looked as if he or she were listening would do.

She had just sneaked past him, and she could see the playground and hear the bell ringing when she heard Bang Bang cry out and start to sob. She closed her eyes for a moment and sighed. Bang Bang was forever cutting himself on the junk that he found, and he never, ever knew what to do about it. He would sit and cry until someone sorted him out. She couldn't just leave him.

She waited to let a car pass, and she crossed the road to him. His shoulders were heaving as he sobbed.

"You OK, Bang Bang?" she asked. "Did you cut yourself on something?"

Bang Bang was holding his injured hand with his good one, and blood ran in a bright red stream from his palm to patter out of sight on the black tarmac of the road. His skin had turned an interesting color from the blood and the years of ground-in dirt, and he raised a shaking finger to point into the tree in front of him.

"It bit me!" wailed Bang Bang. "Something bit me!"

"I don't think so. You probably just cut yourself on a can or a bit of glass," said Maddy.

"Stupid girl!" snarled Bang Bang.

"Hey, take it easy," warned Maddy. "Any more attitude, and you can sort out your hand on your own."

This just made Bang Bang wail even louder, and then he started to suck on his filthy hand to ease the pain from the wound, a sight and a sound that quite honestly turned Maddy's stomach. She turned the leaf litter at her feet over with the toe of her school shoe and frowned. All she could see was more dead vegetation—nothing that could cut skin.

The tree in front of her shivered, and she looked up in time to see a tiny blue-skinned body disappearing into the branches over her head. A nasty little giggle floated down to her.

"See?!" screeched Bang Bang. "There it is, nasty little sneak. I told you. I *told* you it bit me!"

"Can you see that, Bang Bang?" asked Maddy, keeping her eyes fixed on the spot where she had seen the flash of blue and a wicked black eye.

"Course I can," he snapped. "I'm not blind."

Maddy stared at his dirt-creased face, her mouth slack with shock. *Bang Bang has the Sight*, she thought. She got a look at his hand before he jammed it back into his mouth again, and she saw two neat puncture marks in the muscly bit of his palm, right below his thumb. The kind of puncture marks fangs would make.

Suddenly, four of the trees in the row started to shake and shiver, and Maddy saw flashes of blue everywhere as the branches rocked with spiteful laughter. The whole row could be alive with faeries! She panicked and jumped away from the trees, grabbing Bang Bang by the arm as she did so. They narrowly avoided being hit by a car, the horn blaring as the driver swerved to avoid them. She dragged Bang Bang across the road as a bank of dark clouds boiled up from the castle and began to roll across the sky, reaching out for the school. It had gone so dark it was as if someone had flicked a switch, and the air crackled with the threat of lightning. Maddy had learned to recognize the signs of faerie activity, and she would bet money that whatever was hiding in the row of trees opposite the school was going to prove to be the least of her worries in the next half an hour.

She could see the last stragglers going into the school as she dragged Bang Bang up to the gate. Miss Stone, a teacher who wasn't Maddy's biggest fan, was standing there, jiggling the keys impatiently in her hand.

"What on earth is going on, Madeline?" she snapped. "Why are you dragging poor Bang Bang around by his sleeve? Don't torment the poor man!"

"Please, miss," said Maddy, "Bang Bang's hurt his hand. Can he come into the school just for a minute so the nurse can patch it up for him?" She stretched her face into what she hoped was a winning smile, but it cut no ice with Miss Stone.

"Certainly not," she said. "I'm sure Bang Bang can make his own way to the surgery and that he would prefer not to be bothered by little girls." She raised her voice and talked to Bang Bang as if he were deaf. "Isn't that right, dear?"

Poor Bang Bang just continued to sob. Maddy ground her teeth in frustration. "Please, miss," she said in a lower voice. "You know Bang Bang is special. We can't leave him like this."

Miss Stone looked down her long thin nose at Maddy, her pinched mouth pressing into a white line. Her frizzy red hair was beginning to stand on end as the air snapped with ozone, the atmospherics turning it into a parched Afro. "Unauthorized visitors are not allowed on school premises," she said. "And I'm sure 'special' ones would be in breach of Health and Safety. Bang Bang will be fine, but you will be in trouble, young lady, if you do not get yourself to class this instant." She drew herself up and stood to one side, pointing at the school doors with the hand that held the keys.

Maddy looked up at her.

"Well, that's a bit heartless," she said.

"I *beg* your pardon?" said Miss Stone, her pale face flushing so dark with anger it drove her freckles into extinction.

"We can't just leave him!" said Maddy. She flicked a quick glance over her shoulder at the trees, but whatever had bitten Bang Bang was staying hidden. For now. "He's got to come in and get his hand bandaged. And then someone has to walk him home, make sure he's OK."

"Why?" asked Miss Stone.

Because he's been bitten by a faerie.

"Because . . ." said Maddy weakly, as Bang Bang sobbed beside her. "Because he's upset?"

"You will not argue with me, Madeline. I have told you no, and that is that," snapped Miss Stone. "Nor will you speak to me in such a disgraceful way. Let Bang Bang go on his way, and get inside the school *now.*"

Maddy looked around to see if there was anyone who could help, and as she turned her head to the right, she saw a sight that made her blood run cold. Faeries were walking toward the school, using the same route Maddy had just walked, the road the led to the castle, that *ran past her grandparents' house.* They were shrieking and jabbering like a bunch of sixth-graders on a day out. And right at the front was a very familiar figure with a white Mohican.

Fachtna.

Maddy felt her legs turn to jelly with fear and had a sudden urge to pee. She turned back to Miss Stone.

"Please, miss, *please*," she pleaded, her voice low and urgent. "He has to come in."

"Stop being so melodramatic," hissed Miss Stone, oblivious to the howling faeries advancing up the road. "I have no time at all for your histrionics, Madeline. Now, for the last time, leave Bang Bang alone, and *get yourself to class*!"

With tears pricking her eyes, Maddy turned to Bang Bang and yanked on his arm, pulling his injured hand out of his mouth. She grabbed a hank of his dirty yellow beard and forced his head up and in the direction of the faeries.

"Can you see that?" she asked him softly. She knew the answer already because Bang Bang had gone absolutely still, and his eyes bulged from their sockets with fear. "Then walk away," she hissed. "Don't look at them, and don't look back. Just walk away. Find some iron, and hide." She watched him as he turned and fled with his awkward, dragging gait, his coat flapping around his legs.

"At last," said Miss Stone. "I shall be speaking to your grandparents about your attitude, Madeline. It's bad enough you already have one unauthorized visitor on the premises."

Maddy looked at her for a second and then ran past her, her backpack hitting Miss Stone as she scrambled through the gate. She dimly heard the teacher's cry of anger, but she didn't look back as she raced across the playground. Hope surged through her and gave her feet wings. Someone had come, someone had known that Blarney was about to be attacked by a gang of marauding faeries, and they were going to help! She took the steps to the entrance two at a time and burst through the double doors. She didn't know whom she had been expecting, but it wasn't the person sitting outside the school office.

Danny looked up from his cell phone and grinned at her.

"Danny!" she squeaked, not even trying to keep the disappointment from showing on her face as she struggled to get her breath back. "What are you doing here?"

"Well, you know when you can smell a really bad day coming . . ." He looked over her shoulder, and his voice trailed off into silence.

Maddy turned around and looked through the glass of the doors. Miss Stone was still fussing at the gate, completely unaware of the nightmarish assortment of dark faeries that were gathered no more than a breath away from her face, grinning evilly. She double-checked the padlock and then rattled the chain to make absolutely sure the gate was shut fast. She turned to walk away, and then Fachtna stepped forward, drew her sword, and sliced neatly through the hinges. Miss Stone whirled around and gaped at the gate as it lay on the tarmac of the playground, while the gang of faeries slithered around it, side-stepping the iron.

"They're coming!" said Maddy. "What do we do? What the *hell* do we do?"

Danny checked his phone again. "Still no signal. They must be interfering with the transmitter."

"So we're finished?" said Maddy, panic clawing through her stomach.

"Looks like it," said Danny, his face as white as a sheet. "There's really only one thing left to do."

"Which is?" prompted Maddy, as the faeries reached the front steps of the school.

"Panic!" said Danny, as he stood up and picked up the chair he had been sitting on, swinging it hard so it smashed the glass case that housed the fire alarm. The faeries outside stumbled to a halt and clapped their hands over their ears, shrieking with pain as the fire alarm jangled through their senses.

Danny grabbed Maddy's arm. "Now I think we should run."

chapter thirteen

MADDY COULD HEAR MISS STONE SCREAMING AT them as they ran. "I SAW YOU, DANIEL O'SHEA! I SAW YOU SET OFF THAT FIRE ALARM, YOU LITTLE HOOLIGAN!" Her voice swooped over the clanging of the fire alarm, and Maddy could see the bewildered looks on the teachers' faces as they led their pupils out of the classrooms in neat lines. Danny dragged her along behind him as they whipped around the corner, heading for Maddy and Roisin's class. All around them classroom doors were opening, and teachers were telling shuffling children to line up in pairs. There were shouts as Danny and Maddy ran past, but the teachers had their hands full, and nobody gave chase. Miss Rose, Maddy's sweet-faced, soft-spoken teacher, was ushering her class out through the door in a line of twos, and Danny spotted Roisin toward the back of the line, holding hands with another little girl. He elbowed his way past Miss Rose, pulling Maddy in his wake.

"Sorry, miss," he panted as he shoved a girl against the door jamb. Miss Rose's mouth was a perfect O of surprise. "No time to explain."

He grabbed Roisin by her collar at the back of her neck, and this time he hauled both girls back through the classroom door and into the hallway, stepping on feet and bumping into protesting classmates.

"What is going on?" demanded Miss Rose, her face flushing pink. "Let go of those girls at once, and come with me to the playground."

"Can't do that, miss," said Danny.

"And why not?" demanded Miss Rose, just as the demonic squad of dark faeries turned the corner and leered at them.

Roisin's jaw dropped as she gaped at them, the blood draining from her face to leave it paper white. Their classmates began to look confused and peered up the hallway, their eyes looking past the faeries. Fachtna walked up to Miss Rose and loomed over her, baring her shark's teeth at Maddy in an evil grin.

"And why not?" she mimicked, pretending to look confused and shaking her head. The other faeries laughed. Miss Rose looked at the children around her. "Who said that? This is not funny!"

Fachtna unsheathed one of the knives belted across her chest, and she ran the point of the blade against the wall, tearing a thin line through the plaster as she walked toward Maddy.

"What is going on?" squealed Miss Rose, the panic rising in her voice as some of the girls huddled around her began to cry. Fachtna stopped and turned to face the teacher, bending down until her cold, white face was just inches away. Somehow Miss Rose sensed there was something close by that meant her harm, and Maddy watched the fear cloud her eyes as she searched for the source. It was like watching a blind woman trying to feel her way forward to safety while a predator watched her fumble, ready to spring at her throat at a moment's notice.

"Leave her alone," said Maddy.

Fachtna, her red eyes blazing, whipped her head around to Maddy and hissed at her. One dark faerie, its brown lumpen body covered with the spines of thousands of thorns, a long tongue uncurling between needle-sharp teeth, leered at a little girl and pinched her skin between sharp nails. She screamed in pain and surprise, and then she cried as she rubbed at her arm. The whole class was beginning to panic as they realized something horrible was happening, but they did not have a clue what or *where* it was.

"You can leave her alone as well," Maddy warned the thorn faerie as it bared its teeth at her and snarled.

Fachtna weaved her head on her neck like a cobra. "Oh, we will," she said. "As long as you give us a bit of sport."

"Let me guess," said Maddy. "You want us to run."

"Who on earth are you talking to, Maddy?" asked Miss Rose, her voice shaking with fear, while Fachtna's evil smile just widened.

"It's no fun unless you try to escape," said Fachtna.

"Fine," said Maddy. "After a count of three. One, two, . . ." And then she turned and ran, pulling Danny and a stunned Roisin along with her. Behind them, the faeries' howls of joy rose over the jarring clang of the fire alarm. Maddy raced blindly through the corridor, her school shoes slapping dully against the smooth surface of the floor. She nearly staggered as she tried to outrun her own ability, and she didn't dare look back to see how close behind the faeries were. Any second now, she was expecting to feel Fachtna's long white fingers wrap around her neck and yank her off her feet.

She charged blindly ahead, her fingers grabbing at the walls to steady herself as she almost crashed taking the corners too fast. She could see the sports hall ahead of her, and she put on another burst of speed, stretching her hands out to smash the double doors open ahead of her. The hall was empty, and she nearly fell as the soles of her shoes slipped on the waxed wooden floorboards.

She turned back to face the door, her chest ragged with panting and sweat coating her skin greasily underneath her clothes. Danny ran for a stack of molded plastic chairs they used for parents to sit on for assemblies, and he hefted one into the air, holding its metal legs out in front of him. Roisin ran behind the climbing frame and peered out through its curling, primary-colored steel struts with frightened eyes.

Suddenly the fire alarm stopped ringing. The silence it left behind jangled on Maddy's nerves just as loudly as the alarm, but over the roar of her blood pounding in her ears, she could hear slow, soft footsteps, and whispering and snickering.

Only about half of the faeries had followed Fachtna into the sports hall, and Maddy wondered where the others were. Then she heard the sound of smashing glass and the thuds of furniture being thrown against walls, and she realized the rest of the faeries had decided to smash the school up for the sake of it. The ones fanning out behind Fachtna as they eased their way through the swing doors had that hungry, eager look she had learned to dread.

"No tricks, Feral Child?" purred Fachtna as she flipped her knife from hand to hand, twirling the blade through her fingers so that the early-autumn sunlight flashed on its surface. "No iron to swallow?"

"I'll think of something," said Maddy as they circled each other. "But I am wondering why you're not tucked in nice and safe beneath the mound."

"You know why," said Fachtna. "The old bonds are breaking, and we can run free the way we used to." She cocked her head at the sound of splintering furniture. "Time to have some fun." She looked at Maddy. "Time to settle scores."

Maddy slipped her hand into her pocket, flicked the Velcro open with her fingertips, and pulled out the little iron knife.

Fachtna narrowed her eyes. "Do you even know how to use that?"

"Let's see," said Maddy, and she lunged forward, slashing wildly. Fachtna stepped neatly to one side, and Maddy staggered and almost fell. The faeries laughed as Fachtna grabbed Maddy's wrist and twisted it. Maddy yelled with pain, and the knife clattered from her numb fingers to the floor. Fachtna let go of her wrist and shoved her hard, sending her flying across the sports hall to crash against the climbing frame. Maddy looked into Roisin's terrified eyes and then ducked as she felt Fachtna's arm blur over her head, her fist smashing into the bright bars.

She spun and rammed her head as hard as she could into Fachtna's stomach, and she got a tiny bit of satisfaction out of hearing the dark faerie's grunt of pain and the whoosh of her breath as it left her body. Without a pause she curled her fingers into a fist and tried to throw a punch, but Fachtna simply swallowed Maddy's hand in her long fingers. She squeezed, and Maddy shrieked as the pain shot up her arm. She kicked out, hard, and was lucky enough to connect the toe of her shoe with Fachtna's leg just beneath her kneecap. The faerie yelled as she crumpled to the floor, dropping Maddy's hand.

Maddy turned and made a dash to try to retrieve the dull iron knife lying just a few feet away. But it seemed as though she had only taken a couple of steps when Fachtna grabbed her ankle and brought her crashing down, smacking her chin and bruising her chest. She tasted blood where she had bitten her tongue, and she was about to flip on to her back and boot Fachtna in the face when the double doors to the sports hall swung open, and Miss Stone walked in with a face like thunder.

"You really have gone too far this time, Madeline," she barked. "The whole school is standing in the playground, there could be a fire raging through this building for all we know, and your hoodlum friends have caused quite a bit of damage." Miss Stone looked at Fachtna and at the faeries who had stopped advancing on Danny to stare at her in amazement. "I'm warning the lot of you now—the guards are on their way, and your parents are going to know all about this!"

It dawned on Maddy that Miss Stone was seeing *something*. The faeries' behavior was so wild that Miss Stone's brain was registering that something was there. But Maddy didn't think Miss Stone was seeing what she could see. There was a second of stunned silence, and then the faeries roared with laughter.

She's glamoured, realized Maddy. *She has no idea what she is looking at.*

A couple of faeries ran for Miss Stone, who, to her credit, stood her ground and glowered at what her brain was telling her was a bunch of teenagers who had decided to wreck the school and dangle a few primary-school children by their hair. But the faeries were not impressed—they snickered and stretched out long thin hands tipped with razor-sharp talons. They sliced slowly at her skin and circled her like sharks, nostrils flaring at the scent of blood, their eyes feverish with anticipation of the kill.

"Stop it!" yelled Miss Stone, her voice cracking with fear. "Put those knives away right now, and I won't have to tell the guards about them. You're going too far!" The faeries paused, sharp-toothed mouths gaping and eyes glittering, and then they rushed at her, closing the circle in a heartbeat. Miss Stone screamed and beat at them with her hands. Roisin was screaming as well, and Danny, still with the chair in his hand, ran forward to help the teacher, but one of the faeries turned on him, and in seconds he was on the ground, his arm across the faerie's throat, fending off its snapping jaws and long sharp teeth. Miss Stone ran for the break in the circle and raced from the hall, her wails echoing in the empty school. The faeries didn't chase after her. Instead, they swiveled to focus on Danny, as the faerie that pinned him down clawed for his throat, easily avoiding his ineffectual uppercuts and left hooks.

Maddy looked at Fachtna, whose nostrils flared with excitement. "Make them stop!" she cried.

"Now, why would I do that?" asked Fachtna.

"This is between you and me," said Maddy. "You can't involve innocent people like this!"

"Here's the thing, *Madeline*," sneered Fachtna, as she grabbed Maddy by the hair and hauled her up as she got to her feet. "You're not that special. I don't really care what mortal I am hurting. With the barrier failing, it's starting to feel like the old days, when I hunted whatever I wanted. I'll take pleasure in slitting your throat, of course, but not much more than they will his," she said, nodding toward Danny, who was now curled up in a terrified ball as the faeries kicked and rolled him around between them. Fachtna snarled, her eyes wild and bestial. She put the point of her dagger under Maddy's chin. "What do you say to that, Feral Child?"

"You know, you're not leaving me much choice here," said Maddy, as she tried very, very hard not to swallow against the razor-sharp knife tip.

Fachtna frowned. "What are you talking about?"

"For one thousand days, I pledge allegiance," said Maddy.

Fachtna frowned. "What trickery is this? I don't want your fealty!"

"For one thousand days, I pledge allegiance," repeated Maddy, her eyes fixed on Fachtna's face as the faerie hesitated in confusion.

Something big and black collided with Fachtna and hurled her across the hall. Maddy flew from her grip and bounced painfully off the wooden boards again. It was beginning to feel like an extreme PE lesson. The pale faerie screeched as her dagger clattered away across the floor, and she twisted and writhed in the grip of a shaggy black dog with glowing yellow eyes. The doors to the sports hall banged open, and the dark faeries poured in, surrounding Maddy and pulling her to her feet with their long, sharp hands. The dog snarled, and Fachtna screamed with rage as they fought in a blur of white and black, although splashes of red were marking Fachtna's white skin. The sports hall boomed with bangs and scuffles as they threw each other around. Fachtna and the Pooka broke apart, spots of blood from their injuries spattering the ground. They stared at each other, panting, and then with a shriek Fachtna hurled herself at the Pooka just as he sprang for her. There was a crack of bones as they collided and fell into a tangled heap, but when they broke apart, the Pooka had Fachtna by the arm while her free hand groped for the knives belted at her waist. Maddy struggled against the grip of the other faeries, who howled and whooped as they watched the fight, but she couldn't loosen their grip. There was a sharp tang of ozone in the air, and a cold wind rushed through the school, blowing Maddy's hair back from her face. A tiny tornado of autumn leaves advanced into the hall and came to a halt before them. The wind died, and the leaves fell in drifts around the feet of the Queen of Autumn.

Everyone went still as they stared at her, her red hair burning in the gloom and lifting out from her head in a wild static mass of curls. The gold on her skin gleamed, and the whisper of her dress and hair dragging on the ground behind her as she advanced filled the silence.

"Unhand my subject," she demanded, her voice booming loudly in a building that had gone so quiet you could have heard a mouse hiccup. Maddy sagged with relief, but if anything, the faeries that gripped her dug their fingers in harder.

"Our catch," one hissed at the Autumn Queen. "*Our* kill."

Meabh raised one arched auburn eyebrow in surprise, but her green and gold eyes were hard and cold with anger. "Pooka, to me!" she commanded, and the Pooka left off the fight with Fachtna to bound to her side. With his hackles raised and strings of saliva hanging from his huge jaws, he was an intimidating sight, and the group of dark faeries automatically took a step back from his bloody jaws and stinking breath.

Fachtna staggered to her feet and stalked across to Meabh. Her skin was torn and bloody from her fight with the Pooka, but her wings rattled with aggression. "It is not your place to interfere!" she said. "This hunt is for the Winter faeries, and this mortal is subject to no court. I did not accept her oath of allegiance on behalf of my queen."

Meabh laughed, her voice as light as drizzle. "You don't really think that little display of loyalty was for Liadan, do you?" she asked. "Really, I thought you were much cleverer than that, Fachtna." Meabh watched Fachtna's face as realization slowly dawned on it. "That's right, the Feral Child is now part of my court, and as such she is under my protection. Do any of you here really wish to start a blood feud by killing this girl right here and now, no matter how tempting it might be?"

Fachtna glared at Maddy. "A clever trick."

"I thought so," said Maddy, as the Winter faeries let her go.

"Mortals are, at this very moment, trying to break down the front doors of this building to rescue this child and her companions," said Meabh. "Strangely, they find them locked. They will not stay that way forever, and the Sighted will be here soon, so I suggest that any faeries currently on the premises make themselves scarce. As in NOW." That edge of thunder rumbled again in her voice, and the Pooka beside her bared his huge yellow teeth.

Fachtna bared her own teeth at Maddy one last time as the dark faeries ran from the sports hall to climb out through open windows in the classrooms, escaping from the mortal world back into the green fields. "Be careful for your family, Feral Child," said Fachtna. "They don't all have the protection of a Tuatha, do they?" She laughed and walked slowly from the hall, to prove she cared nothing for the mortals who were breaking through the doors at the front of the building.

Meabh listened for a moment to make sure they were all gone. Maddy swallowed at the sound of the doors being kicked open. She was in so much trouble.

"Allegiance for just one thousand days, Maddy?" said Meabh, an amused smile playing about the corners of her red lips. "I do not remember accepting such terms."

"You must have done so," said Maddy, "to send the Pooka to save me."

"Clever, clever girl," purred Meabh. "And with such a sharp tongue. Be careful it does not cut your throat. Very well, I accept your allegiance for one thousand days, and so we play the game."

"What happens now?" asked Maddy.

"Wait and see, my dear," said Meabh with a wink. "Wait and see."

With that, Meabh and the Pooka disappeared in a whirl of leaves.

Maddy sagged with relief and listened to the shouts of angry adults and the thunder of feet running toward her.

chapter fourteen

"A BLACK EYE, BRUISING TO HER RIBS, AND A FEW cuts and grazes—I think that's all. On the whole, I'd say you came off rather well, considering who you were fighting," said Dr. Malloy.

Maddy tried to take a deep breath and stopped it in her throat when it snagged in her chest and gave her that broken-glass feeling again. She groaned softly and pressed the inflamed part of her chest with a grazed palm. Her tongue was swollen and painful, and her left eye had puffed up like a football. Her mouth felt like the floor of a bird cage, and she had a pounding headache. From the look on Granda's face, she was probably going to have a raging earache as soon as Dr. Malloy had gone. Roisin hadn't been touched, and Danny had a shoulder bite, which was painful but not infected and not in need of stitches. He was on the other side of her bedroom door, blearily sitting upright in a chair while Aunt Fionnula screamed at him and then sobbed over him and then screamed at him again. Her bedside manner left a lot to be desired. Maddy was grateful she didn't have to share a room with her. She was exhausted, and her back ached to lie flat on her comfy bed, but Dr. Malloy wasn't done poking and prodding her.

"I really think Danny and Maddy should be taken to the hospital," said Dr. Malloy to Granda. "Have someone check them over thoroughly, just to be safe and keep an eye on them."

"I can do that here," Granda interrupted.

"Think about this, Bat," urged Dr. Malloy. "The hospital is in the middle of the city, surrounded by iron, and the staff can stay with them. It will be a lot easier on you."

"Not if my wife finds out I sent them in," said Granda. "She wants them here, where she can mind them herself, and neither of us wants them moved around. The doors and windows will be locked and bolted; they will be safe enough. Besides—" he looked at Maddy "—they will all be moved into the city tomorrow anyway. Maddy is going to stay with her cousins there. They will be safe enough then."

Dr. Malloy shook his head doubtfully. "Still, I'd be a lot happier if they went into the city tonight. Your wife hasn't the Sight . . ."

"But I do," said Granda. "And nothing is getting into this house tonight." He shot a warning look at Maddy, and she realized Granda hadn't told the doctor about Meabh's visit.

Dr. Malloy sighed. "It's up to you, Bat, but you know what I think. You knew this was going to happen, and we will need to make a decision soon. Drink plenty of water, Maddy, and rest. I mean that—no running around for the next few days, and no school either, although I'm sure you won't find that a hardship."

There was a loud knocking at the front door, and Granda groaned. "Who now?" he asked no one in particular before going into the front room, where Granny was bustling around a visitor. Maddy peered around Dr. Malloy, and her heart sank when she realized it was Sergeant O'Leary. He wasn't one of the Sighted, and while he wasn't very bright, once he got an idea in his head, he was like a dog with a bone. Maddy had made the mistake of telling him last year that a faerie had taken little Stephen Forest when he went missing. Needless to say, he hadn't believed her, and he now considered Maddy to be a troublemaker and an outrageous liar to boot. Which is why Maddy was convinced he was as thick as two short planks—what ten-year-old would make up a story about faeries?

"Come up here, you," she heard Aunt Fionnula say. "We want to have a word."

Maddy didn't need to be told who the "you" was. Things were getting bad if her aunt couldn't even be bothered to use her name. She sighed and eased herself off the bed.

"You should be staying in bed," warned Dr. Malloy.

"She'll just make me get up anyway," said Maddy.

As she walked toward her bedroom door, she could feel her face setting itself hard into the look it always wore when she had to deal with Aunt Fionnula—sullen and bad-tempered. It was like a red rag to a bull as far as her aunt was concerned, and it didn't do her any favors with Sergeant O'Leary either, but Maddy couldn't stomach trying to be the child that Aunt Fionnula wanted her to be. That was Roisin. Maddy loved Roisin, but she didn't have it in her to be that timid or eager to please, not with Aunt Fionnula—just the thought of it made her want to vomit.

So the face that appeared around the bedroom door into the sitting room of her grandparents' cottage was angry and, more importantly, guilty looking—which Maddy knew from the look of triumph in her aunt's eyes.

"We would like you to explain, madam," her aunt said in a quiet, gloating hiss, "how those punks came to the school today and why it was you they beat up."

All of the Sighted ones knew the school had been attacked by Fachtna and a few of her friends out having a good time. But ordinary mortals saw what their brains told them was logical. So the teachers at the school had seen a gang of teenagers breaking in and destroying the place.

Sergeant O'Leary cleared his throat and opened his notebook. "According to one of the teachers, a Miss Stone, you know the gang who broke into the school," he said.

"No," said Maddy, folding her arms.

"What do you mean?" asked Sergeant O'Leary.

"I mean, no, I don't know them," said Maddy.

"But you ran when you saw them coming up the street?" asked Sergeant O'Leary.

"Yeah, well, they didn't look very friendly, and I felt safer inside the school," said Maddy. "Besides, Danny was the one who set off the fire alarm." Danny glared at her as his mother swung around to stare at him, her eyes popping from her head in anger. Maddy felt a stab of guilt about dropping Danny in it, but it did feel good to show up Aunt Fionnula. Let one of *her* kids be Public Enemy Number One for a change.

"Ahem, yes," said Sergeant O'Leary, clearing his throat and looking at his notes again. "Miss Stone did mention that. Danny, could you tell me what you were doing at the girls' primary school in Blarney this morning, when you should have been at the secondary in Cork?"

Danny's face went bright red as everyone in the room stared at him. What with the grandparents, Sergeant O'Leary, Dr. Malloy, Aunt Fionnula, Roisin, Maddy, and himself, it was getting very hot and crowded in the cottage's tiny sitting room. "I, um, I . . ." Danny stammered, his face blazing hotter and hotter. "I just, um . . .

I felt like skipping school this morning. And I wanted to see if Maddy wanted to come with me." He threw her a look. "Maddy skips school off a lot."

"You did *what*?" screeched Aunt Fionnula. "Just wait until I get you home!"

"So why did you set off the fire alarm and run away then, Danny?" asked the sergeant. "And why did they attack you and Maddy?"

"Well, as Maddy said, they didn't look very friendly," said Danny. "I just had a bad feeling."

Which isn't a million miles away from the truth, thought Maddy.

"Can you think of any reason why they would want to hurt you or Maddy or why they attacked Miss Stone?" Sergeant O'Leary asked.

"No, I can't. I'd never seen any of them before in my life," said Danny. "I don't think people like that need a reason."

"What are you going to do about this?" Aunt Fionnula demanded. "My son was very badly hurt—he could have been killed! And I *know* she is at the bottom of it all." She rounded on Maddy and jabbed a sharp finger in her direction. "She always is."

Maddy widened her eyes in mock innocence and watched Aunt Fionnula's face flush with anger.

"The problem I have, Mrs. O'Shea, is that no one seems to know who these teenagers were," said Sergeant O'Leary as he tucked his notebook away inside his jacket.

"Surely some of the teachers must have recognized them! They walked right past them to get into the school," said Granny.

"They did indeed, but again, none of the staff recognized them either, and they ran by so quickly that no one has been able to give me more than a vague description," said Sergeant O'Leary. "Poor Miss Stone was so frightened she really can't remember much. So unless someone can come forward with more detailed information—" he paused and looked hard at Maddy and Danny "—I really do not have much to go on. Maybe after a good night's sleep, something will come to you, eh?" Maddy and Danny looked back at him and said nothing. He sighed. "This is serious business here. We're talking assault, battery, criminal damage, and God only knows what else. Those lads are in big trouble, and so is anyone who tries to protect them or tells me lies. Do you still have nothing to say?" Again, stony silence. "Well, if that's all, I'll be on my way," he said.

Granda walked over to let the sergeant out. "If they think of anything, Bat, anything at all, no matter how small or unimportant it might seem, give me a call straightaway, won't you?" said Sergeant O'Leary as he pulled his hat firmly on to his head.

"I will, Sergeant," said Granda, as Sergeant O'Leary stepped out into the street.

"I'd best be going myself," said Dr. Malloy. "Any problems during the night, give me a call at home. You know the number, don't you?"

"That we do, Doctor. Thanks for coming out," said Granny.

"My pleasure," said Dr. Malloy. "Keep an eye on these two now, and I will see them tomorrow morning in the surgery for a check-up."

They all called their goodbyes as Dr. Malloy left, but as soon as the front door closed, a tense silence descended. Maddy's eyes shifted nervously around as she tried to look anywhere but at Aunt Fionnula.

"There is something funny going on around here," said Aunt Fionnula. "Gangs of teenagers do not just appear out of the blue, vandalize a primary school, and beat up pupils and teachers. And I intend to get to the bottom of it."

"The children have said they know nothing about it," said Granny. "And why should they? I know Maddy doesn't spend her time hanging out with sixteen-year-olds."

"Nor does Danny," said Aunt Fionnula, her glare never leaving Maddy's face.

"It was probably one of those Facebook things—you know, when they tell each other to meet up at a certain place and behave badly," said Granny.

"What do you know about Facebook?" asked Granda.

"I'm not as green as I look, Bartholomew Kiely," warned Granny. "There's plenty of things I know about."

Granda rolled his eyes.

"In Blarney? At nine in the morning?" said Aunt Fionnula.

"Well, what else are you suggesting?" asked Granda, not even bothering to keep the exasperation from his voice.

"I don't know!" shouted Fionnula, her temper finally boiling over. "I haven't a clue what's going on around here, but ever since she turned up, there's been trouble!"

Granny tutted. "You've no proof that Maddy has done anything at all, Fionnula. If you can believe that Danny was hurt for just being there, then I don't see why you would think that gang had a reason for hurting Maddy."

"Because my children behave themselves!" yelled Aunt Fionnula. "My children would not dare do anything to cause trouble like this! They weren't dragged up!"

In the shocked silence that followed, Aunt Fionnula's face went white as she realized that she really had gone too far this time. Everyone stared at her in disbelief, but as her words sank in, Maddy's anger began to boil to the surface.

"Don't you dare . . ." she said, her voice choked with tears of rage. "Don't you dare talk about my parents like that."

"I'm sorry," Fionnula whispered, looking not at Maddy but at Granny and Granda. "I never meant—"

"You never *think*," snapped Granda, while Granny's mouth thinned to a white line of disapproval and disappointment. "That's what you meant to say. You never think about what you're saying because if you did, you'd

know your sister never 'dragged' that child up and nor
have we. We might be old, but we're not finished yet."

"I'm sorry," said Fionnula. "I'm sorry. She just gets
me so angry."

"And ask yourself why that is," said Granny. "Because
it's nothing this child has done. You need to find some
way to have a relationship with your sister's child."

"And soon," said Granda. "Seeing as she'll be coming to stay with you tomorrow."

Maddy looked at him, horrified. "You're not still
sending me to her place, are you?" she asked. "After
everything she's said?"

"It's only going to be for a while, Maddy," said
Granda. "I think it would do you both good to get to
know each other." He looked back at Fionnula. "It's not
right that a family should be fighting like this."

Maddy and Aunt Fionnula glared at each other, and
Maddy could read the same thought in Fionnula's eyes
that was at the front of her mind—*I hate you.* There was
no way she was going to be able to handle five minutes
in this woman's house.

"Look, nothing is going to get sorted out today," said
Granny, as the awkward silence stretched on. "Leave
Danny and Roisin here tonight, and you can pick up
all three of them tomorrow. I think a bit of time spent
together over the Halloween break is just what you
need. I know I can't take much more of this fighting."
She sighed and looked very old for a moment. Maddy
felt a twinge of guilt, and even Aunt Fionnula's face

softened. Aunt Fionnula grabbed her handbag from an armchair and slung it over her shoulder.

"Fine," she said, fidgeting with her car keys. "I'll be back in the morning, and we can talk about this then."

"You really can't expect me to go and stay with her. She's out of her mind!" said Maddy.

"Hey!" yelled Danny and Roisin at the same time.

"That's enough!" roared Granda. "Maddy, you are going to do what you are told and accept that sometimes we know what is best for you, better than you do."

Aunt Fionnula ignored Maddy and the insult. "Have the children ready for me at nine in the morning," she said as she walked out of the front door without a good-bye to anyone.

Maddy didn't bother to watch after her.

"You can't make me go anywhere with her," she told her grandparents in a flat voice. "You can't make me go somewhere where I'm hated."

"Don't you talk about my mom like that," warned Danny.

"You need to go and stay with your aunt for a while," said Granda. "You know you do."

"No," said Maddy, "I don't. And I'm not going to."

She stalked past them all into her bedroom, making sure to give the door a good hard slam.

chapter fifteen

MADDY WAS SO EXHAUSTED FROM THE LAST FEW days that she fell asleep across her quilt, not even bothering to change into pajamas. She slept in her school uniform, the clothes twisting around her and creasing her skin as she tossed and turned in a fitful doze. Dreams tumbled out of her subconscious, chasing each other across the insides of her twitching eyelids. They were filled with fragmented images that often made no sense, as disjointed as viewing the real world through a broken kaleidoscope. She woke up once and saw Danny curled up in a corner of the double bed, facing the wall with his back to her, sleeping deeply. Granda was slipping an iron cuff on her wrist, its weight rough and cool against her skin. She clasped it with her other hand and felt some of the tension draining out of her body. When she fell back asleep, the dreams were sweeter.

She woke up with a rumbling stomach to a dark and sleeping house. The clock ticked away on the mantelpiece in the living room, and she could hear deep, even breathing as Danny's chest rose and fell. Yawning wide enough to make her jaw pop, she staggered over to the bedroom door and peered around it blearily. Granda was asleep on the sofa, snoring slightly through a half-open mouth. Maddy slipped through the door and then went to listen outside her grandparents' bedroom. She could hear two sleepers breathing in there, so Roisin must be sharing Granny's bed.

She tiptoed to the kitchen as her stomach complained loudly, and she raided the cupboards. She made herself a sandwich and wolfed it down as she roved around the kitchen, spilling crumbs on Granny's spotless linoleum. She shoveled in some chocolate cookies and drank milk straight out of the carton while she stood in the light of the fridge. She shivered in the cold air and glanced at the darkness pressed so lovingly against the kitchen window. She could see herself and the room reflected back by the black like a perfect mirror image, apart from a square of light thrown down on the garden lawn. As she gazed at it, half asleep, she spotted a quick movement just on the edge of the square, a flicker that soon disappeared into the border of black.

Maddy narrowed her eyes, and then she felt that all too familiar prickling sensation on the back of her neck. The food she had just eaten churned in her stomach as it clenched. She swallowed hard and crept to the light switch, flicking it off to plunge the room into darkness. She crouched down, close to the floor, her heart hammering against her ribs, and she tried to keep her breathing even and quiet. She waited for a few moments, and then there was another fast flicker against the window, a flash of a twisted and ugly face. She bit her lip to stifle a scream. Then she crawled on all fours to the kitchen counter, lifted her arm over her head and felt along its cool surface for the wooden block where Granny kept her kitchen knives. She gripped the handle of one and eased it out before gently pulling back the bolts on the back door.

The gravel on the garden path crunched beneath her stockinged feet, the stones grinding against the wool of her tights. There was another flurry of movement, darting for the garden wall, a soft gray shadow.

"I know you're there," Maddy called softly, trying not to wake anyone. "I'm getting pretty good at spotting when any of you are around. So you might as well show yourself."

The air went still and quiet. When Maddy strained her eyes, she could see that little smudge of gray against the bluer, velvety black of the night. Whatever it was, it was either taking a long time to think about what she had said or getting ready to attack. Maddy held the kitchen knife out in front of her and shifted her weight slightly so that she was ready to bolt back through the door. Her breath steamed faintly in the early autumn air, and she tensed her body for a blow.

And then the garden breathed out again as the gray shadow uncoiled itself, and a faerie no bigger than an eight-year-old child shuffled into the moonlight. Maddy knew it was rude to stare, never mind gasp with horror, but it really was the ugliest little creature and one of the most frightening faeries she had ever seen.

It was an old hag who scuffed her bare feet across the gravel to stand in front of Maddy. Her skin was as gray as the rags she clutched about herself, and her wrinkled scalp showed through the thin white hair that trailed in limp hanks to the small of her back. The nails on her hands and feet were long and black, and her mouth was sunken. But her black eyes were soft and kind and crinkled with laughter lines at the corners. If it hadn't been for her eyes, Maddy probably would have run back into the kitchen and slammed the door.

Instead, Maddy unglued her tongue from the roof of her mouth, where it had almost dried fast, and said, "You're a banshee, aren't you?" The little faerie woman ducked her head shyly and nodded. Maddy stared at her stupidly, one thought running around her head like a hamster on a wheel.

"Am I dying?"

The banshee giggled, showing one tooth hanging on for dear life in her mouth. "No, Feral Child," she said, her voice as beautiful as her body was ugly. "I came to see the new Hound. It's the blood that calls me."

"I wish you lot would stop going on about blood," said Maddy. "It's horrible. Especially when it's mine you're talking about!"

The banshee flinched as if she had been slapped and lowered her head. "Sorry," she said in a small voice.

Maddy winced. The little faerie made her feel as if she was bullying a pensioner. Which she probably was. The banshee shivered in the cold wind. "Would you like to come in?" asked Maddy. She had no idea why she said it; it just felt like the right thing to do.

The faerie looked up quickly, the black eyes eager, and she shuffled at warp speed past Maddy and into the kitchen, rolling from side to side as if one leg hurt her. Maddy was going to take the horseshoe off the door in case the iron repelled the faerie, but the banshee was past her and nosing around the kitchen before she could reach for it, the smell of damp earth wafting off her as she blinked in the electric light that came on when Maddy flicked the switch.

"The iron doesn't bother you then?" asked Maddy, as she closed the back door quietly.

The banshee shook her head. "I'm a solitary faerie, and one of the types who spends more time with mortals than with faeries," said the little woman. "After a while we get more and more like you, and some things stop bothering us." She pulled a face. "Although I wouldn't like to actually *touch* iron, of course."

"Of course," said Maddy. She watched the little faerie look around the room, her nose snuffling. There was a tiny part of Maddy's brain, a small but rational voice, telling her this wasn't a good idea, that she should probably ask the faerie to leave and hope she would be reasonable about it, but the situation was so bizarre Maddy decided to ignore it. Besides, the reckless, impulsive part of her brain argued, Granda was asleep next door, and if the banshee turned aggressive, Maddy could just yell for help.

"Would you like something to eat?" asked Maddy. From the look of the faerie, it had been a couple of centuries since she had a decent meal.

"Do you have any Cheese & Onion Taytos?" asked the faerie.

"Taytos?" repeated Maddy. "As in, potato chips?" The banshee nodded, her face hopeful. "Yeah, we always have a bag around here somewhere."

Maddy had to root around in the cupboard, but she finally found a family bag Granny always kept for when Maddy felt hungry. Granny had a far more lax approach to sweets and chips than Maddy's parents would have approved of, for which Maddy was truly grateful. She turned with the chips in her hand to see the little banshee wriggling like a puppy in excitement, her gnarled hands reaching for the bag. Maddy held out the chips and sat down in a kitchen chair to watch the faerie lower her head to the bag and shovel the chips into her mouth with fingers tipped with long black nails. Her table manners left a lot to be desired.

"So you're a solitary faerie then? What does that mean?" Maddy asked.

"I don't owe allegiance to any court," said the banshee between mouthfuls. "It's the blood that calls me, and the blood I follow, so I wouldn't be able to offer complete obedience to any monarch. So my kind is left alone. We can visit any court we like, but no one tries to make us stay."

"You keep talking about blood," said Maddy. "Do you smell it or something? Why does it mean so much to you?"

"It's not a smell," said the banshee scornfully, as she crunched gummily with her mouth open. "It's like a song, an irresistible lure that calls to us wherever we are. And the lure is never so strong as when the blood is failing and the body dying. Then it's a light that shines out like a beacon. That's why we follow the blood wherever it goes, even when it leaves these shores. It can go as far as Australia and America. We always follow the blood, and we sing when it passes."

"Why?"

The faerie shrugged her shoulders. "It's what we do, what we've always done. We are one of the last gifts that the Tuatha gave mortals."

"A gift?! Screeching and wailing until someone dies out of pure stress?" asked Maddy.

The faerie looked up at her with a hurt expression. "That's NOT what we do!"

"Sorry," said Maddy, when she realized how hurt the faerie woman was. "How would you describe it then?"

"The Tuatha created my kind and gave them to the families of heroes," said the banshee, lifting her head proudly. "So not only do we mourn and give heroes proper funerals when they die but we also mourn their children and their children's children, until the heroes' lines die out and we fade away. We are a sign of respect from the Tuatha—our wailing lets the world know a mortal of greatness or one descended from greatness, beloved of the Fair Folk, has died. Their passing never goes unnoticed, and a hero is *never* forgotten."

"I still don't get it," said Maddy.

The banshee sighed. "Have you ever been to a funeral when no one turns up to mourn the departed?" she asked.

"I really don't hang out at that many funerals," said Maddy.

"Trust me, it's grim," said the banshee.

"So are you my family's banshee?" Maddy asked.

The little faerie nodded while inspecting the creases of the bag of chips for stray crumbs.

"Did you mourn for my mother?" Maddy asked quietly.

The banshee went still and threw a quick look at Maddy, her eyes filling with tears. She nodded, crumpling the potato chip bag in her hand.

"What . . . ?" Maddy swallowed the hard lump in her throat. "Was she . . . ?"

"She was still breathing when I got to the car, but her eyes were far away," said the banshee softly. "Your father died instantly, but I was there for her. She wasn't alone at the end."

Maddy bent forward, hot tears pouring silently down her face as she cupped her eyes with her palms. "I held her hand," continued the banshee. "I stroked it, and I crooned to her until the light died in her eyes. She wasn't frightened, *a chuisle*, my darling, not one little bit. She didn't see this world at all at the end. She didn't know what had happened. She was looking at something I couldn't see, and then she died as easily as sleeping. It was a good death."

The banshee bent down and squeezed Maddy's arm. "Then I keened for her," she said fiercely. "The whole country heard me mourn your mother."

Maddy looked up at her and nodded, wiping tears and snot away with the back of her hand.

"I don't want to be the Hound," she whispered.

"And yet you are," said the banshee kindly, patting Maddy's hand. "Your blood sings with the joy of being the Hound. It calls out to every faerie close by. Tír na nÓg trembles from its song!"

"I don't believe in fate or destiny," said Maddy.

"Child, you can refuse to believe in a runaway horse, but it will still knock you down and trample you if you stand in its way," said the faerie.

"So you're saying I have to go and find this unicorn hunter?"

"How can you not? We stand on the brink of war and famine. Countless lives will be lost, and still more souls will live and suffer at the end of days. All that you and I love, in this world and in among faerie kind, will be no more. You could stand aside, let this be another's task—" the banshee cocked her head and smiled "—but I don't think it's in you to do that. If it were, you could never be the Hound."

"Meabh said the Hound is nothing more than an empty title, that it doesn't mean anything," said Maddy.

The little banshee wrinkled her nose with contempt, which did nothing to improve her looks. "She would, the devious old witch!"

"Is she right?"

"She is and she isn't," said the banshee. "It's true that it's just a title. But it is bestowed only on the Sighted who are the strongest and the bravest, and it changes them."

"How can it do that?" asked Maddy.

"Kings are flesh and blood and no different than the men they rule," said the banshee. "But call a man a king and he walks taller, feels stronger, and he no longer tries to act like a man; he strives to behave like a king. It's the same when you call the Sighted ones 'Hounds.' They grow into the title, and they are stronger for it—they become real heroes. That's what Meabh fears, girl, that you will get stronger and braver every day and block the Tuatha—block her—at every turn, just like Cú Chulainn. Nor does she want the rest of the Sighted to start feeling brave because they have a Hound again. There is power in words, and don't you forget it."

"What about 'Sticks and stones will break my bones, but names will never hurt me?'" asked Maddy.

"Did you ever wonder why the old magic took the form of a pair of unicorns in the first place?" asked the banshee.

"No, why?"

"Earth magic is everywhere, but we can only see small bits at a time. We could not and cannot grasp how big nature is, so we condensed it down to a single pair of mythical creatures, whose image spread to every country in the world. Because human and faerie believed in them so much, the word was made flesh. So never mock the power of words."

"If the unicorns are earth and nature itself, why did the magic take a form that could be attacked, that could sicken and die?" asked Maddy.

The banshee shrugged. "Perhaps because nature itself, for all its magic, can sicken and die. Nothing can last forever."

Maddy sighed. "Why can't we just wake the Morrighan and let her sort all this out?"

The banshee frowned. "Let the Morrighan dream, girl. We're all safer for it. She has powerful magic and would be a dangerous weapon to wield. Let her sleep until you have no choice but to wake her."

Maddy sighed and rubbed her eyes with the heel of her hand. "What's your name?" she asked the banshee.

"Una," the little faerie woman replied.

"OK, Una, I need you to do me a favor—there's another bag of chips in it for you," said Maddy. "I want you to find Seamus, Cernunnos, or whatever he's manifesting himself as at the moment, and tell him, he wins. I'll find this unicorn hunter for him, and I'll deliver it up to him and the four courts for judgment. But I want the mound open when I get there. I'm walking straight into Tír na nÓg, no messing around."

Una cocked her head and smiled. "And who will I say the message is from?" she asked.

"The Hound," said Maddy grimly, standing up and casting a shadow over the banshee. "You can tell him it's from the Hound."

chapter sixteen

MADDY CREPT BACK THROUGH THE HOUSE TO HER room to change into street clothes. As she tiptoed past Granda, she paused to look into his face. It was slack and soft from sleep and age, and she felt a dull hurt in the pit of her stomach as she looked at him.

Why did you wait? she thought. *Why didn't you surround me with iron as soon as you knew?*

But there was no one to blame for this mess. As much as she denied it, she was beginning to believe in fate. Too many coincidences had brought her to this point.

She crept to the kitchen and stuffed food for herself into a backpack. She had no idea if it was true that eating faerie food trapped you in Tír na nÓg forever, but she wasn't taking any chances. She was planning on getting to the end of the search alive and in one piece.

"You're going then?" said a soft voice behind her. She whirled around to see Granda standing in the kitchen doorway, his face sagging with sadness.

"I have to," she said. "They're not going to stop. They're not going to leave me alone—and people will die."

"Two worlds will end if you don't go, eh?" said Granda, a sad smile twitching at his lips. "Who knew our little Madeline would be so important?"

She smiled back at him, tears beginning to prick her eyes.

He sighed. "I should stop you."

"You should," said Maddy. She grinned at him. "But as Dr. Malloy said, you have loads of other grandchildren to drive you mad." She was horrified as Granda finally broke down and began to sob. She ran over to him and hugged him tight, pressing her face against his crumpled shirt. "I'm sorry," she said, her tears wetting his chest. "That was a really bad joke."

Granda wrapped his arms around her and squeezed the breath from her body. He kissed the top of her head. "You're the child of my heart, Maddy. Don't you ever forget that." He pushed her away from him. "Now go," he said, his voice breaking. "Go, before I keep you here and send us all to hell." She opened the back door and stumbled out into the frosty garden, her vision blurred with tears, and she closed the door gently on the sound of Granda's weeping.

But she wouldn't be completely alone. The last year had taught Maddy that there was one friend she could trust and rely on absolutely, and there was no way she was heading into Tír na nÓg without him. She slipped George's lead from its hook by the back door and crunched down the gravel path to his kennel. The smell of dog blasted her in the face when she bent down to peer in, and George didn't help the aroma when he opened his mouth wide to yawn and added dog breath to the mix. He was warm and sleepy as she pulled him from his kennel, and he was not in the least bit pleased to be going for a walk in the middle of the night. He licked Maddy's face half-heartedly as she tied his little red collar around his neck, the chrome identification tag winking in the moonlight. He huffed and yawned and dragged his feet as she pulled him toward the back gate, the collar riding up to his ears and pushing his face into a mass of wrinkles.

Maddy squatted in front of him, and he looked up at her and wagged his tail unenthusiastically.

"I know you think this is unfair, but I really can't do this all by myself," she whispered. George cocked his head at her and whined. She put her arms around his shoulders and hugged him to her. The old terrier began to squirm with delight as she scratched him on the tickly spot at the base of his tail. He jumped up and butted her cheek with his teeth and began to skip around her as the cold night air woke him up. Maddy giggled. "That's a bit more like it," she said.

They ran as quietly as they could through the sleeping village. The gap in the fence to the castle grounds was still there, and they slipped through, slowing to a walk once they were inside the castle grounds. Maddy took deep breaths to calm herself down. Her footsteps were slow now. She didn't want to get to where she was going too soon.

There was little light to see by. The moon rode on a bank of charcoal clouds, and every now and then one would drift across its surface. Maddy walked cautiously, feeling rather than seeing the path that took her over the darkly rushing river and into the open meadow that ran to the foot of the castle, free of the evergreens that guarded the first half of the path and weakly illuminated by the struggling moon.

She walked through the tunnel that led her into the landscaped gardens that the mound brooded in, George bumping against her calf. It was like another world on the other side of the tunnel. It was an artificial one, created to look as mysterious and faerie-like as possible, but it was still ethereal beneath the wan moonlight. Maddy picked her way through artfully piled rocks and nodding ferns until she came to the mound.

Normally the faerie mound looked exactly as you'd expect—a mound of grass covered with earth. But tonight it yawned wide, a shaft punched through its innards, the wound kept open with a stone doorway. Burning torches guttered in iron brackets bolted into the supports on either side of the doorway and smoked greasily in the breeze.

Tonight Seamus had transformed into Cernunnos. Tonight he was a Tuatha. He stood by the doorway, radiating a dark light that pulsed and shifted like an imploding star. The spread of antlers that arced around his head was huge, and they looked too heavy for his neck to support. His tall frame was covered from neck to feet in a cloak stitched from a patchwork of animal furs. But his face was wreathed in a shadow that the lights of the torches could not penetrate—only his eyes gleamed, silver points that followed every step Maddy and George took toward the mound. In his true Tuatha form, he was a thing apart, different from the other Tuatha. His body hummed with a raw power, and he looked feral and pagan, something much, much closer to nature than the courtly beauty of the monarchs of the four courts.

Maddy swallowed and felt her legs start to go rubbery as she walked toward the Tuatha. She could see now why the ancient Celts had worshiped him. Cernunnos, the Green Man, the Horned God—it was all there in the form of this Tuatha who had named himself Lord of the Forest in Tír na nÓg. It was like walking up to a smoldering volcano. But she squared her shoulders. *I'm the Hound*, she thought. *I am the Hound.*

She stopped a foot away from him and stared into his black hole of a face, locking her green eyes on to the silver stars that floated in his eye sockets. Once it had been moons. What did it mean tonight, that he had picked something so cold and distant to reflect his mood?

"The Hound comes at last," he said, his voice a deep vibration that rang in her ears and rippled through her body. "That was a petty trick you played, girl."

"Yeah, but I bet I had you tied up in knots for a little while," said Maddy. "And just thinking about that gives me a warm, fuzzy feeling inside."

"Careful, child," warned Cernunnos, bending his head toward her so the blast of cold from the light of his eyes could chill her lips to white. "You don't know what you are dealing with."

"I do know," said Maddy, hatred and rage bubbling up and thawing her numbed mouth. "I know exactly what I'm dealing with—I have the scars to remind me."

"But you are a bound mortal now, bound by an oath of fealty to the Autumn Court and the Witch Queen," said Cernunnos. "You do our work now."

"I have a few conditions I need you to agree to first," said Maddy.

Cernunnos threw back his head and roared with laughter, the sound booming around them and trailing away in a rumble of thunder. "What an arrogant pup you are!" he declared. "You would impose conditions on your service to me, a being before whom you should bend the knee?"

"I would," said Maddy.

"What gives you the right to demand such a thing?" asked Cernunnos.

"You need me," said Maddy, the memory of Meabh's smile at the back of her mind. "You need me to walk through that tunnel right now. That gives me leverage."

Cernunnos looked at her for a long moment. "Speak, Hound," he said at last.

"A banshee called Una is watching my family," she said. "If they are in danger at any time, she's to get all the help she needs to keep them safe. And she's not to be touched by mortal or faerie."

"Done."

"When I find this hunter, I want justice," said Maddy. "I want the creature and any faerie it worked with to be punished. Even if that faerie—say, one who is married to you—only gave the order. She's to be punished as hard as whoever struck the blow."

"Justice is a hard thing to ask for," said Cernunnos. "There is a difference between what is just and what is right."

"Not to me there isn't," insisted Maddy. "I'm telling you now—if you want me to do a thorough job of sorting this mess out, then you have to promise me justice at the end of it all."

"You do not know what you ask for," said Cernunnos.

"Yes, I do," said Maddy. "You're just doing that typical faerie thing of confusing everything and not answering the question. Promise me that you will see justice done, even if it has to be done to Liadan, or I'm not setting foot in that mound."

"Then it is so," said Cernunnos. "Remember this moment, Hound, when you get what you ask for. Justice will be meted out to those who hunt the unicorns."

"That's all I want," said Maddy.

Cernunnos shook his head slowly. "You have asked for no small thing."

"I don't want anyone playing favorites, that's all," said Maddy. "Can I expect any help from you this time?"

"You will have help, but for now I stay in the mortal world and guard the gateway," said Cernunnos.

"Fair enough," said Maddy. She rubbed George's lead between her fingers and looked down at him. "Ready for walkies?" He grinned up at her, his tongue lolling from his yellowed teeth, and he wagged his tail. Then she nodded a farewell to Cernunnos, squared her shoulders, and stepped into the mound.

The tunnel yawned ahead of her. The last time she had entered the mound, she had been shoved in unconscious by a weakened Cernunnos, and she had woken in a desert of black sand, forced to find her own way to break through the veil of magic that kept Tír na nÓg separate from the mortal world. Not this time. This time she was going to walk straight in. The entrance was bending to her will, behaving like a regular burial mound. The tunnel opened up into a circular hall, plain and unadorned and lit with more burning torches. Maddy watched her shadow shudder in the torchlight over the packed earth walls, and she stood up straighter. She wished she were just a little taller.

"Maddy! Maddy, wait up!"

She heard familiar voices behind her, and she turned, horrified, to see Roisin and Danny come panting up to her, grinning from ear to ear.

"What are you two doing here?" she asked.

"We woke up, and when we realized you weren't in the house, we checked George's kennel," said Danny, while Roisin leaned on a wall and tried to get her breath back. "It didn't take a genius to figure out where you were going with him at four in the morning."

"Did Granda just let you go?!" she asked.

"He was asleep. He didn't see us leave," said Danny.

"You can't come with me, not this time," said Maddy. "You have to go home. It isn't safe."

"Well, that's gratitude for you," said Roisin.

"If we hadn't come with you last time, you would have been toast," said Danny. "You need us. I'm the brawn, and Ro's the brains."

"What does that make me?"

"The trouble magnet." Roisin grinned. "If we hang around you for long enough, trouble will come find us. Besides, it's hardly safe at home anymore, is it? If war and famine are coming, I'd rather be doing something than sitting around wondering when it's going to happen and not even being able to warn people because they would never believe me."

Maddy shook her head. "You don't get it," she insisted. "Things are different this time. I've got protection, but you two haven't. You need to go home, right now."

Roisin frowned at her. "Yeah, we didn't get a chance to talk about that conversation between you and Meabh. Care to explain?"

Maddy took a deep breath and looked at their faces— they weren't going to take this news well. "I swore fealty to Queen Meabh of the Autumn Court. I said no at first, but she told me I could do it whenever I changed my mind, and it seemed like a good way to avoid getting killed by Fachtna. Technically I'm one of them now, and I can call on their protection as long as I am in the Land. You guys can't though."

"You did WHAT?!" shouted Roisin, while Danny swore. "Are you stupid? Do you have any idea what you've done?"

"I got myself a bit of back-up—that's what I've done," said Maddy, the blood rising into her cheeks.

"You don't make deals with faeries, Maddy. You know that!" said Roisin. "They never make a deal that doesn't suit them in the long run."

"I know," said Maddy miserably. "But it's not forever. My oath holds only for a thousand days."

Danny brightened up. "That's not so bad," he said. He looked at Roisin. "Is it?"

Roisin glared at them both. "That's THREE YEARS, you idiots! Three years you're going to have to do whatever Meabh wants!"

Maddy stared back at her, horror dawning in her eyes. "But that's . . . that's until I'm fourteen."

"Didn't you realize?!" asked Roisin.

"No, well, it didn't sound that long," said Maddy. "I just thought, you know, a thousand sounds good even when you stick 'days' on the end of it, and I thought Meabh would go for it. Which she did . . ."

Roisin narrowed her eyes. "Why would she do that? What's so great about you that she wants an oath of fealty in the first place, and why would she accept one with an expiration date?"

This was going to make Maddy look really stupid, but there was no point in lying. "It turns out I'm the new Hound," she said, blushing furiously now. "And that means a lot to them. They're convinced I can find whoever wants to harm the unicorn and stop this war, and Meabh offered me her help but only if I became part of her court."

Danny and Roisin looked at her and then at each other, their faces frozen in disbelief, and then they started to roar with laughter.

"It's not funny!" said Maddy.

"Oh, it is," gasped Roisin, holding on to her stomach as she laughed. "I mean you—the new Hound? Following in the footsteps of Cú Chulainn, the superhero of Irish mythology, him of the big muscles . . ." She doubled over as another gale of laughter swept through her.

"Not being funny, Maddy," said Danny, "but I've seen bigger muscles on a sparrow's kneecap." The two of them continued to roar with laughter, and despite herself, Maddy found her mouth twitching at the corners.

"It's not funny," she repeated as giggles began to bubble up from her stomach, and before she knew it, she was laughing along with them, with George looking at their faces, confusion in his eyes, wagging his tail and hoping to be let in on the fun.

"Honestly, I don't know why we're laughing," said Roisin.

"We're off to face certain death *again* at the hands of homicidal faeries. What's not to laugh about?" asked Danny.

"It almost makes you long for school trips," said Maddy.

"Not me," said Roisin. "You try being the fat kid on the bus."

"Try being the weird one," said Maddy.

"Touché," said Roisin.

They were silent for a moment as they looked at the dark mouth of the tunnel that would lead them into Tír na nÓg.

"So what's she like then, Queen Meabh?" asked Danny. "Do you think you can trust her?"

Maddy sighed. "You've both met her. I wouldn't trust her as far as I could throw her, but we haven't got much choice."

"Do we ever?" said Roisin.

They looked at each other, the dancing flames of the torches throwing their faces into relief, exaggerating their cheekbones and eye sockets. Roisin and Danny looked older in the torchlight—Maddy wondered if she did too. She wished she were older, say forty-five—then she'd be so old the possibility that she could die in the next twenty-four hours might not be so bad.

"We might as well get on with this," she said, shouldering her backpack.

"Oh good," said Roisin, her face brightening. "You brought food!"

"You didn't?" asked Maddy.

"We didn't have time. We were trying to catch up with you!" said Danny.

Maddy rolled her eyes. "Great, so I have to share the food I brought for one person among three. That'll work."

"That's why we should get in and out of this as fast as we can," said Danny. He gave a short whistle. "Come on, girl, walkies!"

"That is definitely not funny!" said Maddy as Roisin dissolved into giggles again.

Danny grinned at her. "Sorry, I was dying to say that."

"Look, stay behind me, and let me be the first out of the tunnel," said Maddy. "I don't think they are expecting all three of us."

"OK," said Roisin. "Just don't do that funny walk you were doing when we were behind you just now. You looked like you needed to go to the toilet."

Maddy ground her teeth. "Can we just get on with this without any criticism of my general houndness, please?" Danny and Roisin nodded back at her, biting the insides of their cheeks to keep from laughing, while their eyes bulged in their sockets with suppressed glee.

"Fine," said Maddy. She gave George's lead a twitch. "Let's go."

chapter seventeen

IT WAS A SHOCK TO WALK OUT OF THE MOUND AND be bathed in the late golden light of evening. The sun was just beginning to sink, and long shafts of pure gold lay lightly on the Land. Fingers of it touched Maddy's face and warmed her mound-chilled skin. It was a last kiss from summer as it faded away, the air crisp with the bite of autumn. But there was a hint of winter too, in the way the bowl of the sky frosted to an ice blue at its edges, a warning that Autumn's reign was passing quickly and the lean times of hunger and cold would soon be here.

"Oh wow!" said Danny. "I didn't realize we were getting a welcoming committee!"

Maddy's heart sank as she took in the scene in front of them. The pavilions of the four courts were spread out in a meadow that rested between the mound and a brooding forest. Courtiers of every shape, size, and breed of faerie were camped on the grass.

"So much for getting in and out quickly!" said Roisin. "They're all going to be watching us."

"I don't mind their watching us," said Danny. "It's *touching* I object to. Especially since *we* have no protection."

Horses and riders broke away from the main host and galloped up the hill toward them. Jewels flashed in the sun, and Maddy recognized the monarchs, with courtiers riding hard on their heels, pennants streaming behind them.

"They are heading this way!" said Roisin, her voice breaking with panic. "I don't want to meet them, I *really* don't want to meet them."

"It's not like we have a choice," said Maddy, as she wound George's lead tight around her hand to keep him close to her side and eyed the approaching riders.

Meabh led the way, a circlet of gold studded with rough-cut rubies around her head, keeping her tumble of thick red hair away from her face. She burned with a keen light, and the colors of her lips and eyes sparkled hard and cold. It was her time, her season, and the power of Tír na nÓg pulsed through her. But the Winter Queen rode hard by her side, and even in her crippled elfin body, a soft light was beginning to glow as Autumn waned and the power of Winter stirred in her crown of spun crystal.

Maddy squared her shoulders and braced herself against the soft turf of the mound as the monarchs and their escorts swept up to her. She breathed deep the air of Tír na nÓg, air that expanded in her lungs and hummed with a vibrant song in her blood. It made her feel giddy and wildly alive, an intense joy flooding her as the song of the air and the song in her blood joined their voices. She breathed deep again until her head steadied and the fear lessened in her heart. Her hair crackled around her head as the magic of the place seeped in through her pores.

She flinched but stood her ground when it looked as if the monarchs would ride her down, but at the last moment their horses went from a gallop to a halt, their hooves churning up turf as they stopped just two feet away from her. Behind her, she heard Roisin breathe out a sigh of relief.

The horses of the monarchs of Tír na nÓg were huge, far bigger and wider than anything Maddy had seen in the mortal world. Their hides gleamed white, their curling manes hung to their knees, and every single one of them had a golden saddle and silver bridle. Even their hooves were shod with gold. Embarr, Meabh's mount, rolled a huge brown eye at Maddy and snorted hay-sweet breath in her face. She looked back at him and recalled how treacherous he could be to his rider at the command of his mistress. Liadan's elf mount was a different kind of animal. Smaller, leaner, it had a vicious and cunning expression. It bared its teeth at her, revealing long, sharp fangs, and it snarled. It pawed the ground not with a hoof but with a taloned paw. The smell of rotting meat drifted over to Maddy, and she turned her face slightly aside. The mount was the only creature that needed protecting from its rider. Cold poured from Liadan's twisted limbs and splashed all over the silver that protected the mount from her body, leaving patches of frost wherever she touched it. She was a leaking nuclear reactor, and Maddy wondered how she or her court could stand it when Winter's power was at its zenith and it tortured her in its grip. *She must be mad*, thought Maddy, *truly mad to keep such a stranglehold on the crown and the power of being a monarch when it costs her so much. No wonder she wants to break free into the mortal world and feed on all our emotions to strengthen her.*

Meabh nudged Embarr forward with her heels and turned him until he stood alongside Maddy. She smiled, transforming her beautiful face, and stretched out a hand adorned with a blood-red ruby ring.

Instinctively Maddy bent her head and kissed the cold, smooth face of the stone. She heard the other monarchs gasp in shock, and she looked up at Meabh. "You didn't tell them?"

Meabh shrugged. "I like to surprise people. Keep them on their toes."

"What is this?" demanded Sorcha. "Is this child truly the Hound?"

"It would seem so," murmured Meabh. "The Blarney Stone itself has pronounced it."

"What a very young and thin pup it is," said Nuada, a sneer on his handsome face. "Is this the best the mortals can do?"

Meabh shot Maddy a warning look. *Keep your mouth shut.* "Was Cú Chulainn any better in his youth?" she asked Nuada, her voice low and sweet.

"Oh, he was!" breathed Niamh, sounding like a love-struck teenager. "Golden and handsome . . ."

"You should know," said Sorcha nastily. "My point is, if this skinny, half-starved-looking child is indeed the new Hound, then why has she become a part of *your* court? Were it not for the fact that it has to hunt the unicorn hunter, I wouldn't have allowed such a creature out from the mound, after the damage its predecessors have done, and it certainly shouldn't be welcomed into any Tuatha court! You should have discussed this with your fellow regents, Meabh."

"I do not need to discuss with anyone, even the Morrighan herself, whom I accept into my court," said Meabh, her eyes wide with mock innocence. "But even if I had wanted to, I had not the time. The child swore fealty to save her throat from being cut by the captain of the Winter Queen."

"As was my right," said Liadan. "The child has insulted me and my captain grievously. Fachtna was only taking what was her due—until the Pooka interrupted her."

Sorcha gave an irritated twitch of her shoulders. "I couldn't care less who has tried to spill her blood." She turned in the saddle to glare at Liadan. "But it was stupid. And when Winter does it, it looks sinister. This girl has agreed to negotiate with Finn mac Cumhaill on our behalf. We need that dog of his to track the unicorn mare safely. Had Fachtna succeeded in killing this girl, it could have undone everything and brought an eternal Winter. I can't see any of those sniveling, cowering Sighted left in Blarney stepping into her place, no matter what they are threatened with."

Liadan stared hard at Sorcha with her dead white eyes. "Fachtna was hot-headed, but the girl has called my honor into doubt—" at this, Aengus Óg gave a bark of laughter "—and I have a right to demand blood justice."

"And there we have our problem," said Meabh brightly. "We have one court trying to kill the girl, which we all agree would be a bad thing, and no other court, apart from my own, offering her sanctuary, despite the fact that, again, we all agree that the unicorn mare's dying would also be a bad thing. This girl is the one chosen to persuade mac Cumhaill to loosen his grip on that animal of his, and *she* is the one who can walk above and below the mound to track the hunter, so we need her alive and cooperative. Have I got this right so far?"

Liadan inclined her head. Nuada and Aengus Óg shot each other a look, unsure where this was going, and Niamh smiled behind her hand to see how angry

Sorcha was getting. Sorcha's attendant butterflies were beginning to crash into each other as her rage confused them.

"What is your point, Meabh?" Sorcha ground the words out through clenched teeth.

"My point," said Meabh, flicking an imaginary speck of dust from her plaid shoulder, "is that with the Winter Queen not thinking clearly, the girl was in danger and in need of protection. The Autumn Court was the only one to offer it, and in her hour of need, she took it. If Fachtna could have been controlled, there might not have been any need for the girl to enter my court."

"And my point," snarled Sorcha, "is that if that tangle-haired urchin really is the new Hound, then she shouldn't be in *any* court. Hounds have offered the Tuatha nothing but insults. To shelter one is to insult the other courts."

"No one knows that better than I," said Meabh. "I was thinking only of the good of us all." She pouted. "It does sound, dear Sorcha, as if you are accusing me of being dishonest in my dealings with the other courts."

Meabh's warriors bristled and put their hands on their sword hilts at the perceived insult to their queen. The escorts of the other monarchs did likewise, and suddenly the air was charged with aggression and threat.

But Sorcha was cool in the face of it all, and she didn't flinch from Meabh's gaze. She smiled, but it didn't reach her blue eyes. "You misunderstand me. I accuse you of nothing," she said. "You are ever my beloved sister. But that child should not belong to any one of us. Hounds have always been our enemies."

"What harm could this child do?" asked Meabh.

Maddy held her breath and watched Sorcha's face muscles twitch as she fought to control her temper. "I don't know," she said at last, dragging the words reluctantly from her throat. Everyone breathed out, and the escorts put their swords back in their scabbards.

"What about those two?" said Aengus Óg, pointing at Roisin and Danny, his dark eyes hooded. "No one needs them, do they? They don't seem to be worth arguing about."

Maddy looked quickly at her cousins and their pale and frightened faces. "I do," she said. "I need them."

"Why?" asked the Summer King, his voice casual as he dropped his reins and pulled a wicked-looking dagger from his tunic. He began to clean his nails with its tip. "I think they would make magnificent hunting. It's been a while since we hunted mortals."

The other Tuatha laughed at this, their voices sweet and fragile in the cool air. They looked at Danny and Roisin with that hungry expression Maddy was beginning to dread.

"Because she's the brains, and he's the brawn," she said. It was the only reason she could think of under this much pressure. "I'm not going anywhere without them," she added.

"Another condition?" asked Meabh. "Doesn't your little brain overheat thinking them all up?" She looked

Roisin and Danny up and down. "Will you be very upset if we kill them?"

"YES!" they all three shouted at the same time.

"It seems this little pup is hard to control already," said Sorcha, a ghost of a smile hovering about her lips.

Meabh frowned at her and then looked down at Maddy. "Take them then. They will pass through with you unharmed by any faerie, you have my word." She clicked her fingers at her escort. "Horses!"

Three of Meabh's Tuatha dismounted and led their white horses over to the children. Their saddles and bridles were simply leather, but they were beautifully engraved with Celtic patterns.

"You also have an escort of your own, to see you safely to the lands of the Coranied," said Meabh. "Volunteers, no less."

Maddy peered through the legs of her enormous white horse and saw a familiar figure gliding through the Tuatha—a huge black wolf.

"Fenris!" she squealed. She dropped the reins and dodged around the horse's legs to fling herself at him, George barking excitedly as he bounced in her wake, but she stopped short as the wolf sat down and puffed up his chest.

"Please don't hug me," said Fenris. "I'm not a dog."

"I don't mind getting those hugs," said a silvery gray wolf as it padded toward her. His eyes sparkled with mischief, and his tongue lolled over his teeth in a way that made it look as if he could be laughing.

"Nero!" cried Maddy, flinging her arms around his thick ruff and hugging him hard. George jumped up and down on the spot, trying to lick and bite Nero's jaw at the same time. The wolf watched him for a moment, and then he put one huge paw over the little terrier's head and pinned him to the ground.

"He's very sweet, but it is *so* annoying when he does that," he said to no one in particular.

"Hello, Nero," said Danny a little warily. He had met Nero once before, and it hadn't gone well.

"Hello, pup," said Nero cheerfully. "Did I leave any scars?"

"I've got a couple," said Danny.

"That makes us friends then," said Nero, wagging his tail. "I've a couple from stopping you getting your head ripped off."

Danny grinned.

"Hello, Fenris," said Roisin. "Where is Nitaina?"

"At the den, with our pups and the rest of the pack," said Fenris. "This isn't the kind of hunt I would want my young ones at."

"And is it OK if you come with us?" said Maddy with a sidelong glance at Liadan. Technically the wolf pack were allies of the Winter Court, and they had been promised dire punishment for helping Maddy the last time she had gone through the mound. But Liadan gave a dismissive wave of her hand.

"They are free to go with you and protect my interests," she said, although Maddy noticed that both

Fenris and Nero went stiff at the sound of her voice, and they did not look at the Winter Queen. "But there is another who would also go with you, with my blessing."

Maddy watched in horror as the Winter Queen's escort parted to let Fachtna through. The dark faerie strode forward to stand beside her queen.

Maddy looked at Liadan in disbelief. "Do I really need to have this conversation again?" she asked. "I'm not going anywhere with her. I'll be dead before we're out of sight."

Liadan hissed with rage. "You have accused me, Feral Child, of one of the worst crimes known to our kind—namely, raising my hand against a unicorn. My captain and the wolves go with you to make sure that not only do you complete the task entrusted to you but that you do not try, in any way, to implicate me in this crime or falsify evidence against me. Fachtna is my witness."

"I wouldn't do something like that!" said Maddy.

"Your hatred for our kind is overwhelming," said Liadan, fidgeting with her reins as her mount began to sidle and dance on its clawed feet, the creature unnerved by her anger. "It leaks from every pore in you. I can taste it in my mouth. I would be a fool to take the word of a filthy, lying mortal." She looked at the other monarchs. "I *demand* that my captain accompany her!"

"Finn mac Cumhaill will not be tempted out of the Shadowlands so she must go to him. It's a dangerous journey, and she needs a champion," said Niamh.

"For once, Aengus, your charming wife is right," said Meabh.

"We're not going with *her*!" said Danny.

"Well, unless any of my fellow monarchs can spare a warrior or two . . ." Meabh trailed off into silence.

"Out of the question," said Nuada. "I need all my warriors about me in such uncertain times."

"As do we," said Aengus Óg. "This mortal could fail miserably, and then the rest of her kind will be upon us as soon as the barrier between their world and ours is gone."

"Alas," said Meabh, smiling down at Maddy like a cat that has just swallowed a whole mouse, still wriggling, "I too need all the able-bodied faeries in my court by my side. In such troubled times, it is wise to conserve your strength."

Maddy ground her teeth in frustration. She knew exactly what was going on. The Tuatha monarchs were hedging their bets, waiting to see if she failed. Anything could happen over the next couple of days, and they were arming their war bands, testing their strength, and looking to see if they could make a grab for power. Even when faced with an annihilating war, they still could not see further than their own ambitions and petty squabbles.

"You are fortunate that the Winter Queen can spare her captain," said Meabh. Liadan inclined her head graciously, her cold-blasted eyes giving nothing away.

Fachtna bared her filed teeth at Maddy in a parody of a smile.

"Yeah, right." Maddy snorted.

"You do not understand, you rude, willful mortal," snapped Sorcha. "You are a subject of the Autumn Court. The four courts are at peace, and for Fachtna to harm you in any way would be an act of war." Sorcha threw a look at Meabh. "Honestly, how can you deal with such treacherous creatures? Every word from her lips is an insult."

"She has to promise not to hurt me or my cousins," said Maddy. "She has to promise not to touch us or do anything that could result in our being harmed by another. She has to protect us, all of us—Fenris, Nero, and George as well—as if we were her own."

Aengus Óg raised a black eyebrow. "Quite hysterical, isn't it? I cannot believe this is the new Hound."

Meabh sighed. "Swear it, Fachtna, or we will be here all day."

Fachtna looked at Liadan, who gave a slight nod. She looked at Meabh, put a hand on her heart, and bowed. "I so swear, Fachtna of the Winter Court, not to harm the mortal of the Autumn Court or her kin while on this hunt."

"I'd feel better if she had stopped at 'kin,'" said Roisin.

"Come, child, don't be greedy," said Meabh. "I really do think it's the best you can ask for, considering the history between you. Besides, it will be good for you to get to know each other. You have so much in common."

"What's that supposed to mean?" demanded Maddy.

Meabh just smiled her slow, irritating smile. "It's not really my place to say. Perhaps Fachtna will tell you herself one day."

Maddy looked at Fachtna and waited for her to say something, but the dark faerie just looked back at her, her face as still as stone. "Fine. But if she's coming with us, then I want a sword."

"A sword?" asked Meabh.

"A big one, same as hers," said Maddy, pointing at the long blade that hung against Fachtna's thigh.

The Tuatha laughed, but Meabh snapped her fingers, and another warrior stepped forward to unbuckle his weapon.

"Do you even know how to use one?" asked Nuada.

"Yeah, you stick the pointy end in the bad guy," said Maddy. She tried to buckle the belt around her waist, but even on the last hole it still fell around her skinny hips. Maddy blushed and ignored the mocking laughter of the faeries as she tied the leather belt in a big knot around her stomach. The sword was heavy, and she felt as if she were leaning to one side. It also smacked awkwardly against her leg when she took a couple of steps toward her horse.

"Um, I'm not much of a rider," said Danny. "Can't we just walk?"

"Time is short, and you will never keep up with Fachtna if you walk," said Meabh. "Besides, these are faerie horses. They can see in your mind where you want to go, and they will take you there. They never drop their riders."

Unless someone asks them to, thought Maddy. She looked up the vertical sides of her horse. Even the stirrup seemed like a long, long way away. "How are we supposed to get on them?" she asked.

"Give me strength," muttered Meabh as the other Tuatha snickered. She snapped her fingers again, and the warrior who had given Maddy his sword stepped forward, lifted the saddle flap, and unbuckled the stirrup leather, lengthening it until the stirrup hung somewhere around her thigh rather than dangling above her head. Maddy put her foot in it and gripped the leather, climbing hand over hand until she could reach the saddle with her fingers and then pull herself up until her stomach was flat on the seat of the saddle. She clenched her teeth and groaned as her bruised ribs grated, but she managed to swing her leg over and sit upright, sweating from the pain while her stomach muscles cramped. The Tuatha shortened the stirrup leather again so she could reach the stirrup from the saddle. Horse-mad Roisin had already climbed aboard, and she was grinning from ear to ear at the chance to ride, while Danny was already beginning to look travel-sick. Maddy looked down. The ground was a long, long way away. George looked up at her and whined.

"Do me a favor," she said to the Tuatha. "Hand him up to the other girl."

The Tuatha looked down at George, distaste curdling his expression. "Can he not run alongside you?"

"His legs are about six inches long so I think he'll have trouble keeping up, don't you?" said Maddy.

"Just do as she says," snapped Sorcha. "She probably won't go anywhere without *him* either, and time is wasting."

Maddy wasn't impressed at the way the Tuatha picked George up by the scuff of the neck and held him at arm's length as if he had the plague, but the little terrier didn't seem to care. He wagged his tail so hard it was a blur as he was passed into Roisin's arms, and she kissed him on the top of his head and zipped him into her jacket.

Meabh turned Embarr closer to Maddy's mount and passed something over to her. "For Bran," she said. "So she can pick up the scent."

Maddy looked down at her hand to see a small piece of the unicorn mare's mane glittering in her palm.

"For you," said Meabh, pressing a walnut into her hand.

"I don't really like nuts," said Maddy.

Meabh rolled her eyes. "It's not for eating, you stupid girl. Crack it open when the time comes, and you will find a net inside, a soul catcher. My storm hags have worked with me for days and nights weaving spells into the net that will trap the split soul and keep it in the form it has chosen to take. You didn't think you would catch it by throwing a rope around its neck, did you?"

Maddy had not thought that far ahead, but she didn't want to embarrass herself by saying so.

"There is no more time to waste," warned Meabh. "Ride as hard as you can for the Shadowlands, and find mac Cumhaill. For all we know, the split soul is already tracking the unicorn mare, and we need Bran on the hunter's trail if we have any hope of avoiding an eternal winter and the end of days. Remember the consequences for faerie and mortal alike if you fail. Remember your loved ones are depending on you, even if they do not know it."

With those grim words, Meabh pulled Embarr's head about and galloped across the meadow to her pavilion, her fellow monarchs and their escorts cantering in her wake, their banners fluttering in the evening sunshine.

chapter eighteen

MADDY HAD NO IDEA WHOM THE FAERIE HORSES were getting their instructions from, but they took off after Fachtna, who was no more than a blur in front of them. Maddy stood up in the stirrups to avoid the feeling of being smacked on the butt with the saddle as her horse galloped along, and she twined her fingers in its thick blond mane. She clutched the reins in one hand but didn't bother getting a tight grip—she doubted the horse would obey her, no matter how hard she pulled on them.

The wind roared past her ears, making her eyes tear, and the only sound she could distinguish over it was the beat of the horse's hooves, a sound that reverberated through her body. It was cold and lonely, crouched on the horse's back with the wind whipping away every word that left her lips before it could reach the ears of

Danny and Roisin. Maddy sincerely hoped they were not going to gallop the whole way because her body was already aching with the strain of keeping her balance.

Even so, they could not have been riding long when Danny started to pull up his horse. The animal shook its head and fidgeted at the bit as it fought to keep up with its stable mates. The determination of the whole ride began to break up as Danny's horse communicated its distress to the others. Maddy felt her own horse falter beneath her, and she saw Fenris and Nero's smooth bounding strides begin to break and become uncertain as they looked back at the struggling horses.

Eventually the whole ride came to a stuttering halt as Danny kept a hard grip on the reins, refusing to let his horse go forward. The animal stamped and circled, trying to sidle away, but Danny refused to relax his hands and let the animal have its head. Maddy and Roisin's horses turned and trotted back to their mate, blowing gently through their noses with a question in their eyes.

"Why are you stopping?" said Maddy.

"I want to make a quick detour," said Danny, his face set and angry.

"You want to do WHAT?!" said Roisin.

"We haven't got time for this," said Maddy. "What's so important that you want to slow us up from saving the world?"

"Have the two of you forgotten?" demanded Danny, his neck flushing with anger.

"Forgotten what?" asked Maddy, while Roisin looked on with a puzzled expression.

"I bet *she* hasn't," said Danny, nodding to Fachtna, who had turned and half flown, half run back to them, her skin glowing pearly with a fine sheen of sweat. She tipped her head to one side and regarded Danny with an unreadable expression in her red eyes.

Danny looked over his shoulder. "We're out of sight of the Tuatha camp, and the forest is just the other side of the river. I reckon we can swim across."

"The trees won't welcome you, boy," growled Fachtna in her hoarse voice. "You won't last any time at all."

"Oh!" cried Roisin, as she and Maddy remembered at the same time what they should never have forgotten. Maddy swayed in her saddle and closed her eyes against the memory of Fachtna's knife slicing through long silver-green fingers.

"Fionn," she said weakly.

"Fionn," said Danny. He glared at Fachtna. "Did you kill her in the end, for helping us?"

Fachtna smiled lazily at him and slipped a dagger into her hand, tapping its blade against her chin. It looked like a casual enough gesture, but the threat was there. "The dryad was lucky. Queen Liadan commanded me to burn her tree rather than cut it down, and it seems that it is struggling back into life. Green shoots are said to be growing from its blackened stump while its dryad sleeps between its roots."

Maddy swallowed and thought of the pretty little birch dryad, with her black eyes and masses of long silver hair, lying charred and injured beneath the earth, waiting for herself and her tree to grow strong. All because she dared to show them the way to Liadan's tower. Would her fingers ever grow back?

"I need to see her," said Danny, his voice thick with tears. "It was our fault she was hurt."

"She's beyond you, boy," said Fachtna. "She will sleep until she is strong enough to tend her tree again. Don't draw attention to her—be grateful my queen allows the tree to go on living."

"I have to see her," insisted Danny. "I need to make things right."

"I don't know that we can," said Roisin.

But Danny was sliding down from the huge horse anyway, to collapse on the ground in an undignified heap. He dropped the reins and began to walk toward the river.

"Go ahead. I'll catch up," he called over his shoulder.

Fenris looked at Maddy. "Is he serious?" he asked.

"Um . . ."

"Go ahead, boy," called Fachtna. "You're about to find out how little the trees like you."

As soon as Fachtna said those words, the world was silenced. Birds stopped singing, insects stopped buzzing, and a wave of tension seemed to roll over them, a wave that came from the direction of the trees.

Nero sat down and pricked up his ears. "This is going to get messy," he said in a positively cheerful tone of voice.

"Danny, don't do it!" said Roisin.

Danny hesitated and then stepped down into the water. Fenris growled as every tree on the opposite bank leaned toward him, creaking and groaning as they strained against their roots. Then eyes lit up in the trunks of the trees and peered down from their leaves, bright, glistening orbs that shone with hate. Maddy's breath caught in her throat, and Danny stood transfixed in the gaze of hundreds of dryads.

"What are you waiting for?" asked Fachtna. "Swim across to them. I'm sure once you tell them it was all my fault they will welcome you with open arms."

Danny turned to glare at her, but he didn't make a move to go forward or back. Maddy's heart ached for him. She knew he cared for the little silver dryad, but he couldn't make things better. Even if he survived a walk through the trees, there was nothing he could do.

It was Fenris who broke the deadlock. He padded down to the water's edge and nudged Danny with his black nose.

"There is no shame in backing away," he said with a soft growl. "An alpha male needs to know when to make a stand and when to retreat. Now is a time to retreat. Her kin won't be appeased by your guilt—spilled blood never dries."

Maddy breathed a sigh of relief as Danny turned, shame-faced, and went back to his horse. Fachtna waited until he had clambered back into the saddle before she launched herself into the air again, forcing them to kick their horses into a gallop to keep up with her.

After a while, Maddy's legs began to tremble with the effort of standing in the stirrups. The horse must have felt the tremors from her thigh muscles and slowed to a steady canter, allowing her to sit deep and look around her.

The lush, thick turf beneath their horses' hooves was beginning to fade to a poorer soil, full of rocks and stones. The forest on the other side of the river began to peter out as well, until there were only a few stunted saplings struggling to grow on their own. The river grew broader, and its voice changed from a babble to a roar with the force of its current, its white foam coating the stiller waters at the edges of the riverbank.

The barren land and the angry river stretched ahead for about a mile and then disappeared abruptly into a roiling bank of dirty yellow clouds. Maddy leaned back to steady herself as her horse came to a sudden halt, the other mounts pulling up alongside her. Fachtna's wings buzzed as she landed lightly in front of Maddy, while Fenris and Nero flopped down and stretched their long limbs on the thin soil, their tongues flopping from their mouths as they panted.

"What is *that*?" asked Roisin, her eyes fixed on the wall of mist dead ahead.

"*That* is what a mist of dreams looks like," said Fachtna.

"Come again?" said Danny.

"All your dreams, all your hopes, your fears, your darkest desires, your most frightening nightmares . . . it is all in this mist," said Fachtna. "It leaks into the land, or it comes through the Seeing Stones in the mortal world. The Coranied gather it and live within it here in the Shadowlands, distilling it down in their cauldrons so they can feed it to us."

"Wow," said Danny.

"Is it safe to walk through the mist?" asked Roisin nervously.

"No faerie ever tries—well, none but Meabh," said Fachtna. "She walks freely through the Shadowlands. So, is it safe?" Fachtna shrugged. "Some say the mist shifts and can have you lost in the wilderness for years. Some that it is a place where ghosts lurk. We will find out soon enough." She looked at the sinking sun. "But not tonight. Tonight we rest."

Even though it meant more delay, Maddy was relieved she didn't have to brave that mist tonight. The three of them half jumped, half slid down from their mounts. Fachtna began to unbuckle the girth straps that held the saddles in place on the horses' backs.

"We'll untack them and make them comfortable," she said. "The three of you can use the saddles as pillows. I'm not risking a fire this close to the Coranied—who knows what will be attracted to it this close to the mist. So curl up together and keep each other warm. You'll need all your strength in the morning."

———

Maddy must have been exhausted because she didn't even remember falling asleep. But sometime in the night, the sound of splashing woke her up, and she sat bolt upright, terrified something was sneaking up on them from the river. Fenris and Nero lay curled up with their backs touching, their plumed tails draped elegantly over their noses. Danny and Roisin were huddled as tight as they could underneath their jackets, cradling their cheeks with their hands to protect their faces against the stiff leather of the saddles. George lay alongside Roisin's thigh, flat on his back, legs in the air, his rough pink tongue pushing against his teeth as he snored.

Maddy looked toward the river and saw a tall, pale faerie step from the water, her skin glowing. Her white hair hung down to the small of her back and her ice-white face was soft in the moonlight, her lips full and ripe. She walked with a supple grace, and it was only when she uncurled her wet wings, swept her hair back over her shoulders and wrung the water from it with her long hands that Maddy recognized her.

Carefully she climbed to her feet, tied the sword belt around her waist and walked over to the faerie, who had just finished wrapping her linen clothes around her body.

"What happened to you, Fachtna?" she asked softly.

Startled, Fachtna turned to face her, her expression hardening and her lips lifting in a sneer. Free of the stiffening lime that held it in its customary Mohican, her thick, straight mane of hair swirled around her body in a soft white curtain.

"What do you care, Feral Child?" she asked as she bent for her sword belt.

"I don't," said Maddy. "But for a second there, you didn't . . . well, you didn't look like yourself."

Fachtna snorted. "What a stupid thing to say! How can I look like anyone but myself?" she said. "More fuzzy mortal thinking."

"Fine," said Maddy. "You looked, for a second, like someone pleasant—you know, attractive? Like someone you could talk to without being disemboweled."

"Ah, was I beautiful?" asked Fachtna, her sneer still firmly in place.

"I wouldn't go overboard," said Maddy. "You looked *normal*, with all that junk out of your hair and your mouth closed so I couldn't see your teeth. Even with the freaky red eyes. Why do you do that to yourself anyway? Didn't it hurt, filing your teeth down?"

"It did," said Fachtna. "But no one fears beauty on the battlefield. It had to be done."

"Why?"

"Because, Feral Child, someone put steel in my soul, and now I can be no other way," said Fachtna. "Just like you."

"I'm not like you," said Maddy.

"So you say. But you are living in interesting times, and now that you are the Hound . . . well, let's just say life is going to get even more interesting. Pain will forge your soul and bend it in so many ways that one day you won't recognize yourself or the things you've done. I was soft once. I never thought I would be so good at killing or that I would enjoy it so much."

"Is that what Meabh meant when she said we had a lot in common?"

The shutters came down over Fachtna's face. "Perhaps." She drew her sword. "Defend yourself."

"You what?" said Maddy. "You can't touch me, remember?"

"Grow up, girl," hissed Fachtna. "You're safe enough. But it's time you learned to be a proper Hound."

"Meaning?"

"Twice now you've gotten away from me using silly tricks," said Fachtna. "Do you think you will be as lucky a third time? The Hound is meant to be brave, strong, fierce in battle. You don't even know how to use your sword."

"I do!" said Maddy.

"Prove it," said Fachtna.

Maddy drew her sword and lunged at the faerie, the pointed end aimed straight at her stomach. Fachtna twirled her wrist, the silver blades kissed, and then Maddy's sword flew out of her grasp.

"Again," said Fachtna. "Hold your sword up, not dangling down from your fingers. Block me with the flat of your blade. And move your feet! War is a dance."

For the next half-hour, Maddy struggled to lift the sword while Fachtna showed her how to attack, block, and parry. The faerie did make fighting look beautiful, moving as gracefully over the ground as a snake. Maddy lumbered and sweated after her, not once making contact with the tattooed skin.

"Enough," said Fachtna, lowering her sword as Maddy massaged her aching wrist. "Practice, girl, if you want to have a hope of survival." She bent down to stare into Maddy's eyes. "Because the next time we meet, I want to kill a foe worth the fight, not slit the throat of some bawling babe." She straightened and looked at the sky. "The sun is rising. Wake your friends."

Maddy made her way back to the saddles, but when she went to shake Roisin, she found she was already awake and staring at her with her big brown eyes. "Bonding, are we?"

"I have no idea what I'm doing," said Maddy.

chapter nineteen

ROISIN PUT HER HAND OUT AND TWIRLED HER FINgers through the mist as if she were checking the temperature of a bath.

"There's no moisture in it at all," she said. "It's just like smoke."

"Is it going to be safe to breathe it in?" asked Maddy.

"Only one way to find out," said Nero.

"It's all right for you, you're lower down," said Danny.

"What's that got to do with anything?" asked the wolf.

"Smoke rises, which means the taller you are, the quicker it will get to you," said Danny.

Without meaning to, they all looked at Fachtna at the same time. She raised an eyebrow as she stared back at them, but no one said a word.

"I don't think that is going to apply here," said Fenris. "It's not normal smoke, mist, whatever we're going to call it. Besides, the Coranied know we are entering it and why—they would hardly poison us on their borders."

"Our biggest problem is going to be seeing, not breathing," said Fachtna. She thrust her arm deep into the mist, and it was as if it had been swallowed from the elbow down. Maddy couldn't even see a dim outline.

"We'll leave the horses here; it's too dangerous to try walking them through this," Fachtna continued. "If they start to panic in there, it will be hard to hold them, and we do not want to risk getting separated."

"Will they be OK?" asked Roisin.

"They will be fine," said Fachtna. "They will wait for us here until we emerge or their riders call them home."

Maddy picked up George and zipped him into her jacket. She gasped in pain as he wriggled against her sore ribs, and he rasped his rough tongue over her chin by way of an apology.

"Nero and I can smell all of you well enough, but you will have to hold on to each other," warned Fenris. "It will be too easy for someone to get lost and wander away in there."

"We'll have to hold hands," said Roisin. "Fachtna, you lead the way. Maddy, you can hold hands with her, seeing as you are such good friends."

Maddy looked at Roisin, shocked by the spite in her voice, but Roisin just glared at her with a *Yeah, and?* look.

Maddy sighed and held out her hand to Fachtna. Roisin grabbed her other hand, Danny held on to his sister, and together they shuffled forward into the mist.

Maddy had felt a tiny bit stupid, venturing into the unknown holding hands, but once they were inside the mist, it was a different story. She *knew* she was holding Fachtna's creepy triple-jointed fingers and Roisin's pudgy digits because she could feel them, but she couldn't see them. She couldn't see anything. When she looked down, she couldn't even see her own feet.

Panic and claustrophobia clawed at her, and within seconds she found herself fighting the urge to scream. Her breath came in ragged shallow gasps, and in her painful, hitching chest it felt like her lungs were shrinking as rapidly as a salted slug. George picked up on her distress and began to squirm, which only made things worse. Maddy clenched her teeth and felt a tiny trickle of sweat slide down the side of her face, but before she could give in to the panic, a massive wedge-shaped head butted against her side, and she could feel a wet nose nuzzling her hip and she relaxed. She had no idea if it was Nero or Fenris, but just the feeling of the warm, shaggy body padding alongside hers and being surrounded by the sharp scent of wolf calmed her down.

She could hear Danny and Roisin panicking alongside her as their breathing quickened and caught in their chests, and she wished they had enough wolves to go around. She was about to say something when a strange smell tickled her nostrils.

"Can anyone smell that?" asked Danny.

"Is that . . . ," Maddy sniffed, ". . . doughnuts?!"

"I'm getting chocolate cake," said Roisin.

"Pancakes," said Danny. "Definitely pancakes."

Up ahead the mist cleared, and Maddy's mouth dropped open when she saw what was waiting for them.

A cottage crouched in their way, but it wasn't built of bricks and mortar or wood. The whole thing, from the front doorstep to the roof, was made entirely of desserts. The roof tiles were slabs of chocolate cake, the walls were stacks of pancakes mortared with layers of cream and maple syrup, and doughnuts swirled to form a door frame, and from the chocolate-log chimney rose a thin wisp of smoke. The door and the window frames were made from chocolate flakes while the windows were flat translucent sheets of sugar.

"Wow," said Danny.

Maddy hadn't been hungry, but just the sight of that sugary, sweet building made her mouth water. She longed to snap a doughnut off the door frame, cut herself a slice of the pancake wall . . .

"It's a gingerbread house," said Roisin.

"What?" asked Maddy, half in a daze as she imagined how a chocolate-cake roof tile would taste, melting in her mouth.

"It's obvious," said Roisin. "It's the gingerbread house out of 'Hansel and Gretel,' built to tempt passing children so the warty old witch who lives there can snatch them inside and cook them up in her oven."

"Are you sure?" asked Danny. "I can't see any gingerbread."

"Course not," said Roisin. "Who eats gingerbread these days?"

"Can we have some?" said Maddy. Her stomach growled.

"Do you remember what happened to Hansel and Gretel?"

"Oh yeah," said Maddy.

"Let's go around it," said Danny.

"Did the witch do anything to wolves?" asked Nero's voice somewhere near her waist. She could hear both wolves sniffing the air.

"Wolves weren't in the story, but I don't think we should risk it," said Maddy. There was silence for a second, and then Nero said, "Shame," in a quiet voice.

"So do we have a decision?" snapped Fachtna.

"Yeah, we're walking on around it," said Maddy.

"At last," muttered Fachtna, and she strode off, dragging them all in her wake.

They skirted the cottage nervously, and once they were past it, the mist closed over it again. The smell though was all around them, and it didn't seem to be getting any weaker. Maddy, Danny, and Roisin's stomachs growled in the silence, and Maddy had to swallow repeatedly to keep from drooling.

They walked on for a few more minutes, and they found the mist clearing again. The same cottage sat in front of them, waiting for them as contentedly as a cat in the sunshine, and the same lazy trail of smoke was looping into the air from its chocolate chimney.

"I don't believe this!" said Roisin.

"Now can we have some?" asked Nero.

"NO!" they all shouted at the same time.

Fenris sniffed the air. "I don't like this. Let's try to get away from here."

So on they walked, with the smell of all those sugary goodies as strong in their noses as ever, until a few minutes later, there sat the cottage again.

"Are we going in circles or something?" demanded Danny.

"Did you see us take a turn anywhere?" asked Roisin.

"No."

"Well, shut up then!"

"It's not going to let us past," said Fachtna.

"What do you mean?" asked Maddy.

"What I said," she snapped. "It's a creature of the mist. It might be a test set by the Coranied, but whatever it is, it isn't going to go away. You need to deal with it."

"Us?!" said Maddy. "How?"

"I don't know," said Fachtna. "This thing comes from your world, your heads. It's for you to deal with."

"Great," muttered Danny.

"We could just eat our way through?" said Nero hopefully.

Fenris sighed. "Please stop thinking about eating."

"I can't help it. I'm hungry," said Nero. "We really should have hunted last night."

"We need to act out the story," said Roisin.

"What, take a bite and get kidnapped?" said Maddy.

"It's waiting for us, and it's waiting for something to happen," said Roisin. "We have to sort it out before we can move on, so I suggest we act out the story. And when I say we, I mean you two. It only needs a Hansel and a Gretel, and I'd be no good at fighting off scary witches."

"Is this really the only way through?" asked Fenris, a frown creasing his face.

"Unless anyone else can think of another plan," said Roisin. They all looked back at her. "Fine. This is the only way."

Maddy sighed and unzipped her jacket. She handed George over to Roisin. "Keep hold of him, and don't let him run off or we'll never find him again," she said.

"Are you going to take the sword off?" asked Roisin.

"Why?"

"Gretel didn't have a sword," she pointed out.

"Then she was an idiot," said Maddy.

"Just leave it—we've got Fachtna. You might mess the story up," insisted Roisin.

"I'm not involving myself in this," said Fachtna, her long hooked nose wrinkling in distaste.

"I'm definitely bringing my sword," said Maddy. She grabbed Danny by the arm, and the two of them walked up to the cottage. They dug their hands into the flake sticks that made up the rustic front door, broke off handfuls of the brittle chocolate, and shoved it into their mouths. Maddy looked back at everyone else, raised her eyebrows, and shrugged when nothing happened. Danny, cheeks bulging like a hamster, gave a thumbs-up . . . right before the door burst open and a pair of green hands grabbed them both by the arms and yanked them inside.

chapter twenty

Maddy staggered as she was spun around in the doorway and shoved across the room. The sword tangled in her legs, tripping her, and she screamed with pain as she crashed down on the floor, landing on her ribs. Her swollen eye throbbed in the heat of the room.

Inside the cottage was just bare boards, on the floor and on the walls. It was single-room shack that held nothing but a table set for one, a bench with some very wicked-looking hooks and knives on it as well as a massive pie dish, and a huge stone oven. An inferno blazed inside it, and it throbbed from the power of the heat. Flames glared balefully from a small glass door set in the belly of the oven, casting a hellish glow over the shack. It was the only light in the room, and darkness clung as thick as cobwebs in the corners and hung from the rafters of the ceiling.

She heard Danny groan and saw him lying stunned by the bench. Outside the wolves were howling, and a heavy body was throwing itself against the door. Paws scratched at the base of the door, but the chocolate cottage seemed to be impervious to the damage a wolf's granite-hard claws should be able to inflict.

Maddy heard a low chuckle, and she turned her head to look at the witch.

She was straight out of a fairy tale, dressed in black with a hump on her back, and she had green warty skin. Her hands huge and tipped with long black nails, and a tall black pointy hat was on her head. Its brim shadowed her face. She lifted her head to fix her eyes on Maddy, and the flames lit up her face.

Yellow eyes blazed in a green face, and sharp yellow teeth ground and chomped in a wet, slobbering, black-lipped mouth. A long hooked nose and a long hooked chin that almost touched each other completed the picture. She was an echo of Maddy's nightmares, the storybook witch come to eat her flesh and crunch her bones, only this time Maddy wouldn't wake up screaming to find her mother comforting her.

"Naughty little mice, nibbling on my cottage," she said. Even the *voice* was from a book, high and creaking. "Naughty little mice, come to steal from me. Greedy little mice that think they can take what they want without even a please or a thank-you. But now you have to pay for what you took."

There was a movement at one of the windows, and Maddy could see a silvery blur through the cloudy sugar glass as Nero braced his huge front paws against the window sill and tried to peer through into the gloom. The witch saw it too.

"Stupid wolf," she snarled. "Can't it stay in its own story?"

Maddy climbed slowly to her feet. "No one can get in, can they?" she asked.

The witch smiled a ghastly smile at her. "And no one can get out. Not until the story is done."

"You know how the story ends, right?" asked Maddy. The witch hissed at her as Maddy undid the sword belt, wrapped it around the hilt of the sword, and hefted it in her hand like a club. "You do realize I get to shove you head first into an oven?"

"Endings can change," hissed the witch.

"Come on then," said Maddy, grinning and lifting the sword. "Come have a go if you think you're hard enough."

The witch gave a howl of rage and charged. Maddy stood her ground and then spun around at the last second, cracking the witch hard across the back of the head with the flat of her blade and sending her staggering head first into the wall. The witch growled and clambered to her feet.

"Calling yourself a Hound doesn't make it so," the witch said. "Weave a story for yourself if you like, girl—it doesn't mean you can live it. And the ending of every story can change, even this one."

Maddy held the sword over her shoulder like a bat and prepared to swing again. "You're going into that oven, whether you like it or not," she said.

The witch and Maddy circled each other, each looking for an opening, while Roisin screamed their names outside and the steady *thud, thud, thud* at the door told her Fachtna had overcome her reservations and was trying to break in. The witch howled and charged Maddy again, but this time Maddy stepped into her arms and head butted her squarely on the nose. Her head rang, but the witch went down a second time.

Danny managed to grab hold of the bench and pull himself to his feet. Maddy turned to see if he was all right, when the hag climbed to her feet and lunged for the vicious-looking instruments Maddy had noticed when she first entered the room.

"Stop her!" yelled Maddy.

It was not the most elegant intervention. Still woozy from his fall, Danny half fell against the witch, but he managed to pin her arms to her sides in a bear hug. The witch howled with rage and thrashed in his arms. Sweat poured from his face, and the pair nearly fell over backward as she arched her back and pushed off the ground with the pointed heels of her shoes.

"Now what?" he panted, as Maddy advanced on them, her face grim.

"Now you're going to help me shove her in the oven," said Maddy.

"What?!" asked Danny, horrified.

The witch narrowed her eyes to slits and hissed at Maddy through her long teeth.

"That's the end of the story," said Maddy. "You heard her—no one gets out of here until it's over."

Danny hesitated, and the witch took the opportunity to snap her head back and catch him on the nose with her skull. Danny yelled in pain and let go of her, clamping his hand over his face, blood dripping from his nose.

The witch made a run for it and was almost at the door when Maddy caught her. She rapped her hard on the head with the pommel of the sword to daze her, then drew the blade, tossing the scabbard aside. Fachtna came crashing through the door, and the sugar glass exploded as Fenris and Nero leaped in through the windows. The wolves crept forward slowly, their hackles raised, every one of their long sharp teeth exposed in a deep-throated snarl.

"Time's up," Maddy whispered to the witch, who glared up at her. "If they can get in, the story's over." She dragged the witch, who seemed to be a bundle of small bones underneath her dress, over to the oven and flipped the door open, singeing her fingertips.

"Maddy, you can't do this!" said Danny. "You can't burn someone alive!"

"She's not real," said Maddy.

"How do you know?" asked Danny. "She looks real enough to me."

"Maddy's right," said Fachtna. "It's the only way we can get out of here."

"So you're siding with the psycho faerie, are you?" asked Danny, ignoring Fachtna. "This is who you want to be like now, is it?"

"I'm doing what's necessary," said Maddy.

"That sounds familiar," said Fachtna.

Those words were like a bucket of ice water over Maddy. All noise faded in her ears apart from the sounds of her breathing, her heart beating. She could not look at Danny, who was still pleading with her, or meet Fachtna's mocking gaze. She did not want to look down at the struggling witch and see her afraid or pleading. Instead, she looked into Fenris's burning yellow eyes.

A wolf puts its pack first, she thought as the wolf stared back at her and made no move or a sound to either condemn or support her. *A Hound does the same.* She turned away, and the muscles bunched in her arm as she hauled the witch higher, preparing to throw her into the heart of the oven.

"Why didn't you come for me?" said a child's voice.

Maddy looked down and saw her hands were now wrapped firmly around the slender throat of a girl around six years old. She gazed at her in shock. Her shoulder-length black-brown hair was tied up in two braids finished with red ribbon. There was a smattering of freckles across her cheeks, and her face was broad with a snub nose.

"Why didn't you come for *me*?" asked the child again.

"What?" breathed Maddy.

"What good is a Hound that leaves us to suffer?" said the child. "What good is a hero who doesn't come to the rescue? You came for him—why didn't you save ME?!" The child screamed, and Maddy was appalled as her skin began to blacken and shrivel like paper curling in a fire until all she held was a wizened little monstrosity with bulging pale eyes, that bared its fangs at her and clawed her arm until her jacket hung in tatters.

Maddy yelped and tried to shake the thing off, but it shrieked louder and clung on for dear life while all around them the Hansel and Gretel cottage melted away and the mist swirled around them again. There were things in the mist now, things that joined in with tortured wails of their own and angry voices that shouted and jabbered. Fenris and Nero began to shake, their eyes rolling in their heads with fear, their hair standing up on end as they whipped their heads about, looking for an enemy. Danny and Roisin clung together with George held tightly between them, eyes shut, hands clamped over their ears, and all three of them trembled. The noise all around them grew to a deafening roar, and Maddy thought her ears would bleed from the pain of the sound, but then Fachtna stepped forward, grabbed the wizened creature by the back of the neck, and hurled it as far as she could.

It disappeared into the mist with a last despairing screech. The roar of anger that had been all around them was silenced as effectively as if someone had flicked a switch. Maddy sank to her knees as her legs gave way, and over the sound of her ragged breathing, she thought she heard the pattering of bare feet and the high sobs of a child.

"What was that?" asked Roisin, her voice shaking with fear.

"A split soul," said Fachtna grimly.

"*That's* what we are looking for?" said Danny. "Why don't we go after it?"

"Because there could be thousands of split souls lurking in this mist, and we have no way of telling which one attacked the unicorn mare," said Fachtna. "We need to catch it in the act, which means we need to find the mare, which means we need mac Cumhaill to hand over that cursed dog!"

She drew a dagger and grabbed Maddy's hand. "Enough of this messing around," she hissed, and she sliced the blade across Maddy's palm. Maddy yelped with pain and watched, stunned, as Fachtna held her hand down and kneaded her wrist, making the blood pump faster.

"What are you doing?" asked Maddy.

Fachtna grinned at her. "Quickest way to draw Finn mac Cumhaill out is to insult him. He never was the kind of man who could walk away from an insult."

"Couldn't you just call him names?" said Maddy, her stomach churning as she watched her own blood drip into the mist, disappearing from sight before it hit the ground.

Fachtna winked at her. "I spill Fenian blood and call on the Fianna to answer!" she cried, her voice falling dead and flat in the mist that still whispered of hurts and wrongs and vengeance. "I call on Finn mac Cumhaill to answer the call of his tribe and avenge his blood!"

The mist flew apart as if someone had turned an industrial-strength hairdryer on it, and about two hundred yards away a castle not unlike Blarney soared into view, its gateway barred and its windows shuttered.

"At last!" said Fachtna.

chapter twenty-one

"ALL OF YOU, STAY BEHIND ME," SAID FACHTNA.
"Fenris, Nero, guard them on each flank." The wolves
silently padded over to stand on either side of Danny,
Roisin, and Maddy. "Keep that dog quiet, and let me do
the talking."

They walked forward in a defensive huddle until
they stood immediately below the gates to the castle.
There were men on the battlements, men with long
flowing hair, dressed in plaid and breeches. Helms covered their brows and noses, and beards hid the rest.

"Ach," said one as he spat in their direction. "It's a
faerie."

"What do you want, faerie?" called another. "Was it
you that spilled the blood?"

"It was," said Fachtna.

"And why would you go and do a silly thing like that?" said the man.

"To get your attention."

"Aye? Have you come to fight, faerie?"

"No, I've come to parley with mac Cumhaill," said Fachtna. "And to ask for a loan of that dog of his, Bran."

The men on the wall looked at each other in amazement and then started to laugh.

"Then it *is* a fight you've come for, faerie, for it will be a cold day in hell before Finn mac Cumhaill gives up Bran." He laughed. "You have to give me a better reason than a half-daft one to open the gates. Every faerie should know that Finn mac Cumhaill does not parley with your kind. I thought faerie babes took that knowledge in with their mother's milk."

"Will he parley with the Hound of his people?"

The men on the gate began to mutter while the laughing warrior simply smiled down at them. "So it's true then? A faerie traveling with the Hound? Strange company to keep."

"These are strange days," said Fachtna. "And there are ripples in the mortal world and Tír na nÓg alike that will disturb even mac Cumhaill in his fortress. It would be in his best interests to listen to what I have to say."

The warrior grinned down at her. "Mac Cumhaill is a man who knows where his own best interests lie, and I doubt a faerie is going to tell him any differently. But seeing as you come in peace, you are welcome to try to tell mac Cumhaill what's good for him. It has been a while since we had a bit of entertainment around here."

The men laughed, the gates swung open, and they walked into the fortress of the Fianna.

Maddy looked around and shivered. There was no sound to the place, no echo. Their footsteps thudded down on the packed earth with a dull noise that faded from the memory instantly. She listened to every footfall and decided she couldn't describe what the sound was like, even if her life depended on it. There was no sky, no scenery, just that infernal yellow mist pressed against the outside walls and hanging above their heads. There were more men in the courtyard, helmeted and wearing chain mail like the armor worn by the men on the battlements. They stood around in listless groups and watched them go with dull, resentful eyes. Maddy shuddered at their gaze. They were men marooned—the world had gone on without them.

"Are they men or stories or ghosts or what?" she whispered to Roisin.

"Probably a little bit of everything," Roisin whispered back.

Fachtna stopped abruptly and turned around. "I want no whispering or chattering in here," she said, red eyes narrowed. "Say nothing that can give mac Cumhaill or the Fianna any reason to take offense. Understand?"

All three of them nodded at her. She looked at Fenris and Nero. "And no talking at all from the two of you. The

Fianna are a little old-fashioned, so no taking offense at anything they say and drawing attention to yourselves. They might decide that what the place needs is the head of a talking wolf, stuffed and mounted." She prepared to walk on.

"No eating, no talking—this is no fun at all," said Nero, his tongue lolling from his teeth as he grinned. Maddy, Danny, and Roisin choked back giggles as Fenris swept them with his fiery gaze before turning and padding after Fachtna, who strode ahead to a hall set inside the battlements. The huge wooden doors stood open, and she walked through. Maddy practically had to jog to keep up with her supernaturally long strides.

Inside, the hall was dark and oppressive. There were more men lingering in here, in the same silence, the same sullen look in their eyes, and their eyes were only things about them that moved as they sat at long benches that spanned the length of the hall watching them pass. The floor was strewn with rushes that gave off no scent or sound as they walked on them. Shields and banners decorated the stone walls, and at the end of the hall, set on a dais beneath huge arched windows, was a tall wooden throne covered with animal furs. A huge man sat there, his dark curling hair tumbling about his shoulders and a massive sword lying across his knees. There were a few hunting dogs slinking about by the benches, but there was no mistaking the beast that sat at his feet. The wolfhound had piercing blue eyes, and she gazed at Maddy with the haunted expression she remembered from the vision the Coranied had shown her. This had to be Bran. About the throne sat a number of women, all with tears streaming down their faces. Their cheeks were marked with grooves where the water had worn a path. The front of their dresses and their laps were dark and marbled from the salt tide while the rushes at their feet gave off a faint whiff of damp.

"Greetings from the Winter Court, Finn mac Cumhaill," said Fachtna as she bowed her head to the man on the throne. "We have traveled a long way, and we would like to break bread and salt with the Fianna."

The man raised his head to look at them. He looked exhausted and grief-stricken, with deep lines carved into his face. But there was keenness in his eyes his men did not have. He smiled without any real warmth. "What good does it to you to take bread and salt from the living dead, faerie?" he asked in a voice so low that Maddy had to strain to hear it. "No one here eats or drinks anymore. And I wouldn't offer guest rights to one of your kind even if I had the food."

Maddy could see Fachtna's whole body stiffen with anger at the insult, but she kept her voice soft and polite. "Then may we have a private audience?"

Finn mac Cumhaill waved a hand and gave a grunt that Maddy was sure was supposed to be a laugh. It sounded like it found it to be too much effort to make its way up the man's throat. "There is no private here," he said. "The mist tells me why you have come."

"What does it say?" asked Fachtna.

"That you come here to ask for the use of Bran for a little while, to hunt down a unicorn that has fallen far from the eyes of the Tuatha." At the sound of her name, Bran looked up adoringly at her master and thumped her tail a couple of times on the flagstone floor. "The mist should have told you that you are wasting your time. Bran is dearer to me than any child, and I would never let her leave my side, not even if it was my own father who asked for her."

"Our need is urgent . . ." began Fachtna.

"Not to me," said Finn. "What do I care if the outside world is dying? Let it die."

"How can you say that?" asked Maddy, peering around Fachtna's body. The dark faerie looked down at her and bared her teeth in an effort to get Maddy to shut up, but Maddy took no notice. "All the people above the mound, they still tell your stories; you are still a hero. They keep you alive. Isn't that how this place works?"

Finn gave that weird grunting laugh again. "Does this look like life to you, child?"

"Well, it doesn't look like you're having much fun, but—"

"It has been many, many years since I walked in the sun above the mound," Finn interrupted. "The mortal world is a dream to me. What do I care what mortals say? I was flattered when the bards wrote songs about the Fianna and me. They told me my deeds would live on forever in the hearts of men. And so they do, while

I live here in this half-life, a shadow of the man I once was, because I am caught tight in the story and it won't let go. And this place, girl, is where human stories come to die. I wait for my story to end and my memory to fade in the minds of men." He looked at Fachtna with hatred. "But it is enough. I won't pass into the cauldrons of the Coranied and become food for faeries. Now I wait and Bran waits with me." The wolfhound licked at his hand, and he rested it on her head. "You cannot have her."

"You're waiting for your wife, aren't you?" piped up Roisin. "Wait, let me think . . . I remember the story." Finn frowned, and Fachtna looked as if she would happily strangle Roisin. "You went hunting, and Bran found a fawn that turned into a woman when you took her back to your castle. You married her, but one day when you were away fighting, she was lured outside and turned into a fawn again, and you have been looking for her ever since. Is that right?"

Finn's face darkened. "My wife, a faerie woman herself. Cursed to live as a fawn by a Tuatha de Dannan, because she refused to love him," he growled. "But Bran knew her to be a woman in animal form, and she will know her again. My wife is alive still, and Bran is the only dog that I can trust to bring her to me without a scratch on her. So we wait, and we throw our thoughts out to her. The women of my court weep for her endlessly, shedding the tears that I cannot, and she will find her way back to us one day."

Danny spoke up. "There are millions of lives depending on our finding the unicorn mare, and we need Bran to do it," he said. "Are you going to sacrifice all those lives for one woman?"

"Yes," said Finn, stroking Bran's head.

"How can you sit and do nothing?" asked Danny. "I've heard the stories about you. You were the King Arthur of the Irish! The Finn mac Cumhaill I read about would never have turned his back on millions of people and left them to die."

Finn mac Cumhaill fixed him with his dark gaze, and Danny took an involuntary step backward. "I was like you once, boy," he said. "I gloried in the fight, and I stained the ground with the blood of my enemies. I basked in the love of my men and my wife and my child. I felt strong and alive and as if the world were mine." He looked now at Fachtna. "Then faeries took my wife and lured away my son to their lands and to his death, and all was darkness. There was no more laughter, no more joy in the midst of battle, no taste in food and drink. I died in my heart long before my story brought me here, and I live now only to set eyes on my love once more. The mortal world is but a faded memory. I have not shared its concerns for centuries. I wait for my love to return, and Bran and my court wait with me. That is all we live for now. I will not give her up for even a second."

Danny looked over at Maddy and widened his eyes. She knew what he was thinking. She frowned. Yet hadn't Granda made the same decision over her? Didn't he love her enough to be as monstrously selfish as Finn, and hadn't it made her glad, made her ignore the cost? Finn had been waiting here for centuries for the chance to see his wife again. Maybe he was mad. Maybe waiting and hoping for so long with no end in sight would make you a bit bonkers. She looked at the weeping women, whose tears seem to streak down their faces of their own accord. They did not sob or sigh but simply sat there limp and hopeless as their eyes leaked. Maddy shuddered. It seemed that Finn mac Cumhaill had manipulated the magic of Tír na nÓg to make these women grieve every second of their long existence as a tribute to his missing wife. She could only imagine what it must feel like to be weighed down by another's grief and be forced to suffer it.

"But the mist also tells me you bring the Hound," said Finn. "Yet all I see is a skinny, bruised, and battered girl, hardly able to walk with the size of the sword she carries." Maddy held her breath as his gaze settled on her.

"What of it?" asked Fachtna.

"If we had the Hound here, then her blood would call every faerie in the land, every creature under an enchantment, to this castle," said Finn. "You can taste the way the air crackles around her. They won't be able to resist, and perhaps my love might be one of them. If I had the Hound, I would surely see her again."

"Um, hang on a second . . ." said Maddy.

"You cannot have her," said Fachtna.

Finn stood up and flexed his shoulders, his sword in one hand. "You are in my stronghold, faerie," he said as he walked down the steps of the dais toward them. "And I say I can."

Maddy took a step back as Fachtna drew her own sword. "You abuse your rights as a host," she said. "This child's destiny does not lie with you."

Finn grinned at her. And then he charged.

Fachtna dashed forward to meet him, and their swords rang out as they clashed. Finn was a big bear of a man, but Fachtna easily topped his height by a foot, giving her sword arm a longer reach. Maddy realized how much Fachtna had been holding back when she had mock-fought with her. The faerie moved so fast it was impossible to follow what her hands were doing. She blocked, parried, and stabbed at lightning speed, shifting her weight like a dancer, even bending over backward until her hair touched the floor at one point to duck a wild swing from Finn that would have taken her head off. She was toying with the man, fighting him with a sword and a dagger, getting close enough to leave teasing nicks all over his body that stained his clothes with blood, but never went deep enough to really cause him harm. His face flushed—by refusing to inflict a serious wound every time she got the chance, Fachtna was embarrassing him, showing Finn's men she did not think him enough of a threat to finish him quickly.

But of more immediate concern to Maddy and her cousins was the fact that the rest of the Fianna, who up until then had been doing a really good imitation of zombies, were choosing this moment to take a renewed interest in life. As Fachtna and Finn battled each other along the length of the hall, the Fianna got up from their benches and began to sidle toward Maddy, fingering their sword hilts as they did so. More men were creeping in through the double doors at their back, and Fachtna wouldn't be able to handle them all.

Maddy drew her sword and pointed it toward the ground, keeping it loose and relaxed in her fingers, the way the faerie had shown her.

"I think we should stand with our backs to each other," she said, as Fenris and Nero peeled their black lips back from their teeth in a full-throated snarl at the men, who had begun to close in around them.

"I really hope that lesson Fachtna gave you was a good one," said Roisin as George struggled free of her jacket and leaped down to join the wolves, stiff-legged with aggression.

"We're about to find out," said Maddy.

"Touch the Hound, and I'll rip your throat out," said Fenris to one of the warriors, who had gotten too close. The man jumped back with surprise when he realized the huge black wolf could talk. Fenris snapped his teeth menacingly as Nero crouched to leap. "I'm eager to find out if there is still blood in the Fianna veins," Fenris growled.

A loud boom ripped through the hall, the force of it lifting everyone off their feet and throwing them to the ground. Maddy lay stunned, her ears ringing, and then she heard a faint crackling overhead as lightning stabbed down from the rafters and shattered the long tables, filling the air with splinters. She climbed to her feet and watched as men staggered around, some with blood leaking from their ears. She could make out their shouts and cries faintly over the ringing in her own ears, and she could see Danny and Roisin mouthing something at her. Roisin pointed, and Maddy turned to look past Finn and Fachtna, who were getting to their feet, weapons still clutched tight, with a bemused expression on their faces, to the throne at the far end of the hall.

Meabh sat on Finn's throne, her hair puddling around her feet and her ruby crown glowing on her brow. In her lap she held a struggling fawn, which twisted and turned in her hands, its beseeching eyes looking for Finn. The Pooka lay at her feet, and her storm hags guarded the back of the throne. The weeping women had been scattered by the blast, and they were lying unconscious, their eternal tears still welling up beneath closed eyelids to streak down their dusty cheeks.

Meabh locked one arm around the fawn, and she snapped the fingers of her free hand. The ringing in Maddy's ears stopped, and she could hear every sound in the hall clearly.

"My wife . . ." said Finn, taking a step toward the throne. "Is it really . . . ?"

Meabh looked down at the fawn in her lap as it bleated piteously. "Is it? I don't really know. I just saw it on my way here and thought how sweet it looked." She threw a sly glance at Finn. "But I could cut its throat and see if it changes into your lovely wife once it's dead?"

"NO!" cried Finn. "I beg you . . ."

"You beg me?" said Meabh, all pretense at good humor gone from her face, which twisted in anger. "Then give me what I WANT!" she screeched.

"I will not deal with your kind," said Finn, raising his chin in defiance. "Especially with you, Meabh, the well-spring of all my sorrows."

"Fool!" spat Meabh. "There is nothing more unreasonable than a hero who refuses to live *or* die. Fine—sit here and twiddle your thumbs while the worlds burn, but your fortress will burn with them as will your wife. In fact, that sounds rather cruel. Perhaps I will do you a kindness and put your wife out of her misery once and for all . . ."

Finn trembled as he stared at the fawn. "No!" he said.

"Then give Bran to the Hound for as long as she needs her," said Meabh. "She will be returned to you, you have my word."

"Your word means nothing!" said Finn.

"Now, that isn't true, and you know it," said Meabh. "I cannot lie. You, on the other hand, can. So give Bran to the Hound, and you can pretend I was never here.

Soothe your delicate conscience by telling yourself you never helped the Tuatha, only the mortals. Think on it, mac Cumhaill. If your answer is to condemn us all to death, then I will make sure this fawn is the first to die." She tightened her grip on the throat of the little deer, which squealed and kicked in terror.

"I yield, I yield!" shouted Finn. "Peace, Queen Meabh. I will give you what you desire."

Meabh narrowed her eyes at him. "Bran goes with the Hound?"

"Yes, yes," said Finn, his eyes still fixed on the fawn. "Anything."

Meabh smiled beatifically. "See how easy that was?" She glared at Fachtna. "I don't see why you couldn't have handled this without me." Fachtna lowered her eyes. "The whole point of sending the Hound was so that I didn't have to do this myself. Do you know how revolting it is to walk through that mist with all those filthy souls trying to touch me?"

"Please," said Finn, stretching his arms out to the throne. "Give me the fawn."

Meabh looked down at the little creature, which was lying silently now, trembling with fear in her lap. "I think not, mac Cumhaill. I will keep this one as surety for your good behavior. Don't let her down." There was a crack of thunder, and Meabh, the fawn, and her escort disappeared.

You could have heard a pin drop in the silence Meabh left behind. Finn refused to look at Maddy, his shoulders slumped and dejected. He looked like a beaten man.

A Fianna stepped forward. "Do you have something that will give Bran a scent of the unicorn mare?"

Maddy dug around in her pocket and pulled out the handful of mane that Meabh had given her. It shone as bright as a fallen star in the palm of her hand.

chapter twenty-two

IT TOOK A WHILE FOR THE FIANNA TO SADDLE UP
ready to move out. Maddy, Roisin, and Danny were left to
fidget and worry in the great hall while all around them
the stronghold of Finn mac Cumhaill burst into life.

"Can they even leave this place?" she asked a brooding Fachtna, who sat sharpening her sword blade with
a stone.

"I think they could go anywhere they liked, if they
wanted to," said Fachtna. "But they sit here, wrapped in
Finn's despair, and they sink into its mire."

"He's only helping us because he's frightened," said
Roisin.

"If it quickens his blood and helps him to remember
that he is a man, what harm?" said Fachtna.

"Will he get his wife back, for helping us?" asked Maddy.

Fachtna let out a bark of laughter. "She hasn't been seen for centuries."

"So that deer wasn't her?" asked Danny.

"Meabh as good as said she wasn't, and faeries can't lie, remember?" said Fachtna. "It was Finn who wanted to believe it was his wife. He tricked himself."

They all fell silent at that. Roisin sent a glare Maddy's way as if to say, *Can't you see what they're like?*

Maddy did see. It didn't exactly give her a warm, fuzzy feeling inside to exploit a man's grief and pain, but she needed Bran. A lot of people were depending on her getting that dog.

The mist parted before them as they rode out of Finn's stronghold. The Fianna had offered to let them all ride pillion, but Maddy, Danny, and Roisin preferred to walk until they got back to the white horses Meabh had lent them. None of them mentioned it, but Maddy guessed her cousins were as uncomfortable as she was at getting too close to men who seemed like ghosts.

Fachtna had protested when Finn had made it clear that he and the Fianna were going with them.

"This is Tuatha business," she had said. "We need no interference."

"While Bran is on this side of the mound, I will stay with her," said Finn.

"That was not your agreement," Fachtna objected.

"I only agreed to let you use Bran, faerie," Finn warned. "I did not say I would not stay near her. Besides, you might need the help when you find whatever is hunting these unicorns. You would certainly be foolish to refuse it."

Walking among the Fianna and listening to the weeping and wailing in the mist, Maddy was glad Fachtna had finally given in. As the mist parted ahead of Finn mac Cumhaill to give him and his men a clear route to the sun-bathed lands of Tír na nÓg, it was obvious he was still a force to be reckoned with. With the mist pressing around them and above them and the whispering voices brushing against her ears, it took all of Maddy's willpower not to run toward the sunlight that glowed at the end of the tunnel created by the movement of the Fianna. Wispy shreds of the mist seemed to reach out and touch the hem of mac Cumhaill's cloak, but he rode with his eyes fixed straight ahead, and he did not seem to notice the souls that paid him fealty. Maddy did, and she shrank close to the Fianna who rode next to her and was grateful for the warm smell of horse and the creak of leather. The men looked down at her and chuckled. It could have been her imagination, but she thought the Fianna were getting a bit of color in their faces and some spark in their eyes as they left the mist. But Finn mac Cumhaill remained a brooding hunched figure alone on his horse.

The white horses of Tír na nÓg were still waiting patiently, just as Fachtna had promised.

"We don't have long," said Finn. "The light will be gone in a few hours, and we need to pick up the unicorn tracks quickly."

"We must move as fast as we can," said Fachtna. "The hunter may already have a head start."

"Where do we look?" asked Danny.

"The forest, boy," said Finn. "The unicorns would never leave it."

Maddy, Danny, and Roisin struggled on to their horses while the Fianna tried not to laugh. Finn merely raised an eyebrow as he saw how Maddy lengthened the stirrup and then climbed up hand over hand. As soon as they were all mounted, he wheeled his horse about and cantered along the riverbank, heading back toward the mound.

Maddy yelped with fear when the horse she was riding surged forward as the Fianna chased after Finn. They were riding dangerously close to the edge of the bank, and she tried not to look at the ground and the dry, barren earth that crumbled away from her horse's pounding hooves.

As soon as the dark smudge of the forest came into view, Finn stopped and dismounted. He led his horse to the river's edge, and then they both plunged down into the water, which rose to their chests as man and horse struggled against the current. The rest of the Fianna dismounted and followed without a word; even Fenris and Nero threw themselves in and paddled madly for the opposite shore, only their heads visible above the water, long noses pointing to the sky as the river surged over them.

Maddy, Danny, Roisin, and Fachtna were the only ones who hung back. Danny watched with a frown as the wolves and men forged their way through the water.

"Can we do this?" asked Roisin. "Is the forest really going to let us in after what happened to Fionn?"

"Maybe no one blames us?" said Maddy. "Fionn was punished for helping us, and she decided to do that by herself. We didn't make her."

"Fat chance," said Danny. "If the trees figure out we are with the Fianna, they'll have a go at us all right. Let's just hope we can slip past unnoticed." He looked at Fachtna. "But if they do have a go, I hope they get you."

Fachtna twisted her lips in a look of contempt, raised her arms above her head, and shot off into the air. The white horses moved forward as if listening to commands only they could hear, and they slid into the river before any of them could dismount.

Thankfully the horses were so tall that the water only rose to Maddy's feet, and she simply had to raise her legs to keep them dry. Her horse waded through the fast-flowing river with ease, only slipping once or twice when he lost his footing on the wet rocks beneath his hooves. She clutched the reins in one hand and the saddle in the other, and she kept her eyes fixed on the opposite bank, where the Fianna were scrambling on to dry ground, horses and wolves sending up sprays of icy droplets as they shook themselves dry. Maddy wasn't a good swimmer, and she didn't fancy a dunk in the gray water. She looked back over her shoulder at Roisin, who had George wrapped firmly in her jacket. The little terrier had his eyes squeezed shut. Maddy felt sorry for him—he couldn't bear having a bath, much less taking a swim.

After what seemed like an eternity, her horse was lifting his long white front legs from the water and biting deep into the riverbank with his golden hooves as he scratched the dirt to gain traction to pull himself up. She leaned right over his neck to keep her balance as he stood up on his back legs and heaved himself up on to the bank.

The Fianna were busy stripping themselves of their weapons and pulling up handfuls of dirt, which they were rubbing into their horses' coats.

"Get down and prepare your horses," growled Finn.

"What do you mean?" asked Roisin, her forehead puckering with confusion.

"Moonlight will make those white hides gleam," said Finn. "The unicorns—and whatever is hunting them—will see us coming for miles. We don't want to spook the stallion."

Danny half climbed, half fell to the ground as he dismounted, and he looked up at the vast white expanse of his horse.

"You're joking?"

"No," said Finn, scowling.

"But that will take hours!" he said.

"Better get started then," said Finn, before turning on his heel and walking away.

It took them ages to rub enough dirt into the white horses' hides to satisfy the Fianna, and Maddy's back was aching by the time they were finished. Fachtna even smeared her bone-white skin. The Fianna kept themselves busy by wrapping the horses' hooves in cloth and winding tiny scraps of material around buckles and bits.

"What's that for?" Maddy asked a blond bearded man.

"So we don't make even the smallest noise," he said. "We can do nothing to let the unicorns know we are coming or we will lose them."

"Take only what you need," Finn ordered. He pointed at George, who wagged his tail hopefully. "That dog stays here. I don't want him barking."

"We're not just leaving him," said Maddy.

"I'll stay!" said Roisin. "I don't think I'll be much use on a hunt anyway."

"Then it's settled," said Finn. He held out his hand to Maddy. "Give me the scent."

Carefully Maddy drew the piece of mane from her jacket pocket and handed it to him. Finn whistled Bran to his side and crouched down to her, holding the hair beneath her nose. The wolfhound sniffed at it eagerly, her tail wagging madly. Finn put a hand under her hairy chin and lifted her blue eyes to meet his. "Seek it, Bran," he said. "But quietly." Maddy thought that was a bizarre thing to say to a dog. but Bran seemed to understand him—she stopped wagging her tail and cocked her head to one side as she watched his lips.

Finn pointed to Nero and Fenris. "They can be trusted?" he asked Fachtna.

"You can ask me that question yourself," said Fenris. "But the answer is yes. We can help Bran bring the hunter in alive."

Finn frowned at the wolves as they slunk closer to him, but he held out the scent and let them take a deep sniff all the same before he stood up again. "Mount up!" he commanded, as the wolfhound began to sniff the ground and wander into the forest, the wolves loping quietly behind her.

"Will you be OK?" Maddy asked Roisin.

"I really hope so," she said, white in the face, holding a whimpering George by his collar as he strained to chase after Bran and the wolves. "Although I'm not crazy about the idea of being out here on my own when the sun goes down."

"Stay on your horse while you are waiting," said Fachtna. "Any trouble, kick him into a gallop. He will follow his stable mates into the forest and bring you to us."

"What if I get lost?" said Roisin.

"I'll find you," said Fachtna. "I can always find you." She turned away and followed the Fianna into the forest.

"I *hate* the way she says stuff like that," said Roisin. "She always makes it sound like a threat." She smiled weakly at Danny and Maddy. "Good luck."

"You too," said Maddy.

"We'll be back soon," said Danny, "so don't worry."

"Not much chance of that," said Roisin.

Maddy leaned down and squeezed Roisin's shoulder and then ran her hand quickly over George's head. The old terrier licked her hand and looked up at her eagerly, waiting to be taken along.

"Be a good boy and *stay*," she said. She watched his little face fall with disappointment, then she turned her horse toward the brooding forest and urged him on.

chapter twenty-three

THE FOREST WAS STILL AND QUIET AS THEY RODE through it. It was a little too quiet for Maddy's liking. Surely forests should be noisy at night, when the predators come out to feed? She couldn't hear the scurry of small animals through the undergrowth or the bark of a fox. It felt like every living thing around them was holding its breath.

It was warmer beneath the canopy of the trees, out of the autumn wind, and the horses' hooves were muffled not only by the cloth around their metal shoes but by the thick carpet of pine needles on the forest floor. As evergreen trees stretched above them and blocked the moon, the darkness was almost complete. Maddy had no idea how the Fianna were gliding through the trees so confidently. The whole place was making her feel suffocated.

A deep, woody groan reverberated through the forest, as if an old tree was being torn up slowly by its roots. Everyone froze, and the horses threw their heads up and flared their nostrils as they dragged in every scent, searching for a predator. Maddy's hands began to shake on the reins as she watched Fachtna whirl around and scan the trees with her red eyes. The groan came again, closer this time, and the trees around them began to bend and thrash as if their branches were being tossed by gale-force winds.

"They're remembering!" shouted Danny, just as a massive tree leaned down and swiped at him with its branches.

Maddy screamed as his horse was swept off its feet and Danny was thrown from the saddle by the impact. Fachtna shot into the air, while the Fiannas' horses reared and screamed with terror as the trees began to pull their roots free of the ground and close in on them, huge heavy branches swinging like clubs. Maddy sawed on the reins to keep her own horse's head facing forward, and she desperately kicked at his sides. "Come on, MOVE!" she yelled, her cheeks wet with tears of pure terror. She saw a white blur at the corner of her eye, and then Fachtna was hovering by her side, her sword drawn. She whacked the flat of the blade against the horse's rump, and it was as if someone had hit his on switch. The animal jumped forward and began to gallop flat out in a blind panic, and it was infectious. As Maddy tore through the Fianna ranks, every horse fled after hers, whether its rider was still on board or not. The wind in her eyes made it impossible to see where she was going, and she cringed against her horse's neck, waiting for a branch to fall on them.

A loud rumble of thunder sounded overhead even though the evening sky was still bright and clear, and lightning flashed down. Maddy screamed and closed her eyes tight as her lids flared red. There was a stink of burning, and a vegetable scream rose up from the trees around her that she felt rather than heard. Again and again the lightning forked, and the trees shrieked in agony until Maddy was dumb with fear, her face buried in her horse's mane as she blocked out the chaos and the murderous trees around her, her legs numb with exhaustion as she gripped the flanks of her terrified mount who thundered on. Each crack of lightning seared her lids, and her ears began to ring from the noise.

And then it just . . . stopped, and all she could hear was her own ragged breathing, the pounding of her horse's hooves, and the wind roaring in her ears. The Fianna had caught up with her and flowed around her, faces of horses and riders alike drawn with fear. Eventually Maddy was able to grab the reins and pull her horse to a halt. He stood, head hanging and chest heaving. His hide was coated in the foam of his sweat. The Fiannas' horses were no better.

"What in the name of the gods was that about?" barked Finn, his face purple with rage. "Don't bother lying to me, Hound—that had something to do with you. Out with it!"

Maddy stared at Finn with her mouth open and tried desperately to think of a short, quick lie that would keep him on her side. But before she could say anything, they all heard the steady beat of cantering hooves, and Danny rode into the clearing on a cut and bloody Tuatha horse. The animal was trembling, but clearly it took a lot more than an enraged tree to stop one of the giant horses. Danny's face was bruised and swollen, but Maddy was relieved to see he could still sit upright in the saddle. Fachtna flew by his side.

"How fortunate Queen Meabh is watching us all the time," she said, while looking at Finn.

"It was Meabh with the lightning?" When Fachtna simply gazed back at him, Finn spat on the ground. "I should have known. What have these children done that enraged the dryads so?"

"You don't need to know," said Fachtna. "You need to find the unicorns, and quickly—we are running out of time."

Finn opened his mouth to say something, but Bran gave an odd whimper. Her tail was wagging madly, and she seemed to be barking through clenched teeth as she tried to obey Finn's command to keep quiet. When everyone was looking at her, she bounded away, with Nero and Fenris in hot pursuit.

"Well, it seems Bran has picked up the scent," said Fachtna. "Although we may have lost the element of surprise." She flew after the wolfhound without another word. Finn turned to glare at Maddy. She avoided his eyes and kicked her heels against her horse's sides as she followed the faerie.

The exhausted horses could not go faster than a trot. Bran frequently had to stop and wait for them all to catch up, and her frustration was obvious in the way she paced up and down while they struggled to reach her, the wolves watching her with eager expressions. Every muscle in Maddy's body was on fire from being in the saddle for so long, and the trotting jarred her aching bones. She clenched her teeth and tried to fight off exhaustion as the evening deepened into night, and still Bran raced on, nose to the ground.

"Are you OK?" Maddy whispered to Danny. His face was white, and his eyes were shadowed with pain.

"I'll live," he groaned. "But I might have broken a rib."

"Do you want to turn around and head back to Roisin?"

"I think it's a bit late for that," said Danny. He smiled weakly. "Besides, I can't let you have all the fun, can I?"

Suddenly Bran stopped and lay down, her body tense as she stared eagerly into a clearing. Finn held his hand up in the air and then swept it down. In total silence the

Fianna dismounted and walked their horses forward. Maddy and Danny quickly scrambled down from the Tuatha horses and followed them.

There, in the clearing, the two unicorns burned in the moonlight with their intense white skin. The mare was positioned exactly as Maddy had seen her in Blarney but with one crucial difference. Maddy widened her eyes at Fachtna and tapped her own shoulder. Fachtna looked at the mare for a moment and then nodded at Maddy.

In Blarney the mare had been struck by a poisoned dart in her shoulder, and it had been easy to see the wound and the veins around it turning black as the poison spread. In Tír na nÓg, the mare's shoulder was pure, unblemished white. Her body was showing them what world she was hurt in.

Finn tried to step past Fachtna with a length of rope in his hand, but she grabbed his arm and stopped him. She raised an eyebrow at him, and he tried to shrug her off, but she held on as they glared at each other until Finn stepped back, pulling her with him.

"What are you doing?" she hissed at him once they were deeper into the trees.

"I'm going to catch the stallion and lure the hunter to us," said Finn. "We need to move him to a location that will make it easier for us to lay an ambush. We need to make him look like an easy target. I can leave guards with the mare."

"No one touches them!" said Fachtna.

"Besides, there's no need," said Maddy as Finn's face began to turn black with rage again. "The mare was attacked in Blarney, and in the mortal world she's surrounded by Tuatha guards. As the boundary between the worlds is breaking down, they're able to stay with her. If the hunter is both faerie and mortal and is able to move between the worlds, then it makes sense to attack her here, before anyone else finds her, and then finish the stallion. He won't leave her side, the hunter knows that. But the hunter doesn't know we got here first."

Fachtna snorted. "We hope! We made enough noise getting here."

Maddy ignored her.

"All we have to do is wait, *quietly*, and the hunter will come to us," she said.

Finn looked at her for a moment and then nodded. "Fine, we'll go with your plan. I want men on foot to skirt around them and take up a defensive position behind the mare, while mounted soldiers will wait deeper in the forest, ready to chase."

"You'll need this," said Maddy, taking the walnut from her jacket pocket and cracking it open on the pommel of her saddle. A poisonous green net drifted from the shell, hanging on the night air like a cobweb. Sparks of spells glinted in its knots, and the whole thing seemed to whisper as it floated in Maddy's hands.

"What in the name of all that is sacred is *that*?" asked Finn.

"Meabh wove this net to catch the split soul," said Maddy. "The net will hold the soul in the form it chooses to take and trap it in its folds."

"Meabh again," said Finn, his face twisting with hatred. He spat on the ground. "I'll not take anything from the Witch Queen."

Maddy took a deep breath. "I know you have reason to hate her," she said. "I don't blame you. But I need all the help I can get. If you stop arguing with me, this will be over quickly and you can go back to brooding in your castle."

Finn glared at her and fingered his sword hilt. Maddy tensed and waited to see if she had made him angry enough to hit her. It was Fachtna who broke the tension, by ignoring it.

"Go with your foot soldiers in case the hunter is desperate enough to try to fight its way through," said Fachtna. "I'll wait with the horsemen and the Hound." She looked down at Maddy. "In a few more hours, it will all be over, and then you can have the justice you so crave." She smiled a cold, reptilian smile.

Justice. Maddy felt her stomach sour with fear.

chapter twenty-four

DANNY WAS SO EXHAUSTED HE NODDED OFF SIT-
ting upright in the saddle, but Maddy brooded while
they waited for the hunter to make a move. She had been
so convinced that it was a faerie who had attacked the
mare. Now she was not sure. She thought of Cernunnos
and his warning that she did not know what she was
asking for when she had demanded justice. Now, with a
cooler head, she wished she had listened to him.

She thought about what Meabh had said, that sometimes people taken by the faeries did find their way
back to the mortal world, leaving a small part of their
tortured souls behind. Any of the people that she knew
in Blarney could be responsible for this. It could even be
a member of her own family, and she had promised to
hand the person over to the Tuatha. She had demanded

justice. She had no idea what a Tuatha's idea of justice was. What would the faeries do to someone who had dared raise a hand against a creature they considered sacred? She had not thought about this when she had made her demands on Cernunnos. As the faces of aunts, uncles, cousins, and neighbors flashed in front of her eyes, she tried not to think about the fate that her rash words might have condemned one of them to. She thought of that little girl who had stared up at her in the Hansel and Gretel cottage. Who was she in Blarney? Was she old now, or was she a child Maddy didn't recognize? It had all seemed so simple before.

Maddy sighed and bent forward in the saddle to lean against her horse's neck. She could not think about this now. If she had to save someone else, she would come up with a plan when she knew who the hunter was and, more importantly, what was going to be done to him or her. The animal shifted its weight underneath her but did not breathe a sound. She looked through the trees at the clearing where the unicorns slept, blanketed in moonlight, and sighed.

She yawned and rubbed at her eyes. She was longing for a soft bed and a nice thick comforter to snuggle under. Her eyes were dry and itchy from lack of sleep, and she really wanted something hot to eat—Danny and Roisin had polished off all the food in her backpack in one sitting.

Suddenly the unicorn stallion lifted his head and rumbled deep in his throat. His whole body tensed while his sapphire-blue eyes searched the trees to his left. Carefully Maddy eased herself off her horse's neck with one hand until she was sitting upright, and she stretched her legs so they wrapped around the horse's side, ready to grip if she had to kick him into a gallop. The horse was as tense as the unicorn, but he still stayed deathly quiet. She leaned over and shook Danny's arm. He woke with a start, but luckily he did not cry out and spook the stallion. His horse was as tense and eager as Maddy's, and she heard stirrup leathers creak in the dark as Danny adjusted his position and sat deep, ready for the animal to spring forward into a gallop.

There! Maddy's eyes strained against the darkness. Did she see a darker flicker of black in the tossing branches of the trees? A more solid shape among the shivering leaves?

The stallion began to prance before his stricken mate, tossing his head and pawing at the ground in distress. An owl hooted, and Maddy cocked her head in the direction of the sound. It was the Fiannas' signal to get ready for an attack.

An arrow thudded into the ground next to the stallion's feet, and the grass turned black where it touched. The stallion screamed and reared, his front hooves lashing out at empty air. Maddy kicked her horse into a gallop as the Fianna charged into the clearing, swords drawn. Another poisoned arrow sang out heading straight for the stallion's chest, before it was blocked by a Fianna shield. Finn mac Cumhaill's men surrounded the unicorns and locked shields in a protective ring, while Finn strode out to stand in front of the shield wall, sword drawn and his own shield held high. Fachtna landed in front of him, wings spread, searching the trees for something to kill.

Maddy wheeled her horse around in the clearing to look for the attacker just as the tree next to the one the arrows had been fired from started to shudder. It began to bend and shake, and then it stilled as the one next to it began to convulse.

"It's moving," Maddy whispered to herself. "It's moving, and the trees are trying to shake it off." One of the Fianna brought Bran to the base of the first tree the creature had hidden in and let her sniff at it, Fenris and Nero by her side. The wolfhound began to bay as she caught the scent, and the Fianna warrior who was holding her slipped off her leash and let her tear off into the woods, the wolves bounding in her wake, Fachtna running behind them. Maddy's faerie horse raced after them, and she bent close into his neck to avoid low-hanging tree branches that swept just above her skull.

Bran was still baying, and her cries let Maddy hear where she was as she followed the chase through the woods, the sheltering trees blocking nearly all the moonlight from the forest floor. Hooves pounded the ground on either side of her, and she knew Danny and the rest of the Fianna were riding with her. The occasional moonbeam helped her pick out a flash of horse hide, the white of a rolling eye, or the foam that dripped from a mouth to coat a chest. Maddy twined her fingers in the thick mane and gripped hard enough to turn her knuckles white as she fought to keep her seat. She looked down and saw how far away the ground was and how fast it was rolling past. As she felt her body begin to slip over the horse's shoulder, she forced herself to look ahead and sit up straight as the faerie horse charged headlong through the night. She squeezed her eyes shut and prayed the animal knew where he was going because she had no idea how to steer him at this speed.

They sped on through the woods with Bran baying up ahead, and Maddy's balance in her saddle became more and more insecure. Then they burst from the trees into the free air and bright moonlight of a clearing. The faerie horse skidded to a stop so fast that Maddy fell forward on to his neck. When she straightened up, she saw that Bran, Fenris, and Nero had surrounded the split soul.

It cowered flat against the ground, its wizened arms thrown over its bald head to protect it from the bared teeth of the dog and the wolves, and it whimpered like a child into the grass. It was naked, a ropy twist of gray mottled skin and bone, long flat feet and slender fingers tapering into sharp nails. Its head was a grotesque parody of a baby's head, round and hairless and bobbing about on a weak neck. It rolled pale, bulbous eyes, and it squeaked piteously through a tiny rosebud mouth. Maddy jumped from her horse's back as Danny and the Fianna galloped up to it. She gasped from the pain in her chest as her heels hit the ground. One of the Fianna walked toward her as Fachtna bared her teeth at the creature.

"Don't hurt it," she warned the Fianna. The man nodded grimly as they all moved slowly toward the split soul.

It didn't look up as they approached, and it gave no sign that it was even aware they were there. It didn't flinch as Maddy threw the spell net over it, but it squealed in pain as its skin steamed where the net touched it. Fachtna stepped around Bran and grabbed the creature through the net by the shoulders. It offered no resistance as she pulled it to its feet and the Fianna began to drag it toward their horses. Its pale bulging eyes registered nothing and streamed with tears.

It broke Maddy's heart to look at it.

"Was this the same creature that attacked us in the mist?" Maddy asked.

The faerie shrugged. "Who knows? They all look the same."

Maddy walked beside it and stooped a little so she could look up into its face. "Who are you?" she asked it. "Who told you to do this?" But the ugly little thing just cried all the louder.

"This thing can't do anything on its own," she said to Fachtna. "Look at it! It would probably jump off a cliff if you told it to."

"What are you saying?" asked Danny.

"Do you honestly think this thing went after the unicorns with any malice?" said Maddy. "I don't think it's even capable of knowing what it's doing!"

"Don't start feeling sorry for it, child," said Fachtna, a queer smile on her lips. "It attacked a unicorn, and you've promised to hand it over."

Maddy stood up and glared at Fachtna. "It's part of a bigger whole. We need to find the person in Blarney this split soul was tortured out of. Until then, it stays under the protection of the Fianna."

"That is not what you vowed to do," warned Fachtna.

"I haven't finished the job yet," said Maddy. She looked at the Fianna, who had bound the creature. "Look after it. It was one of us, once."

She watched as Bran approached the creature swaddled in the gossamer netting, the wolfhound's nose twitching as she took great snuffling gulps of air.

"What is she doing?" asked Danny.

"She can *smell* it," said Maddy, watching as the spells in the net flared with each sniff of Bran's wet black nose. "Now that the net has it trapped in a physical form, Bran can get a scent. She can lead us right back to the host on the mortal side."

She walked back to her horse and began the laborious climb into the saddle. "We need to get back to the mound," she said, and she turned her horse about to make her way to the river. "Bran, to me," she called, and the wolfhound bounded over to lope at her horse's heels.

She didn't dare turn her head to see whether the others were keeping up with her or if they had decided to ignore her, and she was relieved when Danny brought his horse alongside hers.

"What are you going to do?" he asked.

"I have no idea," she said. "Is Fachtna following us?"

Danny cast a quick look over his shoulder. "She is," he said.

"Are you still taking those boxing lessons?" she asked him quietly.

"Yeah. Why?" he asked her.

"We can't have Fachtna following us through the mound," said Maddy. "She must not be with us when we find the unicorn hunter."

Danny nodded, his face grim.

Roisin looked up eagerly when they came to the river.

"Did you catch it?" she asked.

"We did." Fachtna's harsh voice grated from behind Maddy. "And just as was suspected, it is one of your kind."

Roisin's face fell.

"Now we take the hunt to Blarney," said Fenris.

Maddy looked down at the wolves. "Can you guys go to the mortal world?"

"Of course," said Fenris. "We were of it once. We would have no difficulty crossing back and forth if we chose to."

"We just choose not to," said Nero. "Seeing as how trigger-happy your kind are when it comes to wolves."

"Well, if anyone asks, you're a German shepherd, OK?" said Maddy, grinning at them both.

Fenris looked disgusted while Nero practically spat his own teeth out with indignation. "A dog?" he growled. "You want us to pretend we are *dogs*?" He looked over at George, who was sitting up in front of Roisin, his stubby front legs braced against the pommel of the saddle, and sideways at Bran, who loomed over him. "No offense." George barked and wagged his tail happily while Bran simply looked away with cool indifference.

"Try not to rise to the insults," Fenris said to Nero. "It makes life much easier."

"Enough of this," said Fachtna. "It will be the Samhain Fesh soon, and Cernunnos's patience must be wearing thin."

Just as they turned to set off, Finn mac Cumhaill emerged from the trees. Bran gave a bark of joy and raced to his side, cringing on her belly and licking his hand while whimpering with delight.

"You would still take her from me?" he asked Maddy, as the rest of the Fianna stepped from the gloom of the forest. Their horses nickered and stamped their hooves, their hides steaming with sweat.

"I have to, you know that," said Maddy. "But you have my word I will send her back to you."

"Come with us, and you can stay with her," said Danny. "We really could use the help."

Finn mac Cumhaill smiled sadly. "My love is in this world, not in yours. I can never leave here, even for a moment. While she still breathes the same air as I do, there is hope."

"We'll keep Bran safe and send her home soon," said Roisin.

They turned their backs on the grieving hero and his silent men, and they plunged into the icy river. Bran and the wolves swam across, their heads held high, while Fachtna simply flew to the other side. They cantered across a meadow still blooming with flowers with the moon at their backs until they reached the mound. Its unnatural shadow sat all around it like a barrier, and

Maddy could feel its chill on her cheek as she turned her head to take one last look at the forest.

"We'll leave the horses here," said Fachtna. She held out her arms to help Maddy down, while Danny and Roisin slithered to the ground. "They will attract too much attention mortal-side." She looped their reins around their saddles so the reins were not hanging loose around the horses' legs, and then she slapped them on the rumps. They tossed their heads and cantered for home. Maddy looked at Danny and nodded her head slightly.

"Are you trying to delay us, getting rid of the horses like that?" she asked Fachtna.

"What are you accusing me of?" demanded the faerie, as Danny sidled around behind her and climbed on to a rock.

"It's your queen who wants an eternal winter, a path into the mortal world, so if we don't make it back in time to hand the hunter over, then all of the faeries go to war, and the boundary is too weak to hold them back at the mound," said Maddy. "Your queen benefits if we are late. Halloween is the best time to break through, right, when you are strongest?"

"When time collapses into chaos," said Fachtna. "Yes."

"So a little bit of delay here would hand Liadan her dearest wish, and it would mean that you wouldn't have broken your vow that we would come to no harm."

Fachtna's eyes blazed with rage while her wings rattled a warning. "I swore an oath to the monarchs that I would help you find the hunter, to my queen that I would not allow you to lie about her in the matter, and to you that I would bring you safely home," she barked. "I'm not a treacherous, deceitful, filthy mortal . . ."

"Hey, Fachtna," called Danny, and as the faerie turned toward the sound of his voice, he aimed an upper cut to her face with his fist, catching her right on her pointed chin. The faerie crumpled to the ground without so much as a sigh. They all looked down at her in shock.

"I can't believe that worked!" said Danny as he hopped off the rock, massaging his hand. "But I think I might have broken a finger on her jaw."

"Is she really out for the count?" asked Maddy as George trotted over and swatted the faerie's face gingerly with a paw. Bran cocked her head at him and whimpered as he jumped nervously away from Fachtna.

"Looks like it," said Fenris, his voice quiet with shock.

"It was lucky that rock was there. I would never have gotten enough power to knock her out if I'd had to jump to reach her chin," said Danny.

"What have you done?!" asked Roisin, her eyes wide with fear. "She is going to be so angry when she wakes up!"

"She is, isn't she?" said Nero, his voice quivering with nerves as he backed away toward the mound with his tail tucked between his legs. "Perhaps now would be a good time to get moving?"

They all exchanged looks and then turned and ran through the mound, Maddy calling for Bran as she ducked inside it.

In the light of the torches, their shadows loomed large on the walls. Maddy felt hysterical laughter bubbling up inside her as they sprinted for the mortal world, the dogs and wolves bounding alongside them. They emerged from the tunnel into Blarney and the teeth of a storm. Wind and rain lashed them so hard it drove the breath from Maddy's lungs. and she had to pause for a moment, rain plastering her hair and clothes to her body, as she caught her breath.

"How is Bran supposed to track the hunter in this?" she yelled to Danny over the shriek of the wind. "How will she even pick up the scent?" He shrugged, eyes half closed against the driving rain.

"Maddy!" yelled Roisin behind her. "We've got a really big problem."

"What now?!" yelled Maddy in frustration as she turned to see what Roisin was talking about. Her jaw sagged as she watched Roisin help a shivering, naked old woman with long gray hair up from the grass outside the mound. Fenris and Nero had twined themselves around the woman to protect her from the fury of the weather as she clung to Roisin's side and gazed all around her in terror. Her blue eyes looked very familiar.

"Who *is* that?" asked Danny.

Roisin stared at them with eyes as wide as saucers as the woman trembled and whimpered.

"It's Bran," she said.

chapter twenty-five

"What do you mean, Bran?" yelled Danny, while Maddy sank into a crouch, staring at the old woman, while a dreadful thought strolled nonchalantly into her head and gave her brain a cheery wave.

"Bran was there one minute—the next, her," said Roisin. "Considering that she's stark naked and she has the same eyes as the wolfhound, I think it's safe to say *she* is Bran."

"Oh no," said Danny.

"I've been so stupid," said Maddy.

"What? Why is this about you?" asked Roisin.

"Don't you get it?" said Maddy. "They didn't need me at all. Meabh must have known that Bran would transform on mortal soil and could make her way through Blarney on her own to track the hunter down."

"But she said it was you," said Danny, looking confused.

"No, she said it was 'one such as' me," said Maddy. "I should have listened more carefully to what she said, I should have listened to *every word . . .*"

"But the Coranied said you were the one as well," said Roisin.

"No, everything they said was in the future tense, that it *would* be me," said Maddy. "And they were right—I fell right into Meabh's trap. But they didn't say it *had* to be me. They didn't say it couldn't possibly be done by anyone else—not that I asked."

"Oh, I get it," said Danny. "So basically you just got yourself tied up with the Autumn Court and Meabh—"

"For no good reason," interrupted Maddy, as she rocked on her haunches and jabbed at her head with the heels of her hands. "For no reason at all other than my own pride. I kept asking the wrong questions—even Meabh said that."

"Well, I don't see how it could have been done by poor Bran—she hasn't even got any clothes!" said Roisin. "How's she supposed to track anyone?"

Maddy looked at the shivering woman. "*Una!*" she yelled.

"There's no need to shout," snapped a high voice, and the little banshee came shuffling forward with her odd, rolling gait, a bundle under one arm.

Danny and Roisin stared at her. "Who is *this*?" asked Roisin.

"I'll tell you later," said Maddy. "How did you know we were here?" she asked the little faerie woman.

"I always know where every member of the family is," said the banshee. "That's my job."

She crouched down in front of the sniveling Bran and gently touched her cheek. "Bran, child, it has been too long," she said.

Bran stopped crying for a moment. "Una, is it really you?"

"It is," said the banshee, clasping one of Bran's hands in hers.

"How long has it been?" asked Bran. "How long have I been gone?"

"A long, long time," said the faerie sadly as she opened the bundle and began to wrap Bran in gray rags just like her own. "All you loved are lost to you now. All except Finn mac Cumhaill. Does it hurt to be human again?" asked Una, smoothing Bran's wet gray hair back from her head with her withered hand.

"It does," said Bran. "I want to go back, Una. I want go back to being a wolfhound and forgetting it all. When I am a wolfhound, I don't remember anything about being human."

"I know," said Una, "but there is a job to be done first . . ."

"NO!" Bran recoiled in horror. "Not me. Don't make me do it . . ."

"If you do not find your prey, there will be a war, Bran, a war much like the last one," said Una. "Yet this time I do not think the humans will fare as well. They might not be strong enough against the Tuatha. Would you see these children ruled by the Tuatha as you once were?"

Bran shook her head. "The faeries are cruel over-lords," she said bitterly. "They taught me that."

"It is your fate to be the gentle huntress," soothed Una. "You are the one who always brings her prey back alive and unharmed."

"I live to find mac Cumhaill's love," said Bran. "That is my fate."

"You have not found her yet," said Una. "But right now these children need you. Track your quarry for these children, finish the hunt you started in Tír na nÓg, and then you can find peace in a wolfhound's form again and stay by Finn mac Cumhaill until his wife returns to his side."

Bran nodded and straightened up. She linked her fingers with Roisin's and looked at Una.

"It hurts," she said. "The ground where this hunter trod burns with its curse."

"Then follow it," said Una, squeezing her free hand. "We will walk with you."

Bran began to hobble forward, Fenris and Nero clinging to her sides, causing Roisin to stumble over their huge paws.

"Nero, this is awkward," she said, bending down to push him away. The wolf turned and snarled at her, snapping his teeth at the air, his eyes gleaming turquoise. "What is wrong with you?!" squealed Roisin, as George yelped with fear and ran to cling to Maddy's leg. Nero just carried on snarling at Roisin, his ears pinned back to his head and his black lips peeled to show teeth and gums, while Fenris rumbled on the other side of Bran, his lips twitching from his teeth.

They all eyed the wolves nervously. "I think they've gotten a bit more 'wolfy' this side," said Danny.

"It's probably best to just let them do what they like," said Maddy. White-faced, Roisin nodded her agreement.

It was slow going. The downpour had turned the ground to a slippery muck beneath Maddy's feet. Her jeans were soaked and hung like cardboard from her legs, chafing her cold skin at every step. Gusts of wind drove the rain into her face as hard as a smack while Bran wept and clung to Roisin and Una as they coaxed her along. George trudged alongside Maddy, his head held low and the rain sheeting off his thin spine. Tremors shook his little body. The only ones who seemed to be comfortable in the weather were the wolves, who slitted their eyes against the gale and seemed immune to the rain that dripped from their shaggy coats.

Step by painful step they made their way out of the castle grounds. They had to coax and pull Bran through the gap in the fence, and Maddy gritted her teeth and tried to ignore the old woman's cries of pain. They walked through the village, which was deserted and closed tight against the storm and the lateness of the hour. Maddy breathed a sigh of relief when Bran walked past Granny and Granda's house and again when she failed to take the road that would have led them to Cork city and Aunt Fionnula. The unicorn hunter was no one in her family. But the sick feeling of dread still lingered in her stomach. It was someone here, someone she knew, someone whose kids she went to school with.

They walked out of the village and headed for the countryside, past the brand-new housing estates with their raw landscaping and the identical ornamental boulders with each estate's name carved into them. On they went along the deserted road, the asphalt glistening in the wet and the streetlights hurting Maddy's tired eyes with their sodium glow. Houses were more and more spread out here, until Bran turned down a rutted lane, little more than a dirt track that gave access to a handful of houses crouched behind trees. Bran might be finding every step she took on her bare feet agony, but she was full of purpose as she limped up to the door of a little one-story cottage, not unlike Granny and Granda's, and put her hand flat against the wood.

"Here," she said, her eyes full of sorrow.

Everyone looked at Maddy, even George and the wolves, so she squared her shoulders, stepped up to the door and knocked on it loudly. They all stood and waited, breath held to see who would answer. They waited and waited and waited, and no one came.

"This is ridiculous," said Maddy. She knocked again and cocked her head, listening for footsteps. Hearing none, she tried the door handle, more out of frustration than hope, and she was surprised to find that it turned easily in her hand. The door swung open into a darkened hallway that had a musty, dirty smell.

"Hello?" she called. "Is there anyone home?"

Silence. She took a tentative step on to a grubby and moth-eaten welcome mat.

"Don't, Maddy," whispered Roisin. "We can't just walk into a complete stranger's house!"

"We have to," Maddy whispered back. "We're running out of time. We have to sort this out now! Hello?" she called again, as she stepped further into the house. "We're in trouble here, and we really need some help. Is there anyone home?"

She walked down the hallway and froze as she heard a snuffling noise behind the door to her left. There was faint red light leaking under the door. Someone was here. Maddy drew the sword very, very quietly, splayed her fingers against the cracked and yellowing gloss of the door, and gently pushed it open with the tips of her fingers.

The room was a mess, and it stank of rotting food and unwashed flesh. By the dim light of an electric fire, she could see mounds of trash, old clothes, blankets, newspapers, and empty food cans lying in heaps, piled on top of a ripped sofa and scattered haphazardly around the floor. There was a hunched and scruffy figure sitting on a wooden chair, and he looked up at her as she stepped into the room.

"Bang bang," he said softly. "You're dead."

chapter twenty-six

MADDY STARED AT BANG BANG WHILE UNA
fussed around them all, wrapping them in filthy blankets and trying to drive the chill out of their bones. Fenris and Nero threw themselves down in a corner and
stared in silence, their eyes gleaming in the dim light.
They stank to high heaven of wet wolf, but the smell of
the room was already so bad that the wolf smell could
only make it nudge up a bit. George had parked himself
so close to the electric fire he was in danger of singeing his whiskers. Bran sat bent over double, her long
gray hair curtaining her off from the rest of the room.
Whether she was bowed from grief or exhaustion or
both, Maddy couldn't tell. Roisin and Danny looked at
Bang Bang nervously but said nothing.

Phrases kept running around Maddy's head, little things that people had said that really should have warned her that it was Bang Bang, that should have let her know he was the one, that he needed protecting, before she had made those stupid demands, sworn those oaths.

"He was a lovely lad when he was younger—bright and cheerful and always a smile on him. But he turned funny around the age of twelve, and he's never been right since."

"I'm doing the queen's business, clearing up all this mess."

Bang Bang had been taken at some stage, and he had made it back, but it was too late—he had already been driven out of his mind, perhaps by a dark faerie seeking the nourishment of his pain and distress. Maybe by a queen looking to escape Tír na nÓg or cultivate a willing slave who would do whatever she asked in the mortal world. Bang Bang was so faerie touched that he shared their abhorrence of Christianity. When he had said he was working for a queen, he had been telling the truth; he was tidying up litter for a faerie queen.

But which faerie queen is it that you think you serve, Bang Bang? she wondered. *Which one put the darts in your hand and told you to kill a unicorn?*

"Danny, do me a favor," she said quietly, while Bang Bang chattered nonsense to Una, who listened to him with a kind, interested smile. Danny looked over at her and raised his eyebrows. "Have a look around, and try to find something that will tell us who set up Bang Bang."

"Maddy, that could take hours," protested Danny. "We haven't got time."

"We have to try," she insisted.

Danny nodded, stood up quietly, and slunk out of the room. Bang Bang didn't even notice him leaving.

"You can't hand him over—you know that, don't you?" whispered Roisin.

"I know," said Maddy.

"What are you going to do then?"

"Haven't the foggiest. I was hoping you could come up with a plan."

Roisin sighed and rubbed her temples. "We'll have to split up. One of us has to get Bran back to the mound—I don't think she's going to last much longer as she is. And one of us has to get Bang Bang to the city. He needs to be surrounded by iron."

"How are we going to get him to go though? He gets upset very easily," said Maddy.

Danny came back into the room. Maddy looked at him hopefully, but he shook his head. "The rest of the house is empty. It looks as if he lives in this room," he said.

"We have to find something," warned Roisin. "They are going to catch up with us sooner or later."

"I know," said Maddy. She leaned forward and inter-rupted Bang Bang's childish flow of chatter. "Bang Bang, I need to ask you something."

He stopped talking and turned to look at her, but he didn't say a word.

"Did anyone ask you to do something recently?" she asked. "Did someone give you something special to look after or any presents?"

Bang Bang stayed silent, but a sly gleam came into his eyes.

"Because if someone did, Bang Bang, we really, really need to know," said Maddy. "If you've hidden it, you need to tell us where. We can help you if we have what the person gave you."

Bang Bang pouted at her like a grumpy child. "You're trying to get me into trouble."

"No, I'm not," said Maddy. "I'm trying to help you."

He shook his head. "She said this would happen. She said people would come try to make me tell on her. But I won't, I won't tell on her. She's my beautiful queen, and I love her."

Maddy's heart practically stopped in her chest, and she made an effort to keep her voice light. "Your beautiful queen? That sounds very exciting, Bang Bang. Was her hair black or gold or red?"

"I'm not telling, I'm not telling," sang Bang Bang. Maddy gritted her teeth and resisted the urge to slap him.

"Bang Bang, you *have* to," said Roisin. "You can trust us!"

"My queen will protect me," said Bang Bang.

"She won't, you idiot!" yelled Maddy. "She's got you into a huge mess, and I don't see her riding to the rescue, do you? Now tell us who she is!"

Bang Bang glared at her resentfully. He dropped his head and refused to say another word. Una looked at Maddy and shook her head.

"This is pointless," Maddy sighed in exasperation. "Danny, call Granda, and get him over here. It's time we explained what's been going on, and we need to get Bang Bang into the city."

Danny pulled his cell phone out and frowned at the screen. "It says I've got no signal," he said, just as Maddy felt a familiar prickle on the back of her neck.

"They're here!" she said, jumping to her feet and grabbing her sword as Roisin screamed at a bright eye that peered in at them through a gap in the torn curtains at the window.

The front door banged open, and booted feet marched down the hallway and then stopped outside the door. Fenris and Nero ran to protect Bran as the door swung open and Fachtna, her jaw dark with bruising, stepped into the room, the Pooka at her side.

The faerie had managed to get hold of some more lime, and her hair was stiffened into a Mohican again. Maddy didn't like to think what that said about her mood.

"Playtime is over, Feral Child," she rasped. "It's time to go."

———

Fachtna didn't make them walk far. The glow from the monarchs illuminated them where they were sitting enthroned in a field behind Bang Bang's little house, their courts arrayed behind them. The regents of Summer had thrones made of living oak, thick with soft green leaves. The monarchs of Spring had their thrones of cherry-blossom branches. Liadan and Meabh sat alone, the Winter Queen on her throne of carved crystal and Meabh on a twisted, tortured throne of dead branches. Meabh's chin was cupped in one hand while she drummed the long fingers of the other on the arm of her throne. Cernunnos and the unicorns waited in front of them all. The mare was weak, and her head hung low as she stood next to her mate, but Maddy was relieved to see she was at least beginning to make a recovery. Cernunnos was still wearing his coat of many skins with his face in shadow.

Fear dried Maddy's mouth when she saw how hard and cold the faces were of the Tuatha. They didn't look forgiving.

"Welcome, Bran," said Cernunnos. "You have done well. How can we reward you?"

The woman ducked her head in thanks as she clutched her rags around her. "Let me return to the shape I was," she pleaded, her voice hoarse from weeping. "Let me forget the cruelty and pain. I wish only to live in the blissful ignorance of an animal."

"This is your last word?" asked Cernunnos.

"It is," said Bran.

"Then come to me, daughter," said Cernunnos as he stretched out his arms.

Bran approached him and bowed her head as Cernunnos touched her scalp with his palms. Then she sighed and crumpled to the ground, where her body twisted and shimmered. Gray-brown curly hair sprouted all over her, and eventually it was a wolfhound that stood up and raced away, back to the mound, leaving warm rags on the grass. She was gone without even a backward glance of her haunted blue eyes. Maddy sighed to see her disappear.

"And now, Feral Child, we grant your dearest wish," said Cernunnos. "Justice for the unicorn hunter."

"The hunt isn't over yet," said Maddy.

"I think it is," said Sorcha. "Is that not the hunter standing before us?"

Maddy cast a quick glance at Bang Bang, dirty, disheveled, and hunched over. He was humming tunelessly and looking around himself with a vacant smile. *At least look at one of them!* thought Maddy. *Show us who it is, even if you can't tell us!* But Bang Bang looked at no one and just kept humming nonsense to himself.

"Look at him," said Maddy. "Do you really think he could have done this on his own?"

"We have no reason to believe otherwise," said Sorcha.

"Have you tried looking for one?" asked Maddy, immediately regretting her quick mouth.

"You just cannot bear to think that a human did this," said Niamh, while every other monarch, bar Meabh, bristled. Meabh was examining her nails with a bored expression. "Your hatred for faerie kind has been noted, Feral Child," Niamh continued, "but you cannot find any proof that any faerie had a hand in this crime."

"Even Sorcha suspected the Winter Queen," said Maddy.

"When did you hear me say Queen Liadan had anything to do with the unicorn hunt?" asked Sorcha, her blue eyes flinty.

"Well, you didn't say it as such—" began Maddy.

"Then I did not say it," snapped Sorcha. "Do you have any evidence that Winter aided and abetted this creature in any way to commit this crime?"

Maddy looked at Bang Bang. "Please, Bang Bang," she begged. "You have to tell. Which of these queens told you to hurt the unicorn?"

But Bang Bang just gave her his sly look and shook his head.

"This is serious!" hissed Maddy. "You are going to get hurt, Bang Bang, really badly hurt, if you don't tell us who put you up to this."

He just stuck his tongue out at her and began to pout again.

In desperation, Maddy looked at Cernunnos. "Give me some time . . ."

"There is no more time," he said.

"You can tell he's not well!" Danny burst out. "How can you blame him?"

"He is the only one who stands before us," said Meabh.

"Ask the queens!" said Roisin. "They can't lie, so if they don't reply, well, that tells you it's not just him, doesn't it?"

The Tuatha stood and looked at her and kept their silence. Meabh had a small smile playing about her lips, and Maddy remembered something she had said.

"There is a war coming, but it will come at a time of my choosing and when it benefits my court most."

"You're not going to ask them, are you?" said Roisin, her face crumpling with despair, a silent tear rolling down her cheek.

"Fachtna, speak true," said Cernunnos. "When you traveled with these mortal children, did you find any evidence that any of the Tír na nÓg queens were involved in this?"

Fachtna looked at Maddy for a moment and then back at Cernunnos. "None, my lord."

"Then I will not insult a queen regnant by asking her to answer a charge to a crime there is no reason to suspect she has committed," said Cernunnos.

"Please," said Maddy, her voice breaking up with her tears. "I didn't know what I was asking for."

"I told you that, child," said Cernunnos, "but you would not listen. Now someone else will have to pay the price for your pride and your hatred."

"This isn't right!" shouted Danny.

"What is right and what is just are two completely different things," said Cernunnos. "Hold them!"

The Tuatha guards stepped forward from the ranks and walked over to Maddy, Danny, and Roisin, pinning their arms against their sides. Fenris and Nero growled and snapped, while George cowered in confusion. Una smiled sadly and stroked Bang Bang's face before walking over to stand beside Maddy.

"You cannot stop what is coming," she said. "Be brave, *a chuisle*, and keep your eyes open when he dies. He deserves that from you."

"Bang Bang, run!" screamed Roisin, as she twisted in the Tuatha guard's arms. Bang Bang was clearly upset and confused as he looked about, and then he started muttering and staring at his fingers as they twisted about each other.

Tears streamed down Maddy's face. "Please don't do this," she called to Cernunnos. "Meabh . . . my queen, I beg you, protect him."

But Meabh just smiled at Maddy and ran her fingertips lightly over her ruby red lips.

"As the unicorn is the purest creature on earth, the symbol of righteousness, let him avenge his mate," said Cernunnos.

The unicorn stallion lowered his head and broke into a gallop, his horn pointing straight at Bang Bang. Bang Bang looked up at the sound of thundering hooves, and at the sight of the unicorn, a beatific smile broke over his face, and he held out his arms just as the stallion's horn collided with his chest. There was a dull thud, and Bang Bang was thrown through into the air, to lie still on his back, his open eyes gazing up at the night sky. The unicorn snorted and tossed his head, spattering the grass with beads of blood before returning to the mare's side.

All the feeling left Maddy's legs, and she slid to the ground, her eyes fixed on Bang Bang, as the Tuatha guard stepped away from her. She could hear Roisin screaming and Danny shouting as they ran toward Bang Bang. Stunned, she climbed to her feet and staggered over to join them. He was still breathing, his eyes shining with apparent joy as he said something over and over again. Maddy bent over to put her ear to his lips while Roisin wept and pressed her jacket against his wound.

"So beautiful," Bang Bang whispered. "So, so beautiful."

His eyes began to close, and Maddy shook his shoulder. "Don't go to sleep, Bang Bang. Keep talking to us!"

"So tired . . ." he whispered.

"I know, Bang Bang, but you have to keep talking to me. You've got to stay awake just a little while longer," said Maddy.

"Tell me a bedtime story," said Bang Bang. "A story full of white castles and pretty queens."

The tears were pouring silently down Maddy's cheeks, and she wiped her nose on her sleeve as her voice thickened. "I will, Bang Bang. I'll tell you any story you like, but you have to promise to stay awake." George crept over to him and licked his face. Fenris and

Nero padded over and looked down at the dying man, their eyes crinkled with distress.

"Story . . ." whispered Bang Bang, as his eyelids grew heavier and heavier. "I promise . . ." His eyes closed as his breath faded and his head drooped to one side.

"Bang Bang? Bang Bang, wake up!" Maddy shook him hard by the shoulders, but Bang Bang's head lolled on his neck. Roisin began to cry, huge, hitching sobs that sounded as if they were being torn from her chest. George whimpered, while Danny crouched in the grass, clutching handfuls of his hair in white-knuckled fists and staring at Bang Bang in horror.

Maddy smelled wet leaves and rain carried on the breeze, and she looked up to find Meabh standing over her. The dimming glow told her the other courts were leaving, Bang Bang meaning little more to them than litter left on the ground.

"Why couldn't Cernunnos have shown mercy?" Maddy asked.

"Because you could not," said Meabh. "He swore an oath to you, and he had to give you what you demanded."

"I never wanted this," she said, half blind with tears.

"Yes, you did," said Meabh. "When you thought it was one of us, you did. All that hatred and rage inside of you wanted exactly this. You denied what is inside you, girl, so you were blind to what was guiding you. Those twin snakes whispered in your ear, and you thought you were being *moral* and *righteous*. Tell me, hero, how does it feel now?"

"Bad," Maddy whispered. "But you like the hate and the rage, don't you? It's why you tricked me."

"Aye, girl, I tricked you," said Meabh. "And now that I've collared you and leashed you, I'll stoke those fires in you. And when the time comes and I let loose the dogs of war, the Hound of Ireland will lead my pack, baying for blood."

"Never," said Maddy.

Meabh tipped her head to one side and smiled. "We shall see, Feral Child. I have you for three years. Who knows what I can make you do in that time?" She bent and pressed her lips to Maddy's forehead. "I am your mother now, and I will be seeing you again very, very soon."

A wind blew up from nowhere, and Meabh disappeared in her whirlwind of fiery autumn leaves. Maddy became aware of Roisin pumping Bang Bang's chest and counting. The last of the faeries must have left because Danny had a cell signal. "Hello?" she heard him say. "Granda, we need you to come get us. Something really bad has happened . . ."

Maddy slumped to one side and gazed dry-eyed at the rising sun, wrapping her arms around George as, still whimpering, he cuddled into her chest.

epilogue

THE SIGHTED TOOK BANG BANG'S BODY AWAY.
After all she had done, Maddy felt sick with shame
when people touched her with gentle hands and told
her with kind voices not to worry, that they would sort
everything out. She wanted them to scream and shout
and vilify her for what she had done. Bang Bang was
dead, and it was all her fault. She was going to have to
live with that knowledge forever.

Roisin had been led away sobbing, but Maddy
thought she could hear Danny arguing with someone.
She couldn't be bothered to investigate. She just sat on
the grass, clutching George to her chest like a favorite
soft toy. Familiar feet stopped in front of her, and a man
crouched down to peer up into her face. Granda.

"Thank God, you're all safe," he said.

Maddy looked at him dully, and she didn't say a word.

He sighed. "Things have gone too far. You're leaving for Cork city, Maddy, right now. No arguments. I don't want you to go, love, but it is for the best."

"And what then?" she asked.

"What do you mean?"

"I mean, what do we do when you've packed me off to the city?"

Granda frowned. "Nothing, Maddy."

"Nothing?" she echoed.

"We're going to surround you with iron, and we're going to keep you hidden from the Tuatha. They'll forget about you eventually."

"That's it?" said Maddy, anger rising in her stomach, making her feel light-headed. "Bang Bang is dead, and you are going to do nothing?"

"I've told you before—there is nothing we can do to fight the Tuatha. I thought tonight would have shown you this."

Maddy put George down and climbed slowly to her feet.

"I can do something though, can't I? I can do *plenty*."

She turned and ran, ignoring Granda's shouts behind her. She ran away from the crushed bloody grass where Bang Bang's body had lain, back past the housing estates, through the village, ignoring the people staring at her, and through the grounds of the castle, her breath sawing in and out of her wounded chest, rasping on her ribs like a hand saw. The ground flew beneath her feet, and her blood pounded so hard in her ears she thought her head would burst. She raced over the bridge, through the meadow, and up to the foot of the castle. She briefly glimpsed a gleam of turquoise as a pair of wolves watched her go before they turned to walk through the tunnel that led to the mound. She let them go without a word, running on until she reached the stairs that wound their way through the heart of the castle. She took them two at a time, her hands scratching for traction, her nails breaking against the castle's stone skin. She ran across the battlements while the wind shrieked and pulled her hair.

When she reached her destination, she lay down at the gap in the walls and bent backward to put one hand against the Blarney Stone. She bared her teeth and let her rage and grief boil over and form a hard point in her mind, slamming it into the Stone as it swallowed her hand, making the Stone's consciousness scream with pain. Her mind flew to the Coranied's citadel, and she saw them look up as the shadows swirled around her.

"I know what kind of Hound I am," she said, her voice rich and thick with hate, and anger licking along its edges. She laughed as they got up from their seats and left their cauldrons to look at her. "Do you want to see me as I really am, what I'm like inside?"

But it wasn't a skinny, tangle-haired girl that walked out of the shadows. It was a massive wolfhound, muzzle furrowed in a snarl as it bared its teeth, its eyes brimming with green fire. The creature snapped at the air with fangs like knives as it advanced, turning over cauldrons as it shouldered them aside, toppling piles of books. The raven fluttered on its chain as it struggled to free itself from its perch while the Coranied backed away from the monstrous beast as it swept potions from tables with its tail and ripped leather-bound books to shreds. The black-robed prophets gathered at the farthest end of the room and watched in silence while the animal destroyed their domain and then threw its head back and howled. That cry, so full of rage and pain, reverberated around Tír na nÓg, and it rang in Maddy's ears for long moments after she pulled her hand away from the cowed Stone. She lay on her back in the cold shadow of the castle's battlements and gazed hard-eyed at the sky.

Bang Bang was dead, because of her. All her efforts to play the hero had come to nothing. She thought about what Meabh had said and imagined snakes coiling their way through her stomach and her veins, dripping venom as they went. Was it true? Was she still full of the worst emotions, the things she didn't like to admit to herself? Was it impossible for her to do anything, feel anything, that would not be tainted by the thoughts and feelings that lurked in the darkest corners of her mind, if she wouldn't look them full in the face? Was the real Maddy a much worse girl than the one she saw in the mirror?

She sighed, a deep, gusting breath that belonged in the body of someone much older, and she got to her feet.

The sun was creaking its weary way into the sky, and she turned her face to its rays. It could have been her imagination, but she thought it had regained some of its weak autumn warmth. She walked down the stairs to the entrance of the castle and emerged into a bright morning filled with birdsong. It was hard to believe in the horrors of the previous night, that somewhere nearby Bang Bang's blood was staining the wet grass.

The parking lot of the castle should have been deserted at this time of day, but instead it was full of the silent Sighted ones, who watched with wary eyes as she emerged through the gap in the fence. A taxi waited, its engine idling, pumping out blue fumes into the chill air. Granda stood by the driver's side, and she could see Danny and Roisin's white faces peering out at her from the back seat.

"So this is it, is it? No reprieve?" she asked Granda, her voice hoarse with exhaustion.

"It's for the best, Maddy," said Granda, his face shadowed by his flat cap. "It's too dangerous for you to stay here. One of these days you're going to tangle with the faeries and come off worse. Or dead."

She shivered in the cold air and wrapped her jacket tightly around herself. The driver wouldn't look at her; he just stared straight ahead with his hands clenched on the steering wheel. The rest of the Sighted still had not spoken a word.

"You're doing this for them, aren't you?" she asked Granda, pointing at the silent crowd with her chin.

"They are too frightened for me to stay here. They want me to go away, and all the trouble with it."

"You can't . . ."

". . . blame them, so you keep saying," interrupted Maddy. "But I do, all the same. Because the faeries aren't going to go away, and getting rid of me isn't going to solve anything. Meabh wants her war, and for some reason she wants me in it." She looked over his shoulder at the Sighted. "Are you always going to make me face them alone?" she asked in a louder voice. They still did not break their silence, but she noticed a few of them were embarrassed enough not to meet her eye. She looked back at Granda. "They could do so much more."

"They're only flesh and blood, Maddy, as am I," said Granda. "And you wouldn't have to face the faeries alone if you stopped running after them looking for a fight."

"I did what I had to do," said Maddy, and an image of Fachtna's face twisted into a sneer popped into her head.

Granda nodded. "And now, so am I," he said, opening the back door of the taxi. "I'll hide you, Maddy, until the Tuatha find some other distraction."

She refused to look at Granda as the taxi pulled out of the parking lot, taking her away from Blarney and into the iron heart of the city. "You can't," said Maddy, her eyes dull with defeat.

how to say the characters' names

Aengus Og	*Ain*-gus Ohg
Fachtna	*Foct*-na
Fionnula	Fin-*oo*-la
Meabh	Mayv
Niamh	*Nee*-iv
Nuada	*Noo*-i-da
Roisin	*Roe*-sheen
Seamus	*Shay*-mus
Sorcha	*Sor*-ka
Oisin	*Ush*-een
Una	*Oo*na

exploring the faerie realm

THE UNICORN HUNTER DRAWS ON IRISH MYTH and legend to create a magical world. Read on to find out more about these ancient stories . . .

The Banshees—Banshees follow the great families of Ireland and wail just before a family member's death as a warning. They also wail afterward, so that the world will know someone with hero's blood has passed. Whether they are supposed to act as guardian angels for the families or whether Una simply decided to take this task upon herself, no one is really sure.

Cernunnos (ker-*noo*-nos)—One of the oldest and most powerful of the TUATHA DE DANNAN, he clings to the form he took when he was worshiped in pre-Christian Ireland—that is, as the horned god. But he likes to linger in our world too, so he takes on a human form for the winter months, calls himself Seamus (*"shay*-mus"), and lives in Blarney, County Cork, keeping an eye on the mortal world and any comings and goings from Tír na nÓg.

The Coranied (kor-a-need)—Thousands of years ago, the Coranied, a mysterious race of warlocks, lived in Ireland among the Celts. During this time, the Tuatha de Dannan also roamed freely in the human world. The Celts eventually rose up against the Tuatha and drove all faerie-kind, including the Coranied, beneath the mounds. The Coranied have a unique talent—they can harvest all the bad thoughts and dreams that people have, which is what the dark faeries need to keep nourished. The Morrighan protects the Coranied in return for this talent, and she rations the dark faeries, keeping them too weak to wage war. The Coranied are vital to the Morrighan's ability to keep balance in Tír na nÓg. In turn, they are completely loyal to the Morrighan, and they think only of how to keep the balance. They care for no one and nothing outside of this.

Cú Chulainn (coo cullen)—When he was a child, Cú Chulainn was called Setanta. He gained his better-known name after he killed a fierce guard dog in self-defense. The dog was owned by a man called Culann, and Setanta offered to take the dog's place until a replacement could be reared. "Cú" is the Irish word for a hound, so "Cú Chulainn" means "Cullen's hound." At the age of seventeen, Cú Chulainn defended Ulster single-handedly against the armies of Queen Meabh when she ruled Connacht. It was prophesied that his great deeds would give him everlasting fame but that his life would be a short one. He went on to become known as the Hound of Ulster.

Finn mac Cumhaill (fin mac cool)—The Irish version of King Arthur, Finn mac Cumhaill and his Fenians waged many battles against the TUATHA DE DANNAN in the mortal world before he died and his story and spirit succumbed to the Shadowlands of TÍR NA NÓG. Part man, part story, part ghost, he is kept alive as long as people tell stories about him. The TUATHA, including Meabh, are afraid of him and choose to leave him alone as he broods in the Shadowlands. He is a man who could do so much, yet his grief keeps him looking inward. With no interest in what is happening beyond his castle walls, he sits and broods and waits for a sign that his wife will come back to him. His story is a powerful one, and if he is roused it could see TÍR NA NÓG changed forever.

Fir Dorocha (fir _dor_-ka)—"Fir dorocha" means "dark men" in Irish. These faeries are the embodiment of fear. They spread hatred and terror before them, and they drive mortals crazy. Wherever there is a mob or a riot in progress, the fir dorocha are close by. They have also been known to abduct mortals for the kings and queens they serve. Basically, they do all the nasty jobs LIADAN and the TUATHA DE DANNAN do not want to do themselves. Faeries to avoid at all costs.

The Gancanagh (gan-*cah*-nah)—Maddy is lucky that no matter how gorgeous she thinks Connor is, she's too young to be interested in kissing boys (yuck!). Connor is a gancanagh, a male faerie who has a poison in his skin that makes mortal women fall in love with him forever. When he leaves them, they die pining for him. One kiss is enough.

Liadan (*lee*-ah-dan)—Her name means "gray lady" in Irish. Liadan is an old and powerful elf from the Nordic countries. No one knows why she and her clan came to TÍR NA NÓG seeking sanctuary, but she's as argumentative as the TUATHA DE DANNAN.

The Morrighan (more-*ee*-gan)—In pre-Christian Ireland, the Morrighan was worshiped as a triple-faced goddess. She represents the maiden, the mother, and the hag, and she is the most powerful of the TUATHA DE DANNAN. It is her power that created TÍR NA NÓG, and it is her power alone that maintains the boundaries between the faerie and mortal worlds. The Morrighan is one of the most dangerous of the TUATHA. She is also known as the Raven Queen, and she is the living embodiment of war. Waking the Morrighan is not something that should be done lightly.

Pooka—A Pooka is a malicious faerie that appears in many guises all over Ireland—as a goat, a horse, or a dog—but always jet black with yellow eyes. Some say he is a harbinger of death; according to others, he is just a nuisance that terrorizes travelers upon the road at night. As Meabh's pet, he always appears as a huge black dog.

Samhain Fesh (*sow*-en fesh)—This was the pagan feast that marked the start of winter, when the harvest was gathered in and people got ready to endure the winter months. It is also the time of year when the boundaries between the faerie world, TÍR NA NÓG, and the mortal world wear thin and faeries can cross over to us and we can find ourselves lost in their realm. Christians tried to stamp out Samhain by replacing it with All Hallows' Eve or Halloween, but the old ways are there, underneath it all, even if we have forgotten them. So the next time you go trick-or-treating, put some iron in your pocket. And always be nice to old ladies you meet on the road—you never know whom you are talking to. Faeries never forget a kind deed or a harshly spoken word.

Tír na nÓg (teer na nogue)—This is the Land of Eternal
Youth, and it is also the fabled realm of the Tuatha
de Dannan that exists beneath Ireland's surface, the
place the faeries fled to when they lost their battles
against mortals for control of Ireland. This is where
the Tuatha and the lesser tribes of faeries live.
Many, many people search for ways in, but you need
a faerie guide to enter the realm, and getting out is
never as easy. Something to think about if you have
things urgent to do topside—clear your calendar.

Tuatha de Dannan (*too*-ah day *dah*-nan)—The Tuatha
have many names: the Shining Ones, the Fair Folk,
the Gentry. Some call them faeries, but they call
themselves gods. They used to be in charge of Ireland, until St. Patrick came along, and they have
serious powers. They can control all the elements—
air, water, fire, and earth—cast powerful spells, and
change their form at will. They are vain and short-
tempered, cruel and spiteful. They argue so much
that fighting is practically a hobby for them. They
are the most powerful beings in Tír na nÓg, and
they rule it. It's best not to upset them.